The Legend of the 10 Elemental Masters

By Nick Smith (aka "ulillillia")

A scene from scene 8 in the story – Ivan (left) and Tu (right) watch the "ball", an elemental master, as furry Knuckles (center) views its stats on his spell-created, levitating platform two miles above the ocean under a clear blue sky.

The world map images (on page 112) were originally made by the Visible Earth project by NASA. The image used has been modified in the following ways: to change the projection type, add the latitude and longitude grid, add anything essential to the story, and convert it to grayscale using an algorithm to match the apparent brightness. The original source image is available at http://visibleearth.nasa.gov/view_detail.php?id=7116.

ISBN-13: 978-0-615-34813-1
ISBN-10: 0615348130

First edition
Ninth revision

Preface

I wanted a story that combined as many of my interests as I could – RPGs, science, mysteries, and travel. I also wanted it to be reasonably realistic hence the science fiction aspects.

I got the ideas from several sources. My mind game (a video game played in my mind) and the dreams I get while I sleep are my two primary sources. The party in scene 3 came from a real event and is also where the setting came from. The stats come from RPGs, to mimic them; I include many unique concepts.

I solved a puzzle to name the elemental masters. I wanted catchy names, always starting with "la" and ending with "alent". The puzzle was figuring out what goes in the middle to relate to the element. A "v", for "lava", was for fire, "lavalent". Some, like "larockalent" and "lalightalent", were tricky to decide.

Speed and Knuckles were my imaginary friends from the time. Ivan is one of my top favorite names. I use numbers in almost everything; since Tu is often the second mentioned, she gets her name from "two". Other names were randomly thought of.

From writing my Web site's dream journal, with nearly 1000 dreams (found at www.ulillillia.us), I have a habit of going into great detail describing the scenery since the scenery is often the best recalled. I describe and do things best using numbers since I'm mathematically oriented. Describing color is a good example.

They say a picture is a worth a thousand words. Diagrams, maps, and other images are scattered around to help, converted to grayscale using a brightness-matching algorithm I made.

This is a fictional story. You will first be introduced to the primary protagonist, Knuckles, and dive into the story's first unusual events. Knuckles' real mission and his true power are soon revealed. He must not only solve the mystery as to what is going on in under 55 hours, but also make three ordinary humans become like him, overcoming many obstacles during his quest.

I have three sources for research. The first, and primary, is Wikipedia. If I can't find anything there, then I use Google to search. If neither of these methods worked, I then asked at the forums at www.howwhatwhy.com for assistance as needed.

I did most of the work on my own, though the community at howwhatwhy.com was of great help when it came to research. I was suggested Lulu from an E-mail, which answered my lingering problem with getting my story published.

I began writing in January 1996, inspired by a dream in late 1995 where I went through many states downriver on a log raft. I hand-wrote the stories in a confusing-to-read play format.

This story's history goes back ten years. I hand-wrote it in June of 1999 then typed it soon after. Because it had "useless speak" (character communication with no use to the story), little action, and illogical events (like walking in neck-deep mud on Mount Everest), I rewrote it entirely from scratch during 2002. The new version was 40% as long as I completely changed the plot and got rid of the "useless speak". I wanted to publish but, upon seeing the $300-1200 price tags, I quickly lost interest.

In early 2004, I thought of writing it for a movie since it was free outside about eight dollars for postage. My old play format was not the right format so I spent three months converting my story to the movie format. I liked this format a lot outside its strict, paper-wasting design. I had two requests. One found it to be too complex and the other, strangely, didn't arrive there.

Without success, I went with books. Due to difficulties using quotes and word variety, book format was not motivating. My play format is confusing to read, and movie format was too strict.

I then thought of combining the best of each. Movie format, since it flows well, is my basic design. Instead of wasting lines for actions directly affecting speech (like "one-second pause", "mumbling", or "confused"), I blended it in with the speech like my play format. Other actions and details use the book format.

From 2006, I had difficulty going past scene 4; I didn't resume the day after and I had other side projects. I wrote the full story on April 10, 2008 then halted to update my Web site. It wasn't until October 30, 2008 that I resumed due to my low ambition. I continued at a mad pace until I finished on December 18, 2008 avoiding Web site updates. I waited nine months for copyright to register then released it 10.1 years after I first completed the story. This became my first published story. I prepared my book for sale in bookstores just four months later due to decent sales.

Contents

Act 1: Unexplained events
Scene 1: The jail escapee

May 27, 1999 at 4:07 PM UTC – 54 hours, 52 minutes remaining

    Knuckles glides north 1500 feet above Lake Sakakawea at 800 mph following Highway 83. A small thunderstorm is somewhat visible to the south. The sky is 3/8 scattered with cirrus clouds and 1/8 scattered with altostratus clouds. The wind is 15 mph with gusts to 20 mph. A few small patches of snow in ditches, some with water, are visible but hard to see due to the speed. A 40-second pause in speech occurs while credits display on screen.

    Knuckles resembles a human, but with differences. Knuckles is neither male nor female, though referred to as a "he". Three-quarter-inch-thick dark-violet-colored (FFA000E0) fur covers his entire body. He is only 25 1/3 inches tall, 4 inches wide, and 2.5 inches deep. Knuckles gets his name from his large hands, 40% bigger than a human his size would have. A reflective, glittery, greenish (FFA0FF00) haze a half millimeter across borders his pupil. Knuckles has no nose and a mouth 2/3 as big. Every other aspect of his is that of what a human would have for his size. For details on the numerical colors (in parentheses), see appendix 5.

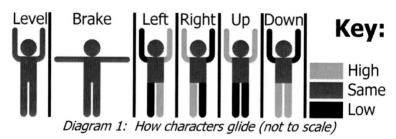
Diagram 1: How characters glide (not to scale)

    When characters glide, they are almost like airplanes. The diagram above illustrates this very well. In level gliding, the body is a long line. A T-shape is used for braking. Braking increases as someone moves more toward the T-shape. For banking and pitching, the body tilts left or right, up or down. The greater the tilt is, the faster the turn, up to 90° per second. When banking, not pitching, turning continues. When level, one descends two feet per second accelerating forward at five mph per second (decelerating when braking), both constant. Acceleration is complicated with pitching – see appendix 6 for details. These orientations can be combined. Gliding cannot exceed 800 mph and fur, shirts, and other loose items aren't affected by the air.

When Knuckles narrates, he sounds louder and clearer than normal. In addition, when Knuckles speaks, he doesn't move his mouth. This is due to a special ability. He can be speaking to a crowd of 100 but allow only 70 of those to hear him with the other 30 completely unaware that he is saying anything. He has almost no emotions so his voice is often quite monotonous.

Knuckles Narrator

Hi. I'm Knuckles. That's me you see gliding at 800 m-p-h. This was the story of my life and I'll never forget it! I'm from Korona, not Earth, though I've been on Earth for almost three Earth years. I'm 314 Earth-years old and thanks to spells and special abilities, I can live almost indefinitely. I came to Earth sensing something bad to occur in about 55 hours though I've been sensing more intermediate events beforehand. This was the first such event that I felt was the start of the whole story.

Knuckles

I'm sensing something going on at Minot Air Force Base, but it's still a few minutes before it'll happen. Normally, I'd be using the teleport spell. Ya know, I've always had the dream of making three ordinary, apparently weak humans become more like me with numerous special abilities. Let's see. (one-second pause) I'll toss on three glides for starters, but I'll need others for it to take effect. (two-second pause) Good to go, now to gain the A-P for it. (one-second pause) I'm getting close now.

"AP" stands for "ability points". Ability points are a common element in RPGs used to learn abilities.

As Knuckles continues gliding, now above Minot, he makes a slight left turn to head directly to the destination, leading away from the highway. Knuckles pitches straight down to dive toward the ground upon arriving at the BX, then leaves the glide landing at just over 800 mph. Knuckles is immune to drag and constantly accelerates at 20 mph per second. Upon landing, he dissipates all the kinetic energy straight up (for safety) in a visible, silent shockwave resembling that from big explosions.

<u>Knuckles</u>
(upon landing) Now that I'm here, about a half minute early, I guess I'll need to wait. (two-second pause) The target, according to what I'm sensing, is someone who escapes from jail. His initial target (one-second pause) is that blue-gray Oldsmobile. Hmm. Minor events, easily sensed. I should get on the roof where I have a clear sight for spell-casting.

Knuckles runs to the roof of the BX building at 15 mph and jumps on top of the highest point then stands, watching the area. Knuckles can move his legs very quickly, making five more steps per second for every ten mph of speed.

Three seconds later, a six-foot-tall, male jail escapee in an orange jump suit comes into view. He runs to the Oldsmobile where a military officer is just starting the car. The escapee arrives and attempts to hijack the car by opening the driver's door. Knuckles casts "glue4" on him, a spell with no effects, of which prevents the escapee from changing his position. A gray "4 immobilized" pops out bouncing like ball three times.

These popups very closely resemble that of the Tahoma font at font size 160 in bold face, but 90% as wide extending a half inch back. Gray popups indicate the addition or intensification of a status effect. Appendix 4 explains more about these popups and their meaning and behavior. "Glue" is the name of the spell series, and the "4" is the spell level. "Glue4" is the spell name. The spell system is explained in appendix 3.

Diagram 2: How characters cast spells, step by step (not to scale)

This diagram shows how human characters cast spells. Spells can be cast anywhere and one starts by bringing the arms, in a fist, up to their forehead and touch it to start "charging" the spell. A faint greenish glow (about 5070B040) 2.5 times the caster's widest part appears around the caster when charging. "Spikes" form around the rim of the glow going straight up 2.5 to 12.5% of the diameter, evenly distributed. The spell power is "focused" after charging. The arm forms a very small angle, smaller than that shown in the diagram, with the elbow pointed back. If right-handed, the caster steps forward with the right leg jerking the right arm forward, to cast the spell. The hand jerk does not need to be toward the target to hit it. The waves seen in the diagram are not present – they travel at the speed of light and don't emit any light. Upon reaching the final step, the spell's effects follow, if any. Not all spells have spell effects.

Knuckles is extremely fast with spells. He casts any spell in at least four nanoseconds, too fast for high-speed cameras. Due to this, Knuckles, from the "normal" state, instantly appears in the "release SP" state (in the diagram). The greenish glow is not seen as its present for only a few nanoseconds.

Knuckles casts teleport on the escapee. The escapee fades away in a quarter second when the spell is cast. The scene changes to that of the jail cell and the escapee fades back in the jail cell in a quarter second. The target is distorted and blurred during the fade, like looking at a scratched mirror. The jail scene remains for three seconds then returns to where Knuckles is.

Knuckles jumps off the building then runs south-southeast, accelerating constantly at 15 mph per second. At 60 mph, he jumps 91 2/3 feet high (with a 50 mph initial velocity decelerating at a constant 20 mph per second). At the top of this jump, he jumps twice more with the same 50 mph initial speed. While in mid-air, he accelerates forward at five mph per second. At the third jump's apex, he starts gliding level. When he reaches Highway 83, he turns slightly to follow above it.

Knuckles
(on the second jump) That was effortless. Next up, it's getting to Erik Ramstad Middle School. That's a ways away yet but I'm not sensing anything urgent anytime soon, so gliding is fine. Just look at those cars down below whizzing by like they were standing still and I'm still accelerating!

Scene 2: A sphere of fire

May 27, 1999 at 4:14 PM UTC – 54 hours, 45 minutes remaining

After another second, the scene skips to where Knuckles is, now going at about 550 mph roughly 100 feet above the ground. Knuckles continues gliding to Minot following Highway 83.

Knuckles narrator
That was a simple event though I was sensing something bigger. I wondered what could've caused his escape since it didn't make any sense. At first, I wasn't too concerned about what I was sensing next, but what a surprise it turned out to be, a sphere like ball lightning, only of pure fire.

Once Knuckles approaches the city's north side on Broadway (which is basically highway 83 continued in a straight line), he drops out of his glide, and, immediately after landing, crashes into a tree leaving both undamaged, even though the impact speed is about 660 mph. The shockwave is sent into a direction away from everything, including the tree. A red "0" pops out from both at the same time, behaving the same way as the gray popup. Red numbers indicate HP damage, with rare exceptions.

<u>Knuckles</u>
Now to figure out where the school is. I guess I'll
just follow the traffic and use the signs. Sensing is
one way, but I need to pass the time somehow....

Knuckles runs into the road and moves somewhat like traffic. The rules of the road are still followed, such as making right turns from a right turn lane, some with a strange twist. If a red light or stop sign is at an intersection, Knuckles jumps over it instead of stopping. Knuckles can make very abrupt turns while running, turning a full circle in one second at 30 mph. If a car's bottom is at least a foot above the ground, he can slip under it.

Throughout the road run, making as few turns as possible (by road), he maintains 30 mph until he reaches his destination. He jumps over the second intersection, which has a red light. Here, a police car is in the right turn lane. In an intersection after this, for the first turn, he slips under a car immediately after an abrupt turn then heads off in the intended direction.

At the school, made of red bricks, Knuckles heads to the right door's center on a collision course with a walking staff member. The doors are black (FF101010) in color and use pneumatic cylinders to close. A 30-foot-tall deciduous tree with large, dense foliage is located to the left of Knuckles' path before. After an abrupt turn to the right six feet from impact, he returns to going to the right door's center. When eight feet from the doors, he slides on the ground to stop decelerating at 100 mph per second. He stops 1.5 feet from center of the right door.

Knuckles casts teleport on himself appearing three feet inside.

There aren't any students in the hallways though there are a few occasional staff members. The staff members go in and out of the office, occasionally to other parts of the school.

If due north was straight ahead of the entrance, the gym is about 15 feet due north. It is behind a pair of polyurethane-coated, thick wooden doors that close via pneumatic cylinders. A second pair of identical doors is 40 feet to the east, both closed.

The cafeteria is to the east. The cafeteria's entrance is five feet east then south of the entrance. Inside, with only ambient light, there are a series of tables four feet in diameter. Six chairs are placed on top of them upside-down in a ring shape. The food is cooked in the eastern part of the cafeteria, closed by wooden blinds. A fenced-in track and unmarked gridiron football field, with goal posts, is outside and further east than the cafeteria. It is oriented the long way from west to east.

The entrance is to the south. It has a pair of an inner and outer set of black (FF101010) doors. About ten feet further south is a sidewalk-like pathway about three feet wide. Cars and school buses pick up students in the unpainted, half-circle, small road five feet south of the pathway. Signs reserve the closest part for buses. Roughly 120 feet due south of the center of the outer doors is where the tree is. The main street, with houses on the other side of it, is about 180 feet south of the entrance.

The classrooms, oriented north to south, are to the west. The seventh grade row is on the eastern side and eighth grade is 50 feet to the west. A hallway with each grades' classrooms lining the sides is about eight feet wide.

In the current, central area, there is a floor-to-ceiling, well-cleaned mirror five feet wide directly to the east. It has a two-inch clearance from the ceiling and three from the floor. Two soda vending machines with seven drinks in each, including one for water, are due west, both 75¢ for a 20-ounce bottle.

The floor uses a carpet of a medium-light teal color (about FF0080A0) with occasional spots of a medium green (about FF208010). The walls are painted a light blue-cyan color (about FF60C0E0) for the lower half and off-white (about FFE0E0E0) for the top half. The ceiling is a false ceiling using two-by-four-foot panels with fluorescent lights in sets of four in every other panel.

On the wall in front of the gym is a small sign printed on standard 8.5x11-inch copy paper. The sign has five lines of text filling the center of the page. All text is bold and of the font Arial. From top to bottom, each line has "Party!" in font size 144 (about two inches high) and red (FFFF0000), "Tonight!" in size 72 and blue (FF0000FF), "9:00 to midnight", "Bring $3", and "Prizes awarded!". The bottom three are size 36 and black (FF000000).

Knuckles

A party? A cost of three dollars? With all the junk
I've sold with the duplicate spell, and freelance
work, that's not a problem, but I'm sensing a
problem with Ivan though. Tu seems fine.

Knuckles turns around and looks at a spot eight feet northeast
of the tree. A two-second pause occurs.

Knuckles

(loudly with frustration) What is that that I'm
sensing out in that field!? (confused) Something's
not right over there, but as far as I can tell, it won't
happen for a few hours yet. (normal) I'm getting
3:22 PM as the time with three-minute error. It's
the primary reason I came here. It's supposed to
be near that tree near the center of the grass.

The scene switches to that of where Ivan is, in the gym
playing matball. Matball is a blend of baseball and kickball. The
pitch is a roll and the bat is a kick. Soft, blue mats four by six
feet and two inches thick are the bases, placed in the corners.

Ivan is a 14-2/3-year-old eighth grade student who is a sports
enthusiast with above average muscle mass. He is a 152-pound
Native American 70 inches tall. He wears short, white (FFFFFFFF)
socks, medium-priced ($40), fairly old running shoes, an orange
(FFFF8000), cotton T-shirt, and dark blue-violet (FF200060),
elastic silk capris (long shorts extending three inches below the
knee). The capris have holes 1/16 inch in diameter forming
equilateral triangles spaced a quarter inch apart (to allow the skin
to breathe). Ivan has bushy black (FF000000) hair two inches
from the head and is five inches long (below the upper neck).

The gym is 60 feet wide and goes 100 feet back (north). A
wooden stage where students wait their turn goes 20 feet further
north. Medium-red (FFC00000), expensive-looking curtains are
on the sides of the stage tied by a darker red (FF800000) ribbon.

A volleyball is stuck between the gutters in the ceiling. The
gutters extend two feet down from the ceiling, four inches wide,

and spaced a foot apart. The upper part uses an area of about eight inches, slightly smaller than a volleyball.

Ivan's opposing team is up for scoring. Three players are on third base, five on second, and two on first. The remaining four stay on the stage in the back.

Ivan

20 to 18, good score and with two out, this is
turning out to be a close game. I like close games.

One of Ivan's teammates rolls the ball toward a kicker and the kicker kicks it causing it to get only three inches above the ground traveling about 20 mph. Someone on third base, of which is where the ball is headed, runs toward home and jumps over the ball (preventing an out). He scores. Those on first base transfer to second but all others stay put. The kicker makes it to first base, to his right but avoids going to second base. The ball is returned to the pitcher since nothing is left to do for the round.

Ivan

Rats, 20 to 19 now.

Another pitch is made. The kick has the ball head to Ivan at 40 mph four feet above the ground. Ivan catches it as someone on third base attempts to go home. The teams start to switch.

Ivan

That was a nice catch, though a bit fast!

The scene changes to where Tu is packing up in earth science class, at 8:13 PM UTC (3:13 PM local). The earth science teacher is handing out report cards and the final test results.

Tu is a 15-year-old African American eighth grade student who is a science whiz. She is 66 inches tall and 140 pounds with below average muscle mass. She wears a V-neck T-shirt and shorts, both cotton and white (FFFFFFFF). Her socks are of the average size. She has new, but cheap, tennis shoes. Tu's black hair is curly and only an inch long.

The science class, instead of desks, has large black tables. Each of the four tables has two sinks evenly spaced and centered in each "half". Each table has six to eight students and four different samples of different rock and mineral types – granite, a geode, talc, halite, quartz, marble (not the ball type), and ten others (totaling 16). The tables don't have the same objects.

If just entering the classroom was due north, the tables and teacher's desk are centered on the north-south orientation. The teacher's desk, cluttered with papers with a handsome, bald, tall male behind it, is due north. The tables are to the east. The northeast corner has a large poster on the north wall. It has the ocean, an erupting volcano, various cloud types, and the layers of the atmosphere and ground, with text labeling the layers. Tu is in the far north of the class and the second table from the west.

Earth science teacher
Tu, your grades are next.

Tu gets up and walks to the teacher. The teacher hands Tu two pieces of paper; the final test is on top. Tu sees that she got an A- on the test with a score of 186 of 200 (93%).

Tu
An A-minus? That's better than I thought I did.

Tu looks at the class grade while walking back to her area and sees that got a B+, or 91%.

Tu
A B-plus? Not bad, though that test helped.

The scene switches to where Knuckles is, now outside the history class where Ivan is. Knuckles waits outside the door 5% opaque (due to a spell he cast, barely visible).

Several school papers, mostly worksheets graded as a B or a C with the occasional A or D and with red marks through the question numbers of wrong answers are on Ivan's desk. He stashes them in his back pack without organizing or being neat. The class report card and final test results are at the bottom. His final test only shows 159 of 200 (79.5%), a C, but his class grade is 85%, a B-. At the very bottom, the last item, is a small three-by-three-inch bright pink-colored (FFFFB0D0) post-it note stating, "See me outside as you leave, Knuckles" in font size 36 Courier New. Upon reaching the last five pages, the bell rings.

Ivan

(upon seeing the pink note) What's this? (reads it) See me outside as you leave, Knuckles. (stops reading; confused) What the!? That seems strange! I'll ask the attendance office about it.

Ivan picks up his large back pack and walks to the attendance office, a short distance due west of the school's entrance. Ivan steps in where two female clerks are working on the Macintosh computers straight ahead. Two female students sit on the cushions against the north wall (based on the school's entrance). Ivan goes to the pretty, short attendance clerk on his left side.

Ivan

Do you know who Knuckles is as I got this strange note from him?

Ivan hands the note over to the clerk and the clerk bumps the mouse to wake the Macintosh computer up from its sleep mode. After a few seconds, a quick search is done but the computer, after a half second, returns no results.

Attendance clerk

Sorry, nothing comes up and I'm not familiar with anyone here with that name. There's world-famous Knuckles, of which I saw looking out the door.

Ivan

Oh well, thanks. It could be a prankster going at it.

Ivan leaves the attendance office. Meanwhile, Knuckles, who is now fully opaque, very closely watches the field. Students

18

head out that direction while leaving, but avoid the area ten feet northeast of the tree following the concrete pathway instead.

Knuckles
(loudly) Uh oh! It's about to happen!

The students, including many staff members, including Ivan but not Tu, look at Knuckles with fear.

Two seconds later, a red (FFFF4000), hot, spherical monster three feet in diameter bursts out of the ground. It, four feet above the ground, stops. The ball emits an obvious heat wave effect as if it was 800°F. It slowly drifts toward the tree.

Knuckles casts teleport to get out of the school while all the students and even the parents in their cars and the school's staff run for cover screaming "monster!" Two seconds after the ball appears, the grass below it catches fire. Knuckles casts water2 on the monster and the fires. A lot of water, as if a full ten-gallon bucket fell over, splashes on both putting the fire out but leaving the monster otherwise untouched although a red "51,170,521" pops out of it, including the commas.

Lavalent		Origin: Virgo supercluster, local group, Milky Way, Sol
Level:	17	Unknown, unknown, unknown
HP:	784,359,083/	
	835,529,604	Strengths: Spell power, hit points, strength, speed, absorbs
SP:	69,045,260/	fire, defense, fear, charmed, sleep, poison, distracted, blind,
	69,046,717	dizzy, confusion, electric, chemical, wind, gravity, stone, dark
Aura:		Weaknesses: Water, ice, intelligence, SP leak, berserk,
		ranged accuracy, light
Age:	2764	

1.3	1.9 ★		1		1.3 ★		1
1.5 ★	0.6		0.9		1.4		1.8 ★
1.1	1.7 ★		1.6 ★		2 ★		1.1
1.1	1.2 ★		1.2		1.7		1.1
2.2 ★	0.7		1 ★		0.9		0.8 ★
0.9 ★	0.4		0.7		1.4 ★		1.7

Physical attack	12,708	Magic attack	58,973	Strength	1,388,950
Melee accuracy	110	Magic efficiency	546,008	Speed	179
Ranged accuracy	89	Magic accuracy	122	Hit points	835,529,604
Physical defense	163,880	Magic defense	271,161	Spell power	69,046,717
Physical evasion	54	Magic evasion	72	Level	17
Actions/second	12	Magic potency	591,692	Experience	853

Figure 1: The monster's stats (scale: 1:3.75)

Knuckles casts "full scan" to view the monster's stats. The grass catches on fire again just two seconds after being put out.

This is what the status window looks like. For details on what all this information means, see appendix 2. The window is 18 inches wide by 12 inches tall, placed two feet from the caster, with the bottom two feet above the ground. The stats show up on a transparent dark gray (40404040) window with text and borders as white (FFFFFFFF). The window is two or three atoms thick. Outside the lack of transparency, the use of grayscale, and being scaled down, the window looks exactly as pictured.

<u>Knuckles</u>
(at the moment the stats window appears) Wow! I haven't seen stats like these for decades! It's still simple though. A lavalent.... Interesting name!

The tree catches on fire three seconds after the window appears. Two seconds later, the window disappears. Knuckles casts "ultimate freeze 6" on both the monster and all fires.

For the spell effects of the "ultimate freeze" series, time stops. The scene, except the monster, grass on fire, and the tree, fades to black completely with Knuckles in the "release SP" state upon starting. A faint, very flat, ring-shaped, blue-cyan (2000B0FF) haze borders the area. The ring is micrometers thin, four inches wide but has an outside diameter of about 700 feet. The ring shrinks accelerating inward like an object being drawn toward a planet gravitationally. When the ring shrinks to being only 20 feet in diameter in two seconds, it becomes fully opaque.

At a foot in diameter, two seconds into the effect shrinking at 160 mph at that time, it expands out at a constant 200 mph with a gigantic ice crystal forming. The ring fades away within one second while it spreads outward. The ice crystal resembles that of a quartz crystal. There are 13 protrusions joining at a common center. There are eight in the outer ring pointing 30° upwards spaced 45° apart, four in the middle ring pointing 60° upwards spaced 90° apart between that of the outer crystals, and the other pointing straight up in the center. Each protrusion is a rectangular box; a four-sided pyramid with 45° slopes caps it.

After a one-second pause, 11 more ice crystals, each 95% as big (on a side), appear inside the previous one in the same spot a third of a second apart from each other. As the ice crystals form, a blue-cyan ring forms and spreads out from it but at a slower speed, relative to the crystal's size, and the same fade duration.

A two-second pause occurs. All ice crystals explode sending numerous ice shards resembling glass shards at 400 mph. A ring spreads out at 500 mph taking two seconds to fade away. After two seconds, the ice shards fade away in one second. A one-second pause occurs then the scene fades back to normal with time resuming after fully returning to normal.

The monster fades away in one second and the fires are gone. The grass and tree are now rock hard. The buildings, students, and other objects are left alone as if nothing happened. A red "942,029,864" pops out of the monster, a red "501,202,708" pops out of the tree and a red "458,447,813" pops out from where the monster appeared above the grass. All three appear at exactly the same time and have the same behavior. Knuckles casts recall on the tree and grass, returning them to normal.

It seems strange that the monster took a lot more damage; take note that the monster is weak against ice meaning that base damage is doubled. Appendix 2 explains this in further detail.

<u>Knuckles</u>
It's been a few years since I last used that spell!

The students and most staff run to Knuckles.

<u>Knuckles</u>
It's also been a few decades since I last saw anything with that much power either. Lavalent. Lava is hot and fire-elemental so that's a good name for it. Planet of origin unknown, plenty of hit points, pure fire-elemental, resistant to many status effects, and incredibly fast and powerful. Level 17? That's unusually low for something like this. Was that what I was sensing? It's only a minor event compared to the big one two days from now.

Ivan
What was that all about? Where did that ball go?

Knuckles
I defeated by casting ultimate freeze 6 on it, a fairly strong ice-elemental spell.

Ivan
I've heard about you and your spell-casting, but I've never seen it.

Knuckles
If you've watched the news any time during the last almost three years, you almost certainly have. That video projection thing I use is actually a spell I have, one of billions.

Ivan stares at Knuckles then the tree.

Earth science teacher
You've really got power! That's truly amazing how you can do that and so quickly! Do you have earth-elemental spells?

Knuckles
Across four series, I've got over 300 spell levels' worth. The two most powerful in the series you can't see the effects of since time stops. Anyway, you should go back to your parents and/or what you were originally doing. I'm not sensing anything for another 16 hours outside basic things like crime and a small tremor in California to occur in about five and a quarter hours, magnitude four dot three.

Scene 3: It's Party Time!

May 28, 1999 at 1:58 AM UTC – 45 hours, 1 minute remaining

The scene fades to that of a pretty sunset in five seconds. The sky is clear except for altostratus clouds 1/4 scattered ten miles to the east. The wind is about ten mph, gusting to 15.

Two seconds later, the scene switches to an area above the southern part of town where Knuckles is gliding around at 180 mph almost randomly about 800 feet above the city looking down. He is first heading northeast west of Broadway but turns left toward the north-northwest a second after crossing over Broadway. Being above everything, the sunset is easily visible.

<u>Knuckles narrator</u>
(a second into the fade) That was the first of the unusual events, but the one involving Puerto Rico was significantly more "powerful". The last time I saw anything with even close to that much H-P was during the Great War a few decades ago. While I wasn't sensing anything but minor things, I took on the role of a policeman patrolling the streets high up. I lost track of time dealing with a brawl and I abruptly headed toward Ivan's house for the party.

Knuckles turns while gliding to head toward the far western area of town where many houses were. After completing the turn, he continues in a straight line. At Ivan's house, Knuckles dives to the ground and redirects the kinetic energy straight up. He lands near a tree and the tree's branches suddenly move as if a gust of wind going 35 mph occurred, but going straight up.

<u>Knuckles</u>
(upon landing) That was a bit close. I'm still a few seconds early though.

Ivan comes out of the door and sees Knuckles waiting. He runs to Knuckles and stops.

Ivan
(running) Knuckles! What you are doing here?

Knuckles
You wanted to go to the party, right?

Ivan
Yes, but I can't – no money nor transportation. The school is quite far for biking and a bit dangerous.

Knuckles
I can't drive either, but what sense is there in using a really slow car when a teleport spell goes....

Ivan
(confused) Teleport spell? You sure that's safe?

Knuckles
With my extremely high magic potency and magic accuracy, I haven't missed or incorrectly cast the spell for more than 250 years.

Ivan
(surprised) 250 years!? You're that old!?

Knuckles
I'm 314 and could live indefinitely, thanks to spells. Anyway, want to go there at the speed of light?

Ivan
Man! That's fast! Sure, why not?

Knuckles
You might feel a bit disoriented due to the sudden place change; it is a weakness of the human mind, conflicting senses, and not a fault with the spell.

Ivan
Okay, but how long does it take to cast it?

Knuckles
Last I checked, it's about 114 nanoseconds, practically instantaneous.

Knuckles casts teleport. From this point onward, unless noted, when this spell is cast, the scene, after the targets disappear, changes to that of the destination. Both Ivan and Knuckles appear ten feet from the main entrance to the school. Ivan, after reacting to the sudden position change, jerks a bit then looks around. Tu, upon the others arriving at the scene, comes on a bike. She gets off, parks it in the bike rack, and walks to them, only noticing them when she's ten feet away.

Ivan

(one second after jerking) Awesome! So, what about the admission fee they charge? The three dollars ya know?

Knuckles

That's not a problem either. Thanks to the duplicate spell to make endless copies of products like fancy ruby-lined desks, toys, computers, refrigerators, and various other items, money isn't a problem for me. Plus, I get paid from the various jobs I do like police work and peace negotiations. Laws forbid me from duplicating actual money and existing products, even though I can make exact atom-by-atom duplicates due to the duplicate spell. I'll give you five dollars for admission and for sodas.

Knuckles digs into his chest. His hand disappears when more than a half of an inch into his fur when he does this. He basically just "reaches in", "grabs" the item he's after, then "pulls it out" with the object completely unaltered. This is a commonly-used special ability Knuckles has. He brings out a real five and a real one dollar bill at the same time. Tu stands watching this.

Knuckles

I see that Tu is interested as well. My chest sort of functions as a bank but more secure than anything humans have ever made. No one can get inside but myself so it's even better than a safety deposit box.

Knuckles hands the five dollar bill to Ivan and the one to Tu who already has four dollars.

Knuckles
I'll be waiting in the cafeteria. Meet me there. State that this money is your allowance.

Knuckles casts teleport and disappears. The scene does not change. Ivan and Tu walk into the school together.

The school looks a little different from the earlier visit. Based on the earlier layout description, a portable corkboard table eight feet north by three feet east using six metallic folding legs for support is to the east. It is covered with a flexible, rubber-like, off-black (about FF202020) cloth with a rippling pattern visible. It is part of the cloth's texture having ten ripples per inch. The entrance area is about 120 lux bright, a bit dark for indoors.

The table has two "sections". The southern section is where the admission fee is taken. The earth science teacher watches a male student who handles the money. The cash is stored in a small chest that folds to reveal two areas. The top area has four slots for bills. From south to north, the first two contain ones, the next contains fives, and the last has tens and the rare twenty. Coins, a few receipts, and a notepad are at the bottom.

Tickets are given in the northern section. There are two rolls of 1000 neon-orange (FFF09030) ticket-pairs each, one unopened starting with "908001" and the other, about a third used starting with "907314". The halves are 1 3/4 inches long by 3/4 inches wide. The top half is placed in a straw basket four inches deep, one foot in diameter, and has input for name, address, and phone number, which isn't filled in. A white, cotton cloth covers the entire inside of the basket. The other half only has the ticket number and is given to the student by a female student.

A dance is going on in the gym. One of the songs played is Scottish dance music, with bagpipes. The music is about 50 dB just inside the entrance; it's 90 dB in the gym. Although the west, right door is open, the walls and great distance muffle the sound. Five colored lights, red (FFFF0000), yellow (FFFFFF00), green (FF00FF00), blue (FF0000FF), and white (FFFFFFFF) move around randomly inside the gym. A second white light shines on a rotating ball of tiny mirrors that gives a glittering look. The gym is 25 lux bright on average where the dancing students are.

A ball from matball is loosely stuck 12 feet north-northwest of the volleyball that was stuck there earlier.

Large speakers 30 inches tall, 12 inches wide, and 8 inches deep are located on the western and eastern side of the stage. A stand like that used by political speakers is located in the center two feet back. On the stand is a small, unattended portable radio that is playing a CD in shuffle mode. It and the speakers are plugged into outlets at the far northern part of the gym.

Four groups of five portable metallic chairs from east to west and eight from north to south are 15 feet from the stage. On the sides and between groups is a four-foot alley for easy walking.

The classrooms are sealed off by a steel gate. They are only accessible through the locked office. The cafeteria's eating area is still accessible. Only ambient light gets into the cafeteria.

Ivan and Tu, together, pay for admission and receive a ticket. Ivan gets ticket number 907314 and Tu gets 907315. For Ivan's five, he gets two ones as change.

Earth science teacher

Hi Ivan, nice seeing you at the graduation party. I didn't think you would come.

Ivan

(stops) I unexpectedly got an allowance for my good grades. I just barely made the minimum B requirement for history, my worst class.

Earth science teacher

Good job getting B's and above. Have fun though.

Ivan and Tu head into the cafeteria. Knuckles is to the left against the north wall ten feet east of the mirror. The cafeteria is dark, just one lux, due only to ambient light.

Tu

What did you want, Knuckles?

Knuckles

I've been sensing for further details on the Puerto Rico event after that lavalent appeared and....

Tu

(confused) Lavalent? What's that?

Knuckles

Didn't you hear about the monster outbreak on the news I reported about?

Tu

Unfortunately, I didn't. I was playing checkers with my mom at the time the news came on.

Knuckles

Anyway, I'll show you with that video projection spell I frequently use.

Knuckles casts "mind thoughts to visual". A 3D holographic image of the lavalent nine inches in diameter rotating 60° per second appears. The heat wave effect is visible, but isn't hot. The image is 50 lumens bright, quite dim, but it sticks out.

Knuckles

This is what the monster looked like at 25% actual size. It's hard to see the heat wave effect in this low light. This is a fire-elemental monster knowing its stats, and seeing it in infrared, it appears to be about 800° Fahrenheit. This is just a projection and won't affect anything in here.

Tu

What an interesting-looking monster! You must be very brave to fight these things.

Knuckles

When you've been in constant battles for centuries, you get used to it and spells are a much better form of ranged weapon although they have unique and interesting downfalls.

The image of the lavalent disappears.

Knuckles
Anyway, now what I was going to say is that I've been sensing further details about the Puerto Rico event. I found a weak relationship between the lavalent that appeared and the flight to Puerto Rico. I know that you're interested in travel and seeing the world so I thought I'd take you on a trip with me, one you probably will never forget.

Ivan
With a monster like that, no way!

Knuckles
I've got all kinds of high-level protective spells too. Unlike beginners which fail and miss often and have little effect, I never miss and my effects last for over 67 minutes, plenty long. If you had the right ability, it would be up to three and a half days. If you do get hurt or die, I have spells to fix that. Revival is best if done within 30 minutes, otherwise I'd need to cast several extra spells beforehand to fix it.

Ivan
Man, you seem to have a spell for everything!

Tu
So then, what about this Puerto Rico flight?

Knuckles
While I can't say what will happen with reasonable certainty, the sense waves are very high amplitude allowing me to sense it months in advance accurate to the minute. Frequencies determine what the event is while amplitude is its intensity or severity. I have a flight to board at 7:42 AM tomorrow. At least, that's the take off time. The actual event is thirty-six-dot-seven-two seconds later.

Ivan
What precision! Anyway, I'd like to go with you.

Tu
Hmm. To travel with a real spell-caster, why not?
I'd like to go, but I don't want to face any monsters!

Knuckles
Remember, I have a spell for pretty much anything.

At 3:00 AM UTC (10:00 PM local) the dancing and music stops. Normal lighting, of 300 lux, is used. Students and staff fill two-thirds of the seats, most in the front, but a few line the back wall. Knuckles hides in the cafeteria and Ivan and Tu are in the gym. The earth science teacher walks to the stand carrying two baskets, one of the tickets, the other of envelopes with a 4x2.5-inch colored coupon inside. The colors are red (FFFFA0A0), yellow (FFFFE0A0) and, most common, green (FFA0E0A0).

Earth science teacher
We are now awarding prizes. Be sure to get your
tickets ready. When your ticket number is called,
you have won a prize. I'll start calling ticket
numbers in about a minute. Thank you.

Ivan and Tu walk to the cafeteria exiting through the gym's eastern doors. They enter the cafeteria seeing Knuckles standing on a nearby table 45° to the left of the entrance. Knuckles jumps a foot high off the table and runs to them at 20 mph.

Knuckles
I'm getting a bad feeling about that ticket-drawing.
If they call your ticket number, they draw the prize
out of the basket rather than you. However, I can
change the arrangements a bit so you can get
either a free go-cart ticket, a free medium pizza at
Pizza Hut, or three free game or movie rentals.

Ivan
Really? Pizza! I want pizza!

Me too!

Knuckles
(two-second pause) Okay, the effect is done. Now
to wait a few seconds....

Two seconds later, the earth science teacher mixes up the top
halves of the tickets in the basket and draws ticket number
"907314" out. A two-second pause occurs.

Earth science teacher
Our first ticket is nine-oh-seven (one-second
pause), three-one-four. Repeat, nine-oh-seven
(one-second pause), three-one-four.

Ivan and Tu look at their tickets while the number is being
read. After the number is first mentioned, Ivan, at six mph, runs
to the stand but walks past the chairs. The earth science teacher
draws an envelope that contains a red coupon.

Earth science teacher
It looks like Ivan is our first winner. Congratulations
on winning!

Ivan shows the ticket to the earth science teacher who hands
the envelope to him.

Earth science teacher
Here's your prize, Ivan.

Ivan
I wonder what I got.

Ivan takes the envelope and opens it. The coupon has "free
one-topping medium pizza" at the top left. It has a grayscale
image of a pepperoni pizza on the top right corner as if looking
30° above it and tilted counterclockwise 20°. The bottom left
area has small text stating, "Limit one coupon per family per day.
Expires 08/31/1999". The bottom right has the Pizza Hut logo. A

solid black line 1/16 inch wide borders the coupon, with eighth-inch margins. The back side has legal stuff written on it in very small text. After looking at it for two seconds, Ivan walks back.

Ivan
(upon getting the coupon) Wow! A free pizza!
Good one!

Tu looks at her ticket expecting the result.

Earth science teacher
Our next draw is ticket number nine-oh-seven (one-second pause), three-one-five. That's nine-oh-seven (one-second pause), three-one-five.

Tu walks to the stage upon first hearing the full number.

Tu
(mumbling) Knuckles was right! Amazing!

Earth science teacher
Tu looks like the winner.

Tu gives the ticket to the earth science teacher who draws two envelopes, one with a red coupon held on tightly, the other is green that falls when the hand is six inches above the basket. Tu hastily takes the envelope with the red coupon then slow-jogs back to the cafeteria at five mph while opening the envelope.

Tu
I got exactly what I hoped for, how nice!

Earth science teacher
The next ticket is nine-oh-seven (one-second pause), five-two-two. That again is nine-oh-seven (one-second pause), five-two-two.

Another student walks to the stand from the seats.

Knuckles

(when Tu enters) See, what did I tell you?

Ivan

That's pretty nice of you to do that. Expires at the end of August.

Knuckles

That's months after the main event I've sensed for years and its this that drew me to Earth. Let's go to my house now so you can get some sleep.

Tu

You have a house? I didn't know that.

Knuckles

It's mostly kept secret. I'll teleport you there.

Knuckles casts teleport on Ivan, Tu, and himself. They appear inside his house, which is pitch black. The house has no windows or doors at all and has no internal lighting.

Knuckles

Since you can't see infrared, I'll brighten it in here.

Knuckles casts "lighten" on the center of the ceiling. The 1200-lumen light provides light 200 lux bright directly below it.

The house, 20 feet long by 12 feet wide, has green-painted walls (about FF20D000) extending up to a white (FFFFFFFF) ceiling 7 1/2 feet tall. There are no appliances, utilities, or carpets but there is a floor of smooth concrete, two beds, a steel red-cushioned bar stool 2 1/2 feet tall 1 1/2 feet in diameter, and a wooden bench with papers in the corner.

If the bench was in the northwest corner, it'd extend seven feet east, nine feet south, 15 inches out from the wall, and three feet above the ground. It resembles scrap as it's painted poorly, leaving exposed pine wood areas. The stool is in the corner of the orange-painted bench (FFFF8000).

Map 1: Knuckles' house upon arriving (1:60 scale)

Papers with waveforms resembling those seen in waveform-editing programs are on the bench. The paper is 8.5x11 inches and has a brightness of 90. The left side has a scale going to 30 with zero in the center. Lines mark every five and ten without a marking. In the image below, the main event (29.5 dB) is on the left and the Puerto Rico event (15.6 dB) is on the right.

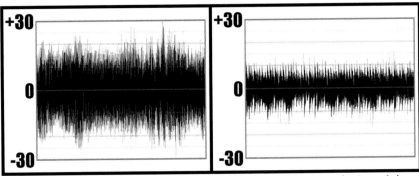

Figure 2: The waveforms Knuckles has on his papers (1:5 scale)

The two twin-sized beds are of the fancy, expensive-looking type. They are four inches from the house's eastern corners and are 7 1/2 feet long by 4 feet wide. The northern bed has a dark blue (FF000080) quilt with an aerial scene of Minot, ND at night 3000 feet above. The southern bed is dark gray (FF404040) and

has an image of cartoon-drawn chemistry lab equipment on it –
flasks, test tubes in a rack, a Bunsen burner, flints and others.

                    Knuckles
Bright enough? Ivan, you get that bed (points to
the northern one) and Tu, you get the other (points
to the southern bed). They are well-suited for you
using favorite designs. I don't need sleep; I'm
immune to it. A special ability called "master status
immunity" provides it, very helpful in battle.

Ivan and Tu walk toward their beds with a smile.

                      Ivan
That's an awesome design you've got. Thanks.

                       Tu
I like it a lot. Wonderful! Chemistry is my favorite!
Thank you! The ceiling could be higher though.

                    Knuckles
That's an easy fix – the edit spell.

   Knuckles casts "edit". The ceiling, wall, and light heights
increase two feet. Nothing else changes, including the bench.

                      Ivan
You really do seem to have a spell for pretty much
anything. What about food, drink, and a bathroom?

                    Knuckles
My house doesn't have any electricity, water, or
gas, since my spells more than do the job,
especially the create spell.

                      Ivan
Can you ever run out of "magic power"?

                    Knuckles
It's called spell power and yes, I can run out. I
have so much though that I won't run out for

millennia, even if I cast the highest level spells possible, higher than needed. I'm very efficient, pretty much the best possible, and I absorb spell power constantly due to other abilities I have. That ultimate freeze 6 spell hardly put a dent in it and so does my ultimate spell, ultimara6. I'll explain more later as we've got a big day tomorrow. I'll be studying sense waves to try and figure things out.

Ivan
(two-second pause) Okay, whatever. I'm not that skilled at science.

Ivan and Tu get into bed.

Act 2: Meeting the villain
Scene 4: Strange quakes

May 28, 1999 at 12:21 PM UTC – 34 hours, 38 minutes remaining

A time lapse lasting 20 seconds starts. Knuckles remains at his desk with papers of the two waveforms being added, of which change very slightly. The low-amplitude one is made ten times as much as the high-amplitude one. The light dims to 25 lumens and moves to straight above the papers. Ivan gets up for a one-minute drink, standing by Knuckles' stool a short while into the time lapse. The light never changes or goes away. The time lapse stops with the stack of papers 2 1/4 inches high. The time is based on that after the time lapse ends. The camera in the southwest corner's top pointing north-northeast doesn't move.

<u>Knuckles narrator</u>
(when the time lapse starts) Throughout that night, I did intensive research on trying to find out what both the Puerto Rico event was going to be and the main event. I focused more toward the Puerto Rico event, but all I could make out was that it involved a flight that I bought tickets for a week earlier, something partially related to the monster, and that of the main event. That of the flight and the main event stuck out far more. I couldn't get any further with the main event though; I wasn't focused on it.

Knuckles casts "create". A sheet of copy paper appears on his desk. In a second, Knuckles draws the waveform for Puerto Rico.
Here, Knuckles speaks to himself at normal volume and due to his "selective speech" ability, Ivan and Tu don't know he was speaking, even if they were awake.

<u>Knuckles</u>
With only a few minutes left, I should have great accuracy, but for some reason, I'm just not able to

make it out. All I know is that it involves a flight to Puerto Rico and that it's also related to the main event. However, there is only a slight hint as to a relationship with that monster outbreak but I'm too uncertain to be confident.

Knuckles looks at Ivan and Tu for a second, who are sleeping.

Knuckles

I've still got about a minute before I need to wake those two. (more loudly) Wait! I just noticed something! (normal) I've noticed a considerable relationship between this flight and that of the main event. What this flight has appears to have a lot of similarities with the main event. Strangely enough, even though it's a few minutes away, I can't tell what it is. I'm getting a feeling it's something I've never experienced before, as, if I have experienced it, I'd know and more readily identify it. I better get ready for battle though, just in case. Then again, I need to wake those two up and feed them.

Knuckles casts "alerten" on Ivan and Tu, which wakes them up and causes a green "sleep" to pop out. They sit upright as if they've been awake for a while.

Green popups rise constantly, unlike red or gray ones. They look exactly the same as well only light green (FF40FF40) instead. They indicate the recovery of hit points or status effects being degraded. See appendix 4 for more details.

Ivan

Hey Knuckles, what's going on?

Tu

Any luck with the Puerto Rico event?

Knuckles

I can't really get much further though I did spot a relationship between this event and the main event thirty-four and a half hours from now. Beyond that, I didn't make any further discoveries.

Ivan
Ya know, if teleport spells are much faster, then why use the slow plane?

Knuckles
This is because the event is to occur on a plane en route to Puerto Rico rather than at Puerto Rico, although I've been sensing something going on there for a few hours. What do you want to eat?

Ivan
What do you have here?

Knuckles
Technically, nothing, but the create spell solves that. This makes the choices and variety unlimited so you can have whatever you dream of having.

Tu
Wow! Talk about a restaurant's menu being a word to a whole library! How about French toast using pentagon-shaped pieces of white bread? No butter, but add cinnamon. How long will it take to make?

Knuckles
I could do that. It only takes about two-dot-six microseconds to make, no big deal.

Ivan
Man, you cast fast! I'll have a waffle in the shape of a VCR though obviously flat and smaller than the size of one.

Knuckles casts create and the meals appear on napkins. For Ivan's meal, the basic text of a fictional VCR is inscribed into the dough after cooking along with darker lines like cartoon drawings.

Ivan
Thanks! I wonder why restaurants don't do that.

A few minutes later, Ivan and Tu are done eating, with Knuckles back at working on his research.

                              Ivan
        That was delicious.

                               Tu
        I agree. Your spells make a good cook any day.

                            Knuckles
        Spells don't have impurities unless you're a beginner
        with a low magic potency. I added extra taste too.
        There's not much time left so we need to get going.

    Knuckles casts teleport. The team – Ivan, Tu, and Knuckles – appears at Minot airport in the waiting room. The waiting room has a TV tuned to CNN Headline News. A piece of torn paper taped on the buttons states, "please do not change the channel". Advertisements play with a car insurance ad first and Knuckles' services second. The Knuckles' services ad, lasting 25 seconds, mentions that it is only for emergency and certain government purposes only. It doesn't mention a way to contact him, but it does mention that he can sense it instead.

                            Knuckles
        Wait in the waiting room while I get the tickets and
        pay for them.

                               Tu
        Okay.

    Knuckles runs at 15 mph to the ticket stand and jumps onto the counter, since he's too short otherwise.

                              Ivan
        (as Knuckles leaves) An ad for Knuckles' services?
        That's interesting!

                            Knuckles
        I've ordered tickets to go to Puerto Rico on May 18,
        1999 in the name of Knuckles.

Airport ticket seller
Ah, Knuckles! That'll be $823.16. Here for that event you sensed?

Knuckles takes eight one hundred dollar bills, a twenty, and a five from his chest. The clerk gives Knuckles the three tickets at the same time Knuckles hands the money over.

Knuckles
Yes, that's what I'm here for. I can already sense strange rumbles. Keep the change though.

Knuckles runs back with the tickets and CNN resumes normal broadcasting. Jimmy Wilson, a male news reporter with short brown hair, a light blue, somewhat big T-shirt, and white shorts wearing sandals, is seen standing on a popular sandy beach near San Juan. The ocean's four-foot, white-cresting waves, with a few surfing them, are 100 feet in the background. Cumulus humilis clouds 1/8 scattered drift above in the gentle four mph breeze. A hovering helicopter is barely visible in the background.

Ivan
Look, CNN is on! (mumbling) So that's what it looks like!

CNN news reporter
We're back with a live report from Puerto Rico with Jimmy Wilson. Jimmy, any new updates on the earthquakes?

Jimmy Wilson
(one-second pause) The quakes have been going on for several hours with no sign of letting up. The four-foot waves visible behind me and the rumbles are a clear sign that earthquake activity is going on. Local seismologists have never seen or encountered anything like it and for so long. We've had reports of magnitude five lasting over four hours and they originate from random areas in the Atlantic Ocean about twelve hundred miles southeast of Bermuda.

Knuckles
Something unusual is causing those quakes!

Those in the waiting room look at Knuckles with fear. A map shows on CNN for five seconds when the location is mentioned. A transparent, red dot (80FF0000) covers an elliptical area from 52 to 65° west longitude and 19 to 30° north latitude.

CNN news reporter
Have seismologists found out what is causing the constant earthquakes?

Jimmy Wilson
(one-second pause) Currently, this information is lacking, though world-renowned Knuckles has predicted this two weeks prior to it happening. Earthquake activity can be felt lining the entire eastern coast of the United States along with most of the Caribbean islands. The activity has been strongest in Puerto Rico though.

Knuckles
I'll need to give details when done. Three minutes!

CNN news reporter
We'll wait for any word from Knuckles about this.

The weather report follows. The weather is not affected by the strange events. Knuckles senses rumbles below him.

Knuckles
Rumbles? Here? Uh oh! I'll need to get everyone on that plane and quickly. Though delayed for a half hour due to refueling problems, it can't wait. I'll cast teleport and use my spells to get going.

Knuckles casts teleport. Everyone going on the flight appear in the plane, most jerk from the sudden place change. Ivan and Tu, Tu in front, are in the window seats next to each other a bit behind the wing edge. The others are randomly placed.

Knuckles
This is an emergency and we must take off. I'm Knuckles, the one that brought you here along with your luggage. We must take off right this minute.

Shaking can be felt on the plane. The passengers buckle up.

Knuckles
Pilot, I'll use my spells to help you take off. Don't worry about further fueling. Put the engine at full throttle, as if taking off.

Pilot
I need clearance from the control tower.

Knuckles
Feel the rumbles? It can't wait!

Knuckles casts teleport appearing on the ground outside the airplane. The runway has one plane accelerating for take off. The sky is clear and there's an eight mph wind.

Knuckles casts "move". The fueling lines are removed and the tank is sealed. Knuckles recasts the spell and the plane rises straight up. At the same time, the engines start roaring. The plane rises up and forward accelerating at a constant 20 mph per second until going 100 mph (five seconds later). The shaking starts to become visible. The plane taking off starts climbing. Knuckles accelerates their plane forward to 173.2 mph.

The shaking is now very intense and the ground starts to crack like spider cracks on a car windshield hit by pebbles. The cracks form random shapes resembling broken safety glass, 1000 to 200,000 square feet typically, averaging 12,000 square feet.

At 173.2 mph, Knuckles casts "barrier 14" on the plane. A water-like (by behavior), very transparent, light gray (10C0C0C0) film forms around it that fades away in a half second the moment it appears. A gray "14 defense up" popup appears then a gray "14 magic shield" pops up 100 milliseconds after it in the same spot. Knuckles casts teleport to return.

Ivan
The ground is cracking apart!

Everyone looks out the window seeing the ground cracking. The cracks get larger and deeper then suddenly cave in where full cracks are. The caving in starts ten seconds after the ground first cracks apart. The ground is replaced by a thick black fog that has a 50-foot visibility. The entire ground caves in with high areas always the first. After it caves in, only a black fog is visible in its place with a light gray fogging effect in the distance due to the air above it, which is unaffected.

Ivan + Tu
(both at the same time) What the!?

Knuckles
I wasn't sensing that (one-second pause), or was I? (half-second pause) I was sensing it! No wonder why I couldn't make out what it was!

Pilot
Now what?

The pilot looks at his instruments. The altimeter rapidly drops at 1800 feet per second at first but slows down quickly stopping at -29,082 then starts climbing back up. The plane is actually climbing quickly and air speed slows down due to a much denser atmosphere. The other gauges, except the compass which has stopped working, work without any problems.

Knuckles
Do not attempt to climb out of this. The air is just much more dense for some reason. Continue your flight as if nothing happened. I'll try to figure out what is going on here.

Scene 5: An unexplained flight

May 28, 1999 at 12:44 PM UTC – 34 hours, 15 minutes remaining

The plane follows a routine as close to normal as possible. Three seconds later, Knuckles views the ground at different parts of the electromagnetic spectrum for two seconds each, from the lowest end to the highest. Microwaves and X-rays rays show nothing. The ground, in infrared, is so bright that the engines appear ice cold. In ultraviolet, the air has a dim glow (from the Sun which is not affected). The colored rim around Knuckles' eye allows him to see from upper microwaves to the low X-rays.

Knuckles narrator

That was the strangest encounter I've ever seen
and it didn't make logical sense. While I looked and
sensed around for clues, I was in for a big surprise.

Knuckles casts "fire shield 8" on the entire plane. A thin film resembling the fire of the lavalent without the heat wave effect appears around the plane fading away in one second upon appearing. A gray "8 fire shield" pops out.

Knuckles

The ground is glowing very strongly in infrared so I
protected the plane with a fire shield spell. The
ground appears to be about twenty-five hundred
degrees Fahrenheit. The outside air at this height is
about a hundred seventy degrees. Why this
happened, I don't know, but don't worry about
running out of fuel or anything as I have spells to
actually create it.

Passenger

How am I going to get home in Puerto Rico?

Knuckles

I don't yet know, but I'm looking into that.

Pilot

Hey Knuckles, come here for a moment.

Knuckles casts teleport and appears inside the cockpit.

Pilot

When I was on the ground, I could've sworn another airplane was taking off. Yet, my radar isn't showing anything at all.

Knuckles

I'm not sensing anything anywhere.

Three seconds pass. The pilot gets out his radio.

Pilot

(into the radio) Pilot to control tower, do you read?

Knuckles

Don't bother as there's nothing around to receive your signal.

Five seconds pass. Ivan sees a small red dot appear out of the ground.

Ivan

(scared) Knuckles!

Knuckles casts teleport and appears by Ivan.

Ivan

(scared) There's a strange red dot below.

Knuckles

(shocked) What the! That's a huge lavalent and it's coming up at 400 m-p-h!

Tu

(scared) A huge lavalent!? Quick, use your spells!

Knuckles casts teleport and appears in the pitch black luggage compartment. Knuckles casts "wind barrier". The gray popup

47

cannot be seen and the spell has no effects. The "delete" spell follows. A hole three by four feet appears and the room lights up. Items here are not sucked out. The "create" spell is cast, creating a cage with a floor three feet below and 24 half-inch bars spaced six inches all around. The cage is entirely made of aluminum. This whole process takes two seconds to do. Knuckles casts teleport to return.

Ivan

(scared) Where'd you go!?

Knuckles

I needed to modify the plane so I could fight it though there's something else beside it that I find suspicious. I can sense its presence, but not see it.

Three seconds pass. The monster bursts above the plane overshooting it. It is a lavalent 30 feet in diameter with a more intense heat wave effect, as if 2400°F. Ivan and Tu hide while Knuckles watches it.

Passenger

(very scared) Ah! Monster!

Knuckles casts teleport and appears in the cage. The monster drops down and looks at Knuckles. The monster has a very low-pitched and fairly loud voice, about 120 Hz at about 80 dB.

Master Lavalent

(in a friendly tone; confused) Hi! I'm the Master Lavalent. Did you call me?

The Master Lavalent jerks though Knuckles doesn't react to it.

Master Lavalent

(in an evil tone) I'll take you out, then the plane!

The Master Lavalent casts "plasma ball 55" on Knuckles. It casts spells without moving and in too short of a time to see.

Time stops. Everything except Knuckles fades completely to black. A small fireball appears over Knuckles fading away in two seconds. Suddenly, the view vibrates violently with eight huge, very loud explosions of dark blue (C0000060) plasma. The first seven explosions fade away in one second and are about 170 dB; the last is 190, fading away in two seconds and is more intense. Knuckles is unaffected. After a one-second pause, the scene fades back to normal and time resumes. A green "1.08756E13" pops out of Knuckles the moment time resumes. He absorbs all elements causing him to get healed instead of injured.

Knuckles casts "ultimate freeze 20" on the Master Lavalent, which has the same effects as before. Spells' effects are highly repetitive so they are explained once. A red "2.1198E10" pops out. The Master Lavalent makes a small jerk but is not defeated.

Knuckles

Whoa, a toughie!

Knuckles casts "stop90". The Master Lavalent abruptly stops all motion while a clock resembling a basic old-style pocket watch scaled to 20 feet in diameter fades in over it in a quarter second. The watch's time, from 3:00, advances 60 minutes per second then abruptly stops after 3/4 of a second passes. The watch fades away in a half second after a half-second pause. The gray "90 stop" pops out at the same time the effects start.

Knuckles casts full scan on it which shows its stats the same way as the lavalent, only with much bigger numbers.

The Master Lavalent's HP is yellow (FFFFF000) because its HP is less than half. It's hard to see in the grayscale version. The two icons to the right of the name are status effect icons.

Knuckles

Yowsers! That's one powerful lavalent! It's just a scaled up version of the lavalent, no big deal.

A green "stop" appears from the Master Lavalent.

Knuckles

What the!? Stop cancelled so soon!?

Master Lavalent	! HP ●	Origin: Virgo Supercluster, Local Group, Milky Way, Sol
Level: 5624		Earth of Fire, unknown, unknown
HP: 1.94724E10/		
4.06704E10		Strengths: Spell power, hit points, strength, intelligence, magic,
SP: 3.96559E09/		defense, speed, absorbs fire,status immunity, hard to find,
4.52899E09		electric, chemical, wind, gravity
Aura:		Weaknesses: Water, ice, ranged accuracy, physical, dark
Age: 1.42953E17		

1.5		5.7 ☆		4.3 ☆		5.2 ☆	3.3 ☆
4.2 ☆		3.4 ☆		4.2 ☆		4.5 ☆	5.6 ☆
3.6		5 ☆		5.8 ☆		3.9 ☆	3.8
5.9 ☆	??	4 ☆		3.8		5.8 ☆	6.2 ☆
5.5 ☆	✳	1.7 ☆	∠	2.5 ☆		2.3	2 ☆
2.2 ☆		1 ☆		4.7		3.5 ☆	1.5

Physical attack	1,709,882	Magic attack	7,869,044	Strength	23,278,101
Melee accuracy	168	Magic efficiency	9.85453E09	Speed	179
Ranged accuracy	113	Magic accuracy	218	Hit points	4.06704E10
Physical defense	3,727,126	Magic defense	5,312,865	Spell power	4.52899E09
Physical evasion	92	Magic evasion	140	Level	5624
Actions/second	136	Magic potency	5.1692E09	Experience	1.91568E15

Figure 3: Master Lavalent's stats (1:3.75 scale)

The window disappears.

Knuckles casts ultimara6 on the Master Lavalent. Time stops and the scene fades completely to black leaving only the Master Lavalent. One second later, a white light appears in the center of the target with rays coming out and a lens flare effect. For five seconds, this light gets brighter at an accelerating rate and the lens flare effect intensifies. At the end, the screen flashes white. Afterwards, the monster instantly disappears and a huge, dark blue (60000080), spherical globe appears spreading out in all directions for four seconds slowing down proportionally to volume. It is a very dark blue as it's a bit into the ultraviolet. The globe fades away in one second a second before coming to a stop. The scene fades back, without the Master Lavalent, and time resumes. A red "5.41957E76468" pops out where the Master Lavalent's center used to be. The ultimara series is the ultimate attack spell dealing damage beyond comprehension (yes, that's 76,469 digits to the left of the decimal).

I haven't had to use that spell since The Great War decades ago! But how did stop cancel so soon? Let me check those stats again....

Master Lavalent ! HP ⊗
Level:	5624
HP:	1.94724E10/
	4.06704E10
SP:	3.96559E09/
	4.52899E09
Aura:	
Age:	1.42953E17

Origin: Virgo Supercluster, Local Group, Milky Way, Sol
Earth of Fire, unknown, unknown

Strengths: Spell power, hit points, strength, intelligence, magic, defense, speed, absorbs fire, status immunity, hard to find, electric, chemical, wind, gravity
Weaknesses: Water, ice, ranged accuracy, physical, dark

	1.5		5.7		4.3		5.2		3.3
	4.2		3.4		4.2		4.5		5.6
	3.6		5		5.8		3.9		3.8
	5.9		4		3.8		5.8		6.2
	5.5		1.7		2.5		2.3		2
	2.2		1		4.7		3.5		1.5

Physical attack	1,709,882	Magic attack	7,869,044	Strength	23,278,101
Melee accuracy	168	Magic efficiency	9.85453E09	Speed	179
Ranged accuracy	113	Magic accuracy	218	Hit points	4.06704E10
Physical defense	3,727,126	Magic defense	5,312,865	Spell power	4.52899E09
Physical evasion	92	Magic evasion	140	Level	5624
Actions/second	136	Magic potency	5.1692E09	Experience	1.91568E15

Figure 4: Master Lavalent's important stats (darkened; Scale: 1:3.75)

The Master Lavalent's stats window appears again. The status effects (right of the name); level, at 5624; hit points, at 4.06704E10; planet of origin, "Earth of Fire"; status resistance to stop, at 3.8; and magic defense, at 5,312,865; are highlighted by having the rest 25% as opaque, simulated in the image.

Level fifty-six twenty-four! Wow that's high! Three dot eight for resistance to stop is nothing nor is its magic defense. Earth of Fire? Strange planet of origin.... It shouldn't have been cancelled that soon ... unless that something I'm sensing healed it.

The status window disappears. A one-second pause occurs.

Knuckles

(shocked) A black dot!? Something pure evil is nearby!

Knuckles casts ultimara6, but nothing happens.

Knuckles

Strange, I can't seem to target it. Nothing popped out, not even a red "missed".

Knuckles casts teleport to appear back where Tu is.

Knuckles

I've defeated the monster, but there's another presence that I cannot see or target.

Just then, the engines start to sputter, as if out of gas. They stop entirely two seconds later.

Pilot

We've run out of gas!

Knuckles casts create and the tank is half full again.

Knuckles

Start your engines again, I've used the create spell to refuel.

The pilot restarts the engines and they start without problems.

Pilot

Good. Thanks. I had a feeling I was going to run out of gas, though not that soon.

Two seconds later, smoke comes from the engines and a fire bursts out of them a second later. Alarms sound in the cockpit.

Pilot

The engines are on fire!

Knuckles casts undo and the fire instantly goes away. The alarms stop.

Knuckles
Easy fix, the undo spell.

Pilot
Was it the fuel you created?

Knuckles
The fuel I created is exactly the same as that of what you had in the tank before. There's something or someone causing it. Yikes!

Knuckles casts teleport. He appears in a fire in the luggage compartment. The hole in the plane does not affect it due to the "wind barrier" spell preventing the outside air from getting in. Knuckles is not affected by the fire but casts "water" on it. The spell has the same effects as water2, though with nine gallons of water instead. The fire is put out. An undo spell repairs the water damage. Knuckles casts teleport to return.

Knuckles
I sensed a fire in the luggage compartment but got rid of it.

Suddenly, the plane starts getting warmer.

Passenger
How come, all of a sudden, it's getting hot in here?

Knuckles
The protective barriers I've added were removed.

Knuckles recasts "fire shield 8" then "barrier 14". The same effects play with the same popups.

Passenger
Thanks, I can feel it getting cooler already.

Out of nowhere, an evil-sounding, low-pitched voice comes out of nowhere. Everyone but Knuckles scream upon hearing it.

Evil force
Ha, ha, ha! You sneaky, smart moron. I'll get you!

Knuckles
(hollering) Come out and fight or are you chicken?
(half-second pause; normal) It apparently left.

The ground returns to normal as if nothing happened. The plane is 41,082 feet above the ocean with Puerto Rico clearly visible. The plane starts to slow down quite a bit then fall a little due to the atmosphere suddenly becoming rather thin.

Ivan
Hey! The ground is back to normal!

Tu
I don't like the sound of that strange voice.

Pilot
Where are we?

Knuckles
Two dot three miles from the Puerto Rican airport.

Pilot
How did we get there in 20 minutes? Are you sure?

Knuckles
I'm definitely certain of the place as I can read the signs down there and I recognize the San Juan airport. I can land the plane for you, though, at this height, it's faster if I just cast the teleport spell instead of the move spell. I'll need to temporarily stop time so the plane doesn't go flying off unexpectedly.

Pilot
Can you see the plane from (checks altimeter; one-second pause) 40,000 feet below? Also, I'll need clearance from the control tower.

Knuckles
If I can barely see the Galileo space craft from here, the plane is simple. I'll get clearance. I don't see any planes taking off; I see one taxiing for take off.

Knuckles casts teleport. He appears on the roof of the airport. Knuckles casts edit twice; the effects aren't seen. Stop follows, without the effects visible, then teleport. After teleport, the plane appears on the ground landed and without the cage add-on, as if it was never there. Knuckles casts "start" on the plane. The spell has the same watch from the "stop" spell but it starts stopped. After a second, it suddenly starts going 60 minutes per second from 3:00 for a second, fading away in a half second after this. A green "stop" pops out. The plane's engines are not running. Knuckles casts teleport to return to the cockpit.

Pilot
Wow! That teleport spell is quite effective.

Knuckles
The ground is solid so the passengers can get out.
I'll give you a hundred-dollar bonus for your efforts.

Knuckles takes out two fifty dollar bills from his chest and gives them to the pilot who takes it and puts it in his wallet.

Pilot
(taking the money) Thank you.

Scene 6: Knuckles, live!

May 28, 1999 at 1:03 PM UTC – 33 hours, 56 minutes remaining

Knuckles casts teleport and the team appears in the airport. Jimmy Wilson and his cameraman are packing up their camera equipment. Upon seeing Knuckles, he immediately hooks up his cameras, taking several seconds. A 15-inch TV is visible 15 feet in the background tuned to CNN Headline News. The TV shows a news report of Knuckles capturing the jail escapee yesterday, complete with videos of the events. The quakes have stopped.

Knuckles narrator

That event was the strangest one I've ever seen and it was my first encounter with the evil presence that's causing the mayhem. I began to understand what was going on in the world at that moment. I knew that news agencies would find the events encountered on the plane an instant top story so I gave a report on both it and the quakes.

Jimmy Wilson

Knuckles! What are you doing here?

Knuckles

I've got a story that will immediately grab attention and it occurred on the flight.

Jimmy Wilson

Like what?

Knuckles

The ground caving in, a huge lavalent, and an evil-sounding voice....

Jimmy Wilson

Huh!? I'll have to report this to headquarters!

Two seconds later, the TV shows "Knuckles news update".

CNN news reporter
We have breaking news from world-renowned
Knuckles. Jimmy is there with him in Puerto Rico.

The TV switches over to that of the camera Jimmy Wilson is getting. Knuckles is centered in the view.

Knuckles
The earthquakes you were reporting about earlier
were not due to normal means, rather, they were
due to what appears to be a landmass breaking
apart from the ocean bottom, a large one. But,
what I came to report was a very unusual event I
just encountered while on a flight to Puerto Rico.
I'll show you the details.

Knuckles steps off the side out of the camera's range and casts "mind thoughts to visual". The window is perpendicular to the camera causing it to appear as a perfect rectangle and is at the top of the screen. The first scene shows Knuckles watching the news report about the earthquakes.

Knuckles
When I first got to the airport, I was watching the
reports about the mysterious earthquakes here, but
right away, I knew that they weren't caused by
natural means. I suddenly heard rumbles.

The window shows everyone on the plane after a teleport spell. The motions of the plane from the move spell and the effects of the barrier spell are also shown, including the popups.

Knuckles
Knowing that I had to quickly get that plane off the
ground, even though it was delayed, I teleported
everyone, including their luggage, into the plane
and their related areas. I got out and made the
plane take off using the move spell and added the
"defense up" and "magic shield" status effects to

protect the plane and its occupants from taking damage or getting hurt. They last 67 minutes.

The window shows the ground cracking apart then caving in. The fire shield spell is shown with its effects and popup visible.

<u>Knuckles</u>
Shortly after the odd take off, the ground cracked apart and caved in revealing a strange fog. I noticed that it was very hot in the infrared so I cast "fire shield 8" on the plane to protect it from heat. The atmosphere was also significantly denser.

The window shows the Master Lavalent when it was first spotted. The modifications Knuckles made to the plane follows.

<u>Knuckles</u>
Then, out of nowhere, I saw a monster that looked exactly like the lavalent encountered at the school, only 30 feet in diameter instead. I needed to prepare for battle so I made changes to the plane to more easily target it.

The window shows the greeting with the Master Lavalent then the battle that followed. Because time stops for the high-level spells, these don't have effects. The stop spell does though. The popups for both do appear.

<u>Knuckles</u>
At first, the monster seemed friendly, but all of a sudden, it started attacking. You can't see the effects of the powerful spells, because time stops while they occur. Some being canceled the stop status effect I added to the monster so I could look at its stats, so I destroyed it with my most powerful attack spell, ultimara6, which obliterates anything.

The window shows the series of strange events that occurred after the battle: the gas running out, the engine and luggage compartment fires, and the removal of the airplane's protective barriers followed by the voice of the evil force.

Knuckles
With the monster defeated, a series of four strange events occurred such as the engines being out of gas, even though the tanks were a quarter full. The engines and luggage compartments caught fire out of nowhere then the plane's protective barriers I added disappeared early causing the plane to get warm on the inside and fast. The scary part was when this strange evil presence actually spoke.

The window shows the ground suddenly returning to normal. The landing part follows.

Knuckles
With the ground back to normal and solid again, I landed the plane and only eighteen dot eight minutes passed from take-off to landing, another thing that seems strange.

The window shows the lavalent's stats for ten seconds then the Master Lavalent's stats, which remain. The transparency effect for these is present – the floor can be seen behind it.

Knuckles
If you do encounter any of these monsters, (with emphasis) do not fight them! (normal) They are incredibly powerful, especially the large ones. (with emphasis) No military should attempt to fight these either. (normal) Bombs and missiles will heal them instead. They are so resistant that they're very hard to scratch even ignoring elemental properties. (with emphasis) Let me deal with them.

Jimmy Wilson
What an unusual event! You really are powerful! Your statement nearly three years ago about having

this kind of power was true! Why did the monster heal you though, knowing the green number?

Knuckles

It cast the plasma ball 55 spell on me and I absorb fire-elemental attacks. That means it cures me. I cast ultimara6 on it, the cause for the big damage.

Jimmy Wilson

I didn't catch that part but oh well. The green one on you distracted me from catching it.

Knuckles

This is all I need to report. You can return to normal broadcasting now.

After a second, the TV resumes normal broadcasting, cutting to advertisements, one for life insurance.

Jimmy Wilson

What a fascinating story! Did you see that thing that caused the voice?

Knuckles

I could only sense its position, not see what it looks like or target it. I tried to get it with ultimara6, but nothing happened, other than wasting spell power. With 467% magic accuracy, missing is extremely unlikely. I need to go to Hawaii though.

Jimmy Wilson

Bye.

Act 3: The real mission
Scene 7: Learning to glide

May 28, 1999 at 1:18 PM UTC – 33 hours, 41 minutes remaining

  Knuckles casts teleport and the team appears at a beach on Maui of Hawaii. The clear night sky is filled with stars and a near-full Moon. The water 20 feet away is calm and there is a very light three mph wind. Ivan and Tu look around. The beach is empty as this is a remote area and 2:18 AM local time.

Knuckles narrator

Although I was sensing another event similar to the Puerto Rico one, it was a few hours away. With time to lose, I decided that, since my abilities were now learned, thanks to those battles, I would give them to Ivan and Tu so they could glide around.

Knuckles

Hey, want to gain the ability to glide?

  Ivan turns around and looks at Knuckles confused. Tu doesn't as she's mesmerized by the water.

Ivan

(confused) Glide? What do you mean?

Knuckles

Glide like I do.

Ivan

Oh, another spell huh?

Knuckles

Actually, it's not a spell; it's the real ability along with a few others so you can in the first place.

Ivan

(confused) The real thing!? How do you do that?

Tu turns around and looks at Knuckles with amazement.

Tu

(scared) Gliding (one-second pause) for real? I'm not sure in that case; I'm not fond of heights.

Knuckles

I use basic glass marbles. Glass seems to have a property that allows easy transferring of abilities. The extras involve gravity manipulation and energy management, both required prerequisites. Another is immunity to drag so you can get beyond about 90 mph, well beyond.

Ivan

Just how fast can you get with it?

Knuckles

Eight hundred m-p-h.

Ivan

That fast!? What about going faster? Why 800?

Knuckles

Strangely enough, that I don't know. Once I got insta-teleport then later the teleport spell, I had no need for its upgrades as I only use it for taking in the scenery, but going too fast with that makes it not as worthy as everything goes by in a blur at even a thousand feet away.

Ivan

How high can you get?

Tu

Good question.

Knuckles

When gliding, you're basically like an unpowered airplane. You control gravity, though the control isn't complete. You constantly descend at two feet per second as well which doesn't seem like much when you're high up, but it really becomes apparent near the ground. Drop below two feet per second and you'll just drop out of the sky. It's a cheap ability compared to insta-teleport, but for starters, it's a great way to get around.

Ivan
I'll take it then, but, uh, how do you use it?

Tu
I'll take it as well. I've always wondered what it's like to go beyond 73 miles per hour though, let alone 800. What's the speed of sound?

Knuckles
It's around seven-sixty-two m-p-h here, though it changes depending on various factors.

Ivan
Wow, eight hundred would mean supersonic!

Knuckles takes four semi-opaque, green (about 8030A010), plain glass marbles a third of an inch in diameter out of his chest. All of the marbles are exactly identical.

Knuckles
I've put the ability in these marbles. All you need to do to receive the ability is just touch them with me and remain touching them until I move my hand away. If you let go, the ability can still be transferred, though there is a ten-second time limit where, afterwards, the abilities are lost for good and I'll have to relearn them which can take days. I have a special ability that prevents transfer to anything evil so that evil presence can't get them nor will it affect the transfer if it gets involved. I'm not sensing it anywhere and the black dot is easily noticed among the oranges, yellows, and greens.

Tu
Black dot? Alright. I'll go first.

Ivan
(disappointed) I wanted to go first, but whatever.

Tu touches the marbles while Knuckles holds them and the green color in them fades away to a clear glass color in three seconds. While fading, small, green (FF00C000), glittering sparkles cover Tu at an average of 20 per square foot almost evenly spaced. The sparkles fade away in one second when the green is gone. When gone, Knuckles puts the marbles back in his chest in the same way as taking something out, but in reverse.

Tu
So, how do I use it now?

Knuckles
I'll show you in a bit. A black dot on my mind radar map means someone is pure evil. It's worse than red which is worse than the neutral yellow. You're both yellow-green which seems to be the norm.

Knuckles gets the same four marbles, now green, again. Ivan touches the marbles and the same glittering effect occurs. When the glittering fades away, the marbles are put back in his chest.

Ivan
(excited) How do you glide now?

Knuckles
Chill out already! I'll give you a demonstration of this using my video projection spell.

Knuckles casts "mind thoughts to visual". The window has a very pretty scene of old, smoothed-out, ice-free low mountains. The mountains have a lot of greenery around and are full of colors and the eight-mile visibility enhances the scene. Knuckles, in the video, is standing on a peak facing toward one 1000 feet higher four miles away. A stream 15 feet wide, moving rapidly left to right, is barely visible due to great distance.

Knuckles

How to glide, (half-second pause) lesson one.
When you get in mid-air.... I forgot to give you
jump 20, an ability that allows you to jump almost
15 feet high as you jump 20 mph upwards.

The window disappears. Knuckles transfers the abilities like
before to Ivan then Tu, only with five sparkles per square foot.

Knuckles

That ability is easy to use – just jump.

Knuckles casts "mind thoughts to visual" again and the
window appears in the same position with the exact same scene.

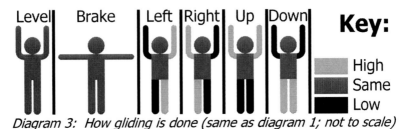

Diagram 3: How gliding is done (same as diagram 1; not to scale)

Knuckles

Back to gliding. After jumping or using some high
place like a roof top as a source of height, form
your body in a straight line.

The window shows Knuckles lying on the ground in the level-
gliding position. He doesn't move.

Knuckles

Have your arms out straight in front of you. While
in this position, assuming you're level, you'll
accelerate at a constant five miles per hour per
second but descend at a constant one and a third.
This is the basic form. If you want to slow down,
just spread your arms out like an airplane's wings.

The window shows Knuckles in the braking form.

For turning, simply tilt your body in the direction
you want to go.

The window shows Knuckles getting back up and standing.
He jumps a half second later 90 feet high, somewhat forward due
to the sloped surface, and starts gliding for the peak ahead.

Knuckles
Although you can't jump this high, gliding still works
the same as shown here. It seems like you're
barely moving, but in just the matter of seconds,
you'll be watching cars go "backwards" as you'll be
going faster than they are and soon, even a race
car would appear to be going the other way. After
two minutes, you're going the speed of airlines and
another forty seconds later, you've reached the
fastest possible. You can already tell that the speed
is pretty high in this video.

The window shows Knuckles pitching up 30°, down 30°, then
turns left 45°, and right 45°. He spends one second doing each
and remains level for two seconds between. The camera in the
window doesn't tilt or roll during this; it just pans. Knuckles
heads toward the peak after the final turn. Two seconds before
and after Knuckles crosses the stream, the camera looks down.

Knuckles
Here, I'll demonstrate pitching. When pitching up,
you'll lose speed, but gain height, useful to avoid
obstacles on the ground. When pitching down,
you'll gain speed, to 800 m-p-h, but lose height.
When turning, you'll continue to accelerate but will
turn at up to about 90 degrees per second, which,
at max speed, will pull about 53 G's. You will be
resistant to this due to the abilities I've given. You
won't be immune, but you'll be very resistant where
53 would feel more like two and a half. You're also

immune to drag to up to 1.4 times the atmosphere's density but you can still swim normally.

Ivan

That is so awesome!

Knuckles

Also, don't fall from a height any higher than about 600 feet or you'll get hurt. That's about a hundred thirty m-p-h impact or so. This isn't a crash course.

The forests in the window start to have noticeable textures.

Knuckles

At these speeds in mountainous areas, you need to watch out for high peaks and trees.

The trees in the window can be individually resolved but Knuckles pitches up a fifth of a second early barely avoiding impact. He levels out a second later and continues gliding whizzing over the top of the peak with a few feet to spare. A second later, the window disappears.

Knuckles

That's all there is to it. Simple huh?

Ivan

That was fast!

Knuckles

Try it by gliding out over the ocean and dropping in.

Ivan

Alright!

Ivan jumps 13 feet and Tu jumps 11, both at the same time. They start gliding over the ocean at the top of the jump. Both speed up until they skim the ocean surface, Ivan at 32 mph and Tu at 27, slowing down quickly making a big splash. They get into an upright position and tread water after stopping. Their immunity to drag does not affect swimming – water is about 830 times denser than air, well beyond the 1.4 limit.

Tu

This water is a bit chilly.

Ivan

(with Tu) That was fun!

Knuckles

Practice your gliding skills as I have a feeling you're going to need them.

Ivan and Tu swim back to shore. Ivan goes underwater and swims one mph faster than Tu. Near shore, they both walk in the water back to dry land.

Knuckles

Ya know, I think, after you get into gliding, you should be protected. I'll add the "defense up" and "magic shield" status effects on you.

Ivan

(confused) Huh? Status effect?

Knuckles

A status effect is something that changes the property of something, whether for good or for bad. The "defense up" one makes you more resistant to physical damage and "magic shield" does the same for magical damage. This way, if you land going 200 mph, you won't get hurt from sliding on even rough surfaces or crashing into a tree. Also, if something casts a spell on you, you won't be affected nearly as much. Be careful though as the effect expires after 67 minutes and you don't know what that evil force will do.

Tu

Speaking of which, where is he?

Knuckles

That I don't know. I don't sense him within a million miles around, which is a bit strange.

Tu

Good! I don't like that thing anyway! What about monsters?

Knuckles

One won't occur for another five hours and its out over the ocean about 13 miles.

Tu

Whew!

Knuckles casts "barrier 40" on both Ivan and Tu. A gray "26 defense up" and "26 magic shield" pops out of both. It's not a gray "40" because the 14 was present before – the status effect was upgraded in intensity by 26 – that's what the popups mean.

Knuckles

It appeared as if you already had the effect, but I refreshed it and used a higher spell level to further increase the resistance by increasing the intensity. Stay clear of the volcano, as lava will still hurt you. Also, I forgot to mention, if you slow down to two feet per second, you'll just drop out of the sky no longer gliding until you aim the glide in the direction you are going. Watch out for that. Go ahead and explore all you want, but don't get into trouble. I can sense what is going on and where you are at any time. Have fun!

Scene 8: A large sphere of water

May 28, 1999 at 6:24 PM UTC – 28 hours, 35 minutes remaining

Ivan repeats the glide over the ocean then pitches 10° up when near the surface. He nearly loses all speed and drops. Tu repeats it twice. Next, they do it over the beach and head into a forest after a left turn. A time lapse occurs lasting five seconds for five hours where the sun can be seen rising. Ivan never appears during the time lapse. Tu swims in the ocean for the last second. During the last 100 milliseconds, Tu, wet, is sitting on the beach next to Knuckles. Ivan is nowhere to be seen. There is a 12 mph wind and 3/4 broken stratus clouds 500 feet above.

Knuckles narrator
(a second into the second glide) With Ivan and Tu practicing gliding, I resumed studying the upcoming events. While I got no closer to resolving the main event twenty-eight-dot-six hours later, I found a strong relationship between the Master Lavalent encounter and the event ten minutes away. I also, unexpectedly, learned something new with gliding that I never knew in the 280 years I had it.

Tu
What about this monster you're sensing?

Knuckles
I'm not saying that it is a monster like the Master Lavalent, what I am saying is that the event about ten minutes from now appears to have a very close relationship with it. The amplitude is slightly lower and the frequencies are about the same.

Tu
How on Earth do you make these predictions?

Knuckles
I've got centuries of experience. Toss in a very high-level sense ability, I've become a master at it.

The problem is, if I've never experienced anything similar, as the case is with the main event, I cannot tell what is going to happen. I pick out parts that I can make out for things I have experienced, of which there's plenty of; it's just not distinguishable.

Tu looks around for Ivan. A one-second pause occurs.

Tu
Where's Ivan? I haven't seen him for three hours.

The scene switches to that of where Ivan is. He is gliding 800 mph southeast 35,000 feet above the ocean five miles due north of Hawaii Island paralleling the coast. Ivan pitches straight up for ten seconds a second later then levels off 11,000 feet higher. He accelerates for 45 seconds, reaching 800 mph in 40, and repeats.

Ivan
(two seconds after the scene change) That diving board trick really did work! Now, I'm lost and who knows how high. I want to get into outer space, if it's possible. I wonder how high I am and how high I could get. (looks around for three seconds) Hey, isn't that the large island of Hawaii that I'm over? I recognize the three peaks, but aren't those the three volcanoes? So much water, so little time! (one-second pause) I wonder if there are any monsters up here. I, hopefully, could easily escape at this speed, but that big monster seemed to go really fast. Here we go with another climb!

Ivan pitches straight up and climbs for ten seconds.

Ivan
The sky is really getting dark. Daytime is supposed to be bright, but this seems too dark for daytime. I should look around again.

Ivan levels out. He is now 57,000 feet high.

Ivan

That big island sure got quite a bit smaller after that and the sky a bit darker. Why is that? Strange.

The scene switches back to where Knuckles and Tu are.

Tu

Didn't Ivan ask about getting four bucks for pool admission ten minutes ago?

Knuckles

He did. It involves a diving board but he's nowhere near any pools on this island that I can see. Only eight minutes remain!

Tu

Did he... (one-second pause) die?

Knuckles

(shocked) What the!? How on earth did he get up over 57,000 feet high!?

Tu

(shocked) Huh!? I know diving boards can't get you up that high, not even close!

Knuckles

(amazed) Oh, I see his trick now. He used the diving board, nearly busting it, for a great source of height, nearly 70 feet, and glides until near the ocean surface pitching up. He levels out before stopping and gets to 800 m-p-h then pitches to go straight up for ten seconds. He levels off to accelerate again then repeats. I never knew you could do that with the glide ability! Oh well.

The scene returns to where Ivan is, now 68,000 feet high going 700 mph and accelerating. One second later, the stop spell's effects play on him. His motion abruptly stops; a gray "1 stop" pops out. The teleport spell makes Ivan disappear, reappearing on the beach lying in the sand. Knuckles casts "start" with the same effects as before. A green "stop" appears. Ivan becomes shocked then disappointed.

> Ivan
> (shocked; confused) What the!? How did I return to the ground suddenly?

> Knuckles
> I'm surprised you figured out something with the glide ability that I never knew about. You were almost 200 miles to the southeast and nearly twelve dot five miles high!

Rumbles start to become audible, but not visible. The ocean's waves are not affected.

> Ivan
> So that's how high I was! I was trying to get into outer space and I was also lost.

> Knuckles
> Now that I know about that, I can tell you with certainty that you could indeed get into outer space, but acceleration will decrease as you climb due to weaker gravity. We've got a monster to deal with and we need to be together again. (shocked) Uh oh! Rumbles! (normal) I'll need to make some sort of platform we can use to get around with.

Knuckles casts create. A square-shaped object eight feet on a side and a foot high appears in the sand. The platform has light reddish-gray (FFE08070) bricks 8x3x3 inches. Three four-feet-tall seats, made only of right angles, with armrests are a foot from the edges. The part sat on is 20 inches above. Two are in the southern corners, the west for Ivan and the east for Tu. The other, for Knuckles, centered east to west, is a third the size.

Knuckles casts "barrier89" on the platform, Ivan, and Tu. A gray "89 defense up" and "89 magic shield" pop out of the platform and a gray "49 defense up" and "49 magic shield" pop out of Ivan and Tu. He casts "levitate16" on the platform. A pair of bright blue-to-magenta-colored, sparkling, fully opaque wings comes out from the center of the platform. They have three-inch-long feathers, span five feet each, and are shaped like a bird's wing. The wings fade in in a quarter second and flap twice, once a second. On the third flap's start, they fade away in a half second. A gray "16 levitating" pops out when the effects start. Knuckles casts "wind barrier" around the platform with a gray "1 blocking wind" popping out. This spell has no effects.

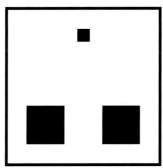

Map 2: Platform layout (Scale: 1:60)

<u>Knuckles</u>
All set to go. Let's go!

Everyone gets on the platform and seated. Within a foot of the platform, the wind stops blowing due to the wind barrier.

The platform rises, accelerating constantly to 200 mph at 20 mph per second. At 8500 feet, the platform decelerates vertically to a full stop but accelerates horizontally over the ocean at the same acceleration rate, stopping at 200 mph. The platform is rotated horizontally so that the seats face the direction of travel. All movement in terms of acceleration, top speed, and rotation from this point onward are the same, unless noted.

<u>Knuckles</u>
We're good to go. Wait!

Knuckles casts "fire shield 88", on Ivan, Tu, and the platform. A gray "88 fire shield" pops out of each.

Knuckles
(continuous) Knowing the previous case where it was hot outside, I've added this extra layer of protection at the highest levels I can use.

Ivan
What now?

Knuckles
Knowing the previous case, the ground should crack apart and cave in.

The ground cracks apart the same way it did for the Master Lavalent encounter. The platform slows to a stop and hovers.

Knuckles
A thick black mist should appear replacing it and a large monster should pop out soon after.

Tu
I wished there was a hiding place.

Knuckles
You won't be able to hide; they can sense your presence anyway.

The ground caves in. It is replaced by water of a strong blue color. The stratus clouds fade away in a second a second earlier.

Knuckles
It should be caving in at any moment now.

Ivan
What about that strange voice?

Knuckles
I don't know. I'm sensing that black dot now. For some odd reason though, the ground hasn't caved in yet. Did that evil presence delay or cancel it?

Suddenly, a monster like the Master Lavalent bursts out of the water straight down in a big splash rising 400 mph. It is entirely of water and is of the blue color of the water below (FF5080F0).

Knuckles
There's something strange here.

Knuckles jumps on top of his seat and turns around, with the camera, a full circle in four seconds. No land is visible anywhere.

Knuckles
That's odd. No land and we aren't that far out from land. All water... there must be a water-elemental monster instead.

The monster rises above the platform at 100 mph slowing down at 100 mph per second. It heads back down looking at the team. Knuckles casts "full scan" on it the moment he could first visually see it and a window appears showing its stats.

Master Laqualent		Origin: Virgo Supercluster, Local Group, Milky Way, Sol
Level:	5624	Earth of Water, unknown, unknown
HP:	4.06704E10/	
	4.06704E10	Strengths: Spell power, hit points, strength, intelligence, magic,
SP:	4.30336E09/	defense, speed, absorbs water, status immunity, hard to find,
	4.52899E09	earth, wind
Aura:		Weaknesses: Electric, ranged accuracy, physical, dark
Age:	1.42953E17	

	1.5		5.7		4.3		5.2		3.3
	4.2		3.4		4.2		4.5		5.6
	3.6		5		5.8		3.9		3.8
	5.9		4		3.8		5.8		6.2
	2.4		2.4		1		4.6		2.9
	4.6		5.5		4.7		3.4		1.5

Physical attack	1,709,882	Magic attack	7,869,044	Strength	23,278,101
Melee accuracy	168	Magic efficiency	9.85453E09	Speed	179
Ranged accuracy	113	Magic accuracy	218	Hit points	4.06704E10
Physical defense	3,727,126	Magic defense	5,312,865	Spell power	4.52899E09
Physical evasion	92	Magic evasion	140	Level	5624
Actions/second	136	Magic potency	5.1692E09	Experience	1.91568E15

Figure 5: Master Laqualent's stats (Scale: 1:3.75)

Knuckles

A water one indeed!

Evil force

Get them or you'll die!

The window disappears.

Knuckles

(confused) Huh!? That voice again, and it's threatening someone.

Evil force

Get them, now!

Master Laqualent

(scared) What for? They're good!

Evil force

(mad) I said get them, or you'll die! Now!

Master Laqualent

(scared) Is "megaflood55" okay?

Evil force

(with Knuckles) Anything to get rid of them!

Knuckles

(with the evil force) Is that monster (one-second pause) friendly?

The stats window appears again. The Master Laqualent casts megaflood55 on Knuckles, Ivan, and Tu.

Time stops. The scene completely fades to black, except the targets. A second later, a clear, still ocean appears with the team at the surface. A water bubble 50 feet in diameter forms around Knuckles, 140 for the others. A 7000-foot tsunami appears in the distance whizzing over the team four seconds later at 1200 mph leaving them underwater. When it hits, the bubbles collapse in on the team enveloping them tightly so only an eighth of an inch of water surrounds them. The ocean fades away in two seconds. The bubbles expand for two seconds at 400 mph in all directions, without gravity, thinning out. After a second, the scene fades back and time resumes. Three popups appear. Knuckles has a green "1.09277E13", Ivan a red "1.06414E13", and Tu a red "1.10196E13". Ivan and Tu fall over like rag dolls.

Knuckles casts "life-cure" on Ivan and Tu. Time stops again and the scene fades 3/4 of the way to black. A yellow angel, emitting white light at 500 lumens, appears five feet above Ivan's and Tu's highest point with a wand, one for each. They resemble a human girl doll 15 inches tall and have a dress that widens at the bottom. The angels descend one foot per second for three seconds tapping the wand two seconds in. Blue (FF0000FF) sparkles appear behaving the same way as that of ability transfers with a density of ten per square foot. A green "fatal" and "1" pops out when the sparkles start fading away.

A large, white-light-emitting sparkle at 200 lumens an inch in diameter appears; it starts at the bottom and spirals upward. The sparkle, making two full circles while spiraling up, emits smaller, falling, white (FFFFFFFF) sparkles 100 lumens bright the same size as the blue ones ten times a second for three seconds. The large sparkle moves to the center of each in a half second, grows to two feet in diameter in a second, and shrinks to nothing in another second. The angel rises a foot per second and fades away in one second. The scene fades back to normal and time resumes. A green "306" pops out of Ivan and a green "272" pops out of Tu. Ivan and Tu get back up as if nothing happened.

Evil force
I'm beginning to hate that pink idiot!

The evil force casts ultimara3 on Knuckles. The effects are the same as ultimara6 except Knuckles doesn't disappear at the end and the globe is brighter (C0000080). A red "0" pops out.

Evil force
(surprised) What the!? Immune to that! (growls; very mad) Try to find a way to get to me 1800 years into the future. Bye!

Knuckles
(confused) 1800 years? That's way further than
my original prediction three years ago!

Knuckles looks at the Master Laqualent.

Master Laqualent
(scared) Really, I'm friendly.

Knuckles
I see that you are a light green dot and the aura in
my stats shows it. I forget to check this often. You
attack, I attack. You support, I support. That's the
way I'm used to. What is this all about anyway?

The window disappears.

Master Laqualent
(a little scared) I don't know. Some strange
presence with a scary-looking black dot came out of
nowhere and somehow entered our world. I don't
know how he figured that out.

Knuckles
(confused) Entered your world? I'm not sensing
that thing now nor anything within a million miles.

Master Laqualent
Fortunately for me, you're pure good. I can sense
it. (amazed) Wow! Over level 9000!? No way!

Knuckles
My level has been unchanged since the Great War
ended. I saw you in the stats from the full scan
spell at the same level as the Master Lavalent with
pretty much the same stats.

Master Laqualent
You've encountered the Master Lavalent too?

Knuckles
Yeah, but I defeated him with ultimara6 not knowing that the evil presence possessed him. I also didn't check my radar or the aura stat.

Master Laqualent
He'll automatically get revived due to exposure to his element so you don't have to worry, hopefully anyway. Ya know, I have a gift I'd like to give, though it's not much. It's an extra experience plus.

Knuckles
Unfortunately, I'm maxed with 20, almost 21.

Master Laqualent
(shocked) That many!? Oh well. It was a try.

Knuckles
No problem. Anyway, how do you get the ground to return to normal?

Master Laqualent
I can't be outside my own element or I'll die and can't be revived outside revival spells. Do you have a way to keep me constantly in water so I'm safe?

Knuckles
Hmm. My chest is about all I can think of.

Master Laqualent
Your chest? That's strange.

Knuckles
I have a special ability, "chest matter compress", which compresses matter significantly. Another special ability prevents anything but myself from getting in, except targets I allow, of which must be better than a green dot. You meet this criteria so it'll work. This means that that evil presence can't get to you at all. I could throw a few beneficial status effects on you too for safe measures.

                    Master Laqualent
Okay, thanks.

Knuckles casts "barrier89" on the Master Laqualent with the same effects and popups appearing.

                    Master Laqualent
(shocked) Wow! Level 89! You're really amazing!
                       Knuckles
It's the highest level I have for that spell. I don't use it myself because I'm immune to damage. It'll last either 67 minutes or three days.

                    Master Laqualent
Ya know, you should be our main support. There are ten elemental masters like me out there. You're seeing me and you've already met the one for fire. There are eight others, but I haven't had any contact with the Master Ladarkalent in about a day by now, which is odd.

Knuckles puts the Master Laqualent in his chest, disappearing instantly when Knuckles reaches his hand out.

                       Knuckles
I've put you into my special area of water. It's not big, but it should be good enough until I resolve this mystery. What about the ground though?
                    Master Laqualent
I should be fine here and it's plenty big. As to the ground (hollering), Laqualent land to normal!

The ground instantly returns to normal like nothing happened.

                    Master Laqualent
Good?

Knuckles
Thank you. I'll do whatever it takes to protect and save the other elemental masters.

Scene 9: The military factory rescue

May 28, 1999 at 6:47 PM UTC – 28 hours, 12 minutes remaining

The platform moves back to land going forward 160 mph and down 120 mph. It remains until 600 feet from impact. Here, the platform slows to a stop vertically but speeds up horizontally until 1450 feet from shore slowing down to a stop over the same beach. It gently lowers to land. The team gets off of it.

Knuckles narrator
(as the platform moves) Now things were starting to make some sense. I found that the evil force was attempting to use the masters of the elements for something, but I had no idea what. I also discovered a conflict as it makes no sense on how he could be 1800 years into the future when the main event I predicted three years ago is still more than 28 hours away, far less. I knew I was in need of more clues, but that is now put off to the side due to a new mission. That new mission was to somehow find and save all eight remaining elemental masters, but I had no idea how to find or access their elemental worlds. Even with all the spells I have, I was not able to find out. I had to put off the mission of finding the elemental masters as I had a new emergency to deal with in which that evil presence was involved with.

Knuckles
I'll likely need this platform later, so I'll just put it in my chest instead of deleting it with the delete spell. (shocked) Yikes! I need to get to Nevada and fast!

The platform disappears. Knuckles casts teleport. The team appears in the desert by a factory (at the map's southern X) guarded by a fence and military guards (as light dots). A 400-foot-long, orange-colored, 15-foot-tall brick building is 100 feet north. A fence standing 12 feet high with barbed wire at the top borders the building. A four-foot-wide walkway of two-by-two-foot concrete slabs leads northward to the building. Two guards in military uniforms "decorated" based on a mid-range rank stand guard side by side straight ahead. A small shack 10x15 feet has a small guard inside and a few cupboards at the floor storing typical military weapons like grenades and machine guns.

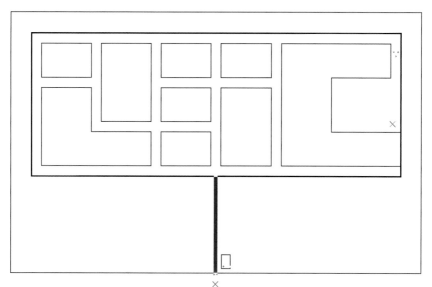

Map 3: The factory's basic layout (Scale: 1:1200)

Knuckles
(confused) The military? What does the military have to do with this? Something's fishy here.

Guard 1
(the southwest guard (left)) Hi Knuckles, what brings you here?

Knuckles
Someone is about to die in that building over there, a young adventurer.

The guards suddenly make a small jerk, as if possessed.

Guard 1

(in a mean voice) Get out of here! This is not your business!

Knuckles

(surprised) What the!? Something has apparently possessed the guards!

Knuckles casts "possession blocker 82" on the two guards. The spell has no spell effects. A gray "82 blocking possession" pops out of both. "Barrier89" is cast on them and a gray "89 defense up" and "89 magic shield" pop out of both.

Guard 1

What happened?

Knuckles

Something apparently possessed you and it's evil.

Guard 2

(the southeast guard (right)) An evil spirit? Here!?

Knuckles

It's a mystery I'm trying to solve and someone is in there about to die. I cast a spell on you to prevent it from possessing you again and another spell to drastically boost your resistance even further as that evil force is powerful, very powerful.

Guard 2

Thank you for the protection. You may pass, but, don't let those two go into any of the classified rooms, but if needed, do not let them get into any classified material.

Knuckles

Yes, and I know which ones those are. The target is not in any classified room or area, however.

The guards move off the side to allow the team to pass through. After passing through, they move back and watch.

Knuckles
You heard the guards now. Just follow me, I know
the path. I can sense your moves, remember?

The team runs to the building's entrance; Tu tries opening the door but finds it locked.

Knuckles
Oh great, a locked door. Easy fix.

Knuckles casts edit on the door, the spell effects can't be seen. Tu opens the door, holding it to let the others walk in.
The building has a grid-like layout, best explained by the map. In general, the rooms, sometimes "joined", are 54 by 36 feet with hallways ten feet wide. A metallic, brown-painted (FF804020) closed door with frosted glass is on each side of a "block". Below the knob is a keypad with 16 buttons. Each door's window has black stickers spelling "room X" on it – X is a number starting with 100. Fluorescent lights light the area to a rather bright 600 lux. The walls are light gray (FFD0D0D0) and the ceiling is smooth. No natural light gets in; there are no windows to the outside.
The team runs north, turning right when at the north then east wall. Three guards block the way; the closest two carry a grenade. The guards, upon turning the corner, remove the pin and throw the grenades straight across. Knuckles casts "stop" on the grenades when they stop moving. Two watches appear with the same effects, one for each grenade. A gray "1 stop" pops out of both. They're frozen in time and don't explode.
On the left, where the third guard is, a red "emergency" button is built into the wall. To the south past the guards is a large, empty room. Tyler is to the south (the eastern X) chained up on a steel platform lowering an inch per second two feet above a pool of molten aluminum 12 feet on a side.
Tyler is a 27-year-old Caucasian male 73 inches tall with an eastern European accent. He is 170 pounds with average muscle

mass (above average for his legs). He's generally dressed for desert travel. Tyler wears a light blue (FF4080FF), cotton, long-sleeve shirt, denim jeans of the standard blue color, leather sandals, standard-height, white (FFFFFFFF) cotton socks, and light-weight clothing. He has blonde, spiky hair two inches long.

Knuckles casts "possession blocker 82" on all three guards. Following that is "barrier89" with the effects played on all three, including the related popups.

Guard 3
(the south guard; confused) What happened? How did I get here?

Knuckles
An evil presence possessed you. I cast a spell on you to prevent that from happening and another for added resistance. Someone is in danger over there.

The guards turn around to see Tyler. When they do, Knuckles casts "fire shield 88" on Tyler; a gray "88 fire shield" pops out.

Knuckles
Fire shield spell, first line of defense. Do not enter that room!

Knuckles casts delete on the chains bounding Tyler. The platform suddenly falls taking Tyler with it. Teleport follows and Tyler appears with the team. The platform splashes in the pool of molten aluminum spraying it all over. Tyler is not affected by the aluminum during the teleport spell's effects.

Guard 4
Man are you fast! I never knew that guy was there!

Evil force
It's time to burn!

Knuckles casts teleport on all seven. The team, Tyler, and the three guards appear outside the gate.

Guard 3
(scared) That was scary sounding!

Knuckles
That's that evil force.

The building morphs into a gorilla-shaped ball of blue flame 30 feet wide, 20 feet back, and 50 feet tall in four seconds. Knuckles casts full scan on it, showing its stats.

Flameingo		Origin: Virgo supercluster, local group, Milky Way, Sol Earth, United States, Nevada
Level:	1	
HP:	738,424/ 738,424	Strengths: Hit points, spell power, magic defense, attack, defense, absorbs fire, vanish, fear, sleep, immobilized, poison, doomed, stone, fatal, electric, chemical, wind, gravity, strength
SP:	46,887/ 46,887	
Aura:		Weaknesses: Level, confusion, dizzy, water, intelligence, action rate, light, distraction, ice, charmed
Age:	1	

	1.7 ★		1.8 ★		1		1		1.7
	2 ★		1.3		1.5		1.8 ★		2 ★
	1.2		0.7		1.5		0.4		1.2
	2.6 ★		0.3		1		2.4 ★		2.6 ★
	2.7 ★		0.8		1.3 ★		1.2		1 ★
	1.1 ★		0.5		0.7		1.8 ★		2.1

Physical attack	5216	Magic attack	5278	Strength	162
Melee accuracy	108	Magic efficiency	60	Speed	11
Ranged accuracy	104	Magic accuracy	114	Hit points	738,424
Physical defense	3844	Magic defense	6686	Spell power	46,887
Physical evasion	9	Magic evasion	24	Level	1
Actions/second	2	Magic potency	418	Experience	3

Figure 6: Flameingo's stats (Scale: 1:3.75)

Knuckles
(shocked; confused) What the!?

Evil force
Meet Flameingo! Burn Knuckles to a crisp!

The evil force casts "flare18" on Knuckles. A flame 18 inches wide by 27 inches tall like that of a torch with a red (FFFF0000) outside and blue (FF0000FF) center, erupts violently remaining for three seconds then fades away. The intense heat turns the desert sand into glass. The scene jiggles up and down violently five times a second. A green "1.01417E10" pops out of Knuckles the moment the effects start.

Flameingo casts "fire" after this, taking 450 milliseconds. Knuckles casts "ultimate freeze" 200 milliseconds into this on Flameingo and goes first. A blue "530,664,773" pops out. Blue popups, indicating critical hits (hits that deal more damage than normal), behave the same way as red and gray popups.

Flameingo fades away in a half second after the spell's effects. Flameingo's cast doesn't take effect since it wasn't completed. The fence and shack remain, but the building is gone.

Evil force
(mad) You fool! Err I hate you!

Knuckles

That thing is gone now.

Guard 1

That thing really must be mad! It's so scary, let alone that monster! Good thing we have you around to fight them!

Guard 5

But (one-second pause) what about the building?

Knuckles

That's an easy fix.

Knuckles casts "recall". The building instantly reappears as if nothing happened.

Knuckles

Good thing for the teleport spell and status effects.

Guard 5

Thank you. Your services are always welcomed.

Knuckles

I'm not sensing anything for a while yet so I'd like to do some research on new clues I've obtained from encounters with that evil force. Your protective status effects, if the evil force doesn't remove them, will last for 67 minutes. Bye.

<u>All guards</u>
(all five guards at once) Bye!

Knuckles casts teleport. The team, including Tyler, appears at a beach in an open area near Australia's Great Barrier Reef. It is night and the near-full moon is blocked by the 7/8 broken (almost overcast) clouds of the altostratus and cirrocumulus types. Storm clouds, cumulonimbus, are visible far out over the ocean. A 15 mph wind blows over the brilliant blue water causing one-foot waves. A few beachgoers are around, some windsurfing, and others swimming. A few boats of all types, mostly as yachts but no commercial ships, are out at sea. A few law enforcement officers are scattered around patrolling the area.

<u>Knuckles</u>
What are you doing, Tyler?

<u>Tyler</u>
How did you know my name? Who are you three?

<u>Knuckles</u>
I'm world-renowned Knuckles, the spell-casting alien. I can sense anyone's name with ease.

<u>Tyler</u>
I was just trying to get to rocks in the desert for a report I was doing and all of a sudden, I was placed in that strange, hot area chained up. I don't know how it happened, but man that scary, evil-sounding voice really spooked me when I heard it, upon you arriving! What about you?

<u>Knuckles</u>
I'm after getting rid of that evil force, even though it's apparently very powerful.

<u>Tyler</u>
Where are you going though?

90

Knuckles

Right now, we're in northeastern Australia, the area where I'm sensing the next event. I'm going wherever my sense ability tells me danger lurks.

Tyler

(very excited) Woohoo! More travel, and more adventures! Yeehah! Can I join you?

Knuckles

If you don't mind seeing powerful monsters, sure. Of course, I can add many beneficial status effects to protect you as much as possible and if that fails, I've got spells to cure or revive anyone.

Tyler

All right, I'll join you.

Knuckles

I have some abilities I'd like to transfer to you that those two have.

Knuckles takes out five of those green marbles from his chest.

Knuckles

To get them, just touch these marbles and you'll get it. Don't worry, it's perfectly safe and the evil force can't get them due to special abilities I have. I'll remove my hand when the transfer is complete, but don't you do it or it'll mess things up.

Tyler

Okay.

The ability transfer effect occurs on Tyler, with 25 sparkles per square foot. Knuckles puts the marbles back when done.

Knuckles

The others already have glide available and could teach you. I have research I'd like to do with the many new clues I've got.

Knuckles casts "barrier89" on Ivan, Tu, and Tyler. A gray "0 defense up" and "0 magic shield" pop out of Ivan and Tu, but a red "no effect" pops out of Tyler. The zero is because the effect is present, but the duration is reset. The randomness of spells causes the duration to be less than what remains with Tyler.

Knuckles

Oh, oops, you already have the status effects. This significantly reduces physical and magical damage.

Ivan

I'd love to teach him what fun it is gliding around and reaching for space.

Race operator

(on the megaphone; in an Australian accent) The triathlon race will begin in two hours. Thank you.

Knuckles

And that's the same time the next sensed event will occur.... Well, one-dot-eight minutes earlier.

Ivan

Uh oh, not again!

Act 4: Monster Mayhem
Scene 10: Monster outbreak

May 28, 1999 at 8:58 PM UTC – 26 hours, 1 minute remaining

Ivan, Tu, and Tyler walk to the water. They speak with each other for 30 seconds. Tyler jumps 12 feet high and glides over the ocean. Ivan and Tu do the same two seconds later, only with 14-foot jumps. They remain in the water treading. A time lapse occurs where two hours pass in five seconds. As time goes on, the number of boats, jet skis, and beachgoers increases, the fastest at the end. Four seconds in, a police car with flashing lights is seen for 200 milliseconds 50 feet away. Knuckles assists taking someone away. The time is when the time lapse finishes.

<u>Knuckles narrator</u>
(when the humans walk to the water) With Tyler added and numerous clues available to scour over, I spent nearly two hours finding more clues with what I had. I was now certain that the jail escapee more than a day earlier escaped with the help of this evil force. The monster at the school, the quakes near Puerto Rico, the Master Lavalent encounter, and now the Master Laqualent encounter were all caused by the same thing. But strangely, the 1800 years into the future clue never fit into anything except, perhaps, the fact I can't see it, but sense it but that was only a wild guess. Between saving the elemental masters, of which I had no idea how to get to them in the first place, and figuring out how to get to that evil force, wherever it is, I was caught between a rock and a hard spot.

<u>Race operator</u>
(into the megaphone) The triathlon race will begin in two minutes. Please come to the stand for your briefing. Thank you.

Ivan
I want to join the race!

Knuckles
Unfortunately, you won't be able to. You're not of the athletic type and this is a practice race for the year 2000 Olympics, if they actually happen.

Ivan
(disappointed) Well, what about the gliding?

Knuckles
I have a strong feeling that they'll consider it under my influence, cheating; I'm banned from all races. I'm only banned because no human can approach my top running speed of 846 m-p-h, let alone just 40 m-p-h, and that's without speed pluses or the hasten spell, which puts this over 10,000. At that speed, I can run a 26-mile marathon in nine, or a hundred ten, seconds, instead of four hours.

Ivan
That is incredible! I didn't know you were that fast!

Tyler
You are amazing! What about car racing?

Knuckles
I'm too small to drive cars and I still can't.

Tyler
Oh, oh well.

Race operator
(into the megaphone) The race will begin in one minute. It begins with a three-kilometer run along the beach then a five-kilometer bike ride along the streets. At the end, you'll see a flag. Swim one kilometer out to a waiting ship. The first to arrive wins. The winner will receive a ten-thousand-dollar prize. Please get to your starting line.

Knuckles
I'm afraid that I'm going to have to postpone that race for five minutes.

Knuckles casts teleport and appears by the tall, male race operator on top of a wooden stand with a microphone on a small portable platform. Two speakers 16 inches tall, 9 inches wide, and 6 inches deep are on the sides of the platform in front and are aimed toward the 80 athletes nearby. The volume where the athletes are is 75 dB with the bass reduced some.

Knuckles
I'm Knuckles with a warning.

Race operator
Uh oh! What is it?

Knuckles
I'm sensing something similar to an earlier event I encountered and it's something only I can deal with. I ask that you postpone the race for a few minutes so I can deal with it.

Race operator
Okay, but what will happen and how long will the delay be?

Knuckles
I'm sensing a monster outbreak similar to that of what occurred at a school in Minot, North Dakota.

Race operator
A monster outbreak? That would be reasonable enough to postpone the race, but how long?

Knuckles
I don't know, but it shouldn't be more than ten minutes, five from what I'm sensing.

Athlete
(in a southern US accent) Hey Knuckles, why not get the police or military involved?

Knuckles

Apparently you haven't seen my recent CNN news warning. These monsters are extremely powerful and basic military weapons won't scratch them.

A lampalent bursts out of the ground. It looks exactly like the lavalent, only electricity as easily-seen, 1200-lumen-bright sparks.

Knuckles

It's starting!

Knuckles casts "megaflood6" on the monster. A red "972,437,250" pops out of it and the monster disappears. Everyone in the area becomes scared, some scream.

Knuckles

That's apparently the smaller of the electric-elemental ones but it's not over.

Evil force

You are a skilled caster, but try figuring this one out! Come out and fight!

Almost everyone screams in terror upon hearing the evil force. Five of the braver athletes watch while taking cover.

Bursting out of the ground are 153 monsters of various types. Lachalents are 20% opaque clear ice balls. Larockalents look like sandstone with distinct layers. Lachemalents are a 60% opaque green slime. The light blue (104080FF) lairalents are hard to see. Lalightalents are all white (FFFFFFFF). Gray (20808080) Lagravalents bend light around them without drawing anything in. All monsters are three feet in diameter. The 17 lavalents, 20 lachalents, 16 lampalents, 21 larockalents, 19 lachemalents, 22 lairalents, 17 lalightalents, and 21 lagravalents burst out of the ground everywhere at 70 mph no closer than a foot to anyone.

When the monsters appear, everyone, except the team, flee screaming. Knuckles casts "hypernova9" on the monsters. Time stops. The scene, except the monsters, fades completely to black in one second. A close-up scene of the star Eta Carinae fades in a second later. One second later, the star collapses, taking one second, and explodes as a hypernova. After two seconds, the monsters are enveloped in the explosion and the scene vibrates extremely violently. Three seconds into the exposure, the scene fades away in one second and the original scene returns in one second. When the main scene returns, time starts and the monsters fade away in one second.

A bunch of red, blue, and white numbers pop out of the monsters, one each. White numbers behave the same way as red, blue, and gray ones and indicate supercritical hits. They all pop out at the same time but have different values. The base value is from "893,586,774" to "987,648,540". The 113 red numbers use this range with equal probability for each value. The 39 blue ones have a range of "1.34038E09" to "3.95059E09" with the low end being more common. See appendix 6 for how the ranges are distributed. The white one is "3.3023E09".

Evil force

How dare you, defeating my friends! I'm getting the master of earth and you'd better stay away!

Knuckles

You can now resume your race.

Race operator

What was that scary voice?

Knuckles

That, unfortunately, I don't know, and it's causing mayhem. It's why I came to Earth in the first place.

Athlete

Thank you for defending us.

Knuckles

Another outbreak may occur but I'm not sensing anything major here before the main event.

All master monsters also have selective speech and, while in Knuckles' chest, they can only speak to Knuckles.

Master Laqualent
(only to Knuckles) The Master Larockalent is in a forest in India near the Ganges River.

Knuckles
(to the Master Laqualent) I'm on it. (normal) I'll need to go to India apparently.

Race operator
Okay, bye. Take it safe!

Scene 11: A large sphere of rock

May 28, 1999 at 9:10 PM UTC – 25 hours, 49 minutes remaining

Knuckles casts teleport. The team appears in a jungle 40 feet from a calm area of the Ganges River at night. There is a light rainstorm and, at the tree tops, a 20 mph wind, gusting to 30.

Knuckles narrator
That event was surprisingly brief and the race did go on as planned, though the athletes, frightened, didn't perform as well as they would've done. I was in need of getting to the earth elemental master.

Master Laqualent
That looks like the spot.

Knuckles
I can sense rumbles.

Master Laqualent
Oh, that means you're about to enter an elemental master's world from someone else entering earlier.

Rumbling becomes audible. The team walks to the river. Knuckles takes out the platform from his chest; it instantly appears then Knuckles drops it into the river causing a big splash.

With three present, I need to modify this platform,
and re-add the status effects.

Knuckles casts "edit". The platform is resized to a ten-foot square. The seats, now cushioned and fancier, are arranged like a baseball diamond but are still a foot from the edges. Knuckles takes the north seat, Ivan takes the west, Tu takes the east, and Tyler takes the south. The platform is otherwise unchanged.

Knuckles casts "barrier89" on the platform and a gray "89 defense up" and "89 magic shield" pop out. "Levitate74" follows and a gray "74 levitating" pops out.

The rumbles become visible.

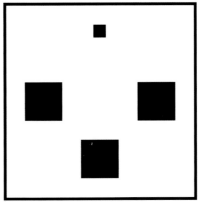

Map 4: Platform layout after modification (Scale: 1:60)

Knuckles
Quick, get on the platform.

The team gets seated on the platform. The platform rises, stopping at 5000 feet. Three seconds into this, the ground cracks apart then caves in ten seconds later. The rainstorm fades away in one second a second before caving in. An endless canyon-like area extending infinitely in all directions with infinite visibility replaces the ground. There are large, steep hills, cliffs, and valleys two to five miles deep. High, iceless mountains are barely visible (small) due to being 40 miles away. No water is in sight.

Knuckles

(before the ground caves in) I wonder what the earth master's realm looks like. Rocks I would suppose. (after the ground caves in) Canyons, large, vast ones at that. So, now what?

The Master Larockalent bursts through the rocks below going up at 400 mph. It looks exactly like the larockalent, only, like the other elemental masters, 30 feet in diameter instead.

Evil force

Why, if it isn't the master of earth! You'll see an orchid-colored spell-casting dweebo above you. Defeat him and you'll live, if not, you'll die.

Master Larockalent

Who are you?

Evil force

I'm your new master.

Knuckles

(to self; confused) New master?

Master Larockalent

(with Knuckles) I don't need a master.

The Master Larockalent appears in front of Knuckles.

Master Larockalent

They are good, not evil!

Evil force

What did I just tell you? Defeat that orchid-colored thing and you'll live. Do it now!

Knuckles casts "barrier89" then "possession blocker 82" on the Master Larockalent, both with the same popups as before.

Knuckles

That'll help protect you.

A green "focus", "defense up", "magic shield", and "blocking possession" appear out of the Master Larockalent a half second later. The moment this appears, the monster disappears. The popups are still present.

Master Larockalent

What the!? Where am I?

Knuckles

I put you in my chest before that evil force can possess you. You're completely safe in there.

Evil force

So that's your trick! Status effects and protection in your chest eh? (two-second pause) Why you dirty little thing! Blocking me out huh? Why don't you visit Atlantis some time, especially my house?

Knuckles

I will. You're such a wimp!

The evil force casts "hypernova60" on Knuckles. A red "0" pops out. It casts "stop52" on him a quarter second after the scenery fades back. A red "immune" pops out. It casts "sleep56" and a red "missed!" pops out of Knuckles instead of spell effects.

The evil force tries again. A black sphere with dim, 20-lumen stars at the top ten inches in diameter fades in in a half second surrounding Knuckles. Blue (FF0000C0) sparkles fall from the stars like a snow globe for two seconds. The objects fade away in one second. A red "immune" pops out when the effects start.

The evil force casts "enrage48". A red (FFFF0000) sphere 60 inches in diameter fades in in a quarter second collapsing to 27 inches in a quarter second. Red beams strike Knuckles from the sphere while the sphere vibrates to up to eight inches in diameter and returns, doing this 12 times in two seconds. The beams stop and the sphere fades away in a half second. Another red "immune" pops out of Knuckles when the effects start.

Evil force

What are you not immune to?

102

Knuckles
You're just wasting spell power. You also don't seem to know how to hit either.

Evil force
(mad) Grr. I hate you. I'll find something for you, a nice treat.

Knuckles
I don't eat. (half-second pause) Oh, he left.

Master Larockalent
Thank goodness. I've underestimated you.

Knuckles
I'm immune to all negative and neutral status effects and if you're in my chest, you'll be as well. So, how about returning the ground to normal?

Master Larockalent
I was wondering why I wasn't getting hit by those I'm not immune to, stop for example. As to the ground, (hollering) Larockalent land to normal!

The ground returns to normal and the rainstorm returns, although the team is in the clouds.

Knuckles
I've noticed a pattern with how to get the ground back. It's elemental-master's name (one-second pause), land to normal.

Master Larockalent
You are correct on that. Go to the top of Mount Everest as that's where the Master Lavalent told me to tell you to go for two more.

Knuckles
The Master Lavalent told you?

Master Larockalent
What's odd is that he is coming into our elemental worlds to tell us when he knows that it's dangerous.

Knuckles
So the Master Lavalent did revive! Good! I defeated him not knowing that that evil force was behind it. I was worried about that when I encountered the Master Laqualent.

Scene 12: Everest double trouble

May 28, 1999 at 9:20 PM UTC – 25 hours, 39 minutes remaining

Knuckles narrator
Two down, eight to go! That evil force was starting to get very mad and seemed very desperate. Why he was after the elemental masters was still a mystery. I had two more elemental masters on the way with a nasty surprise thrown in.

Master Laqualent
You'd better hurry!

Knuckles
Alright, I will!

Knuckles casts teleport. The team appears a mile from the peak 3000 feet below. Altostratus clouds below obscure the view. A fluffy, dark gray cloud (FF303030) 1000 feet in diameter is above the peak. It randomly changes shape keeping the same volume. The widths vary from 800 to 1250 feet.

Knuckles
That's odd! I targeted the peak, not this spot.

Evil force
Ha ha! You fell for my trap! I placed a teleport barrier here!

The platform moves straight to the peak, stopping above it.

Master Laqualent
The teleport barrier part is true, but the two masters are still here.

Knuckles
(to the Master Laqualent) Two? This'll be fun.

Ivan
That's a strange-looking cloud there over the peak.

Knuckles
Don't worry. It's just very dense water with lots of dust, though it is odd in terms of location and looks.

When above the peak, the ground cracks apart.

Knuckles
Here we go with round three, well, four.

Ten seconds after the ground cracks apart, it caves in with the highest parts first becoming endless sky without clouds. A 20 mph wind increases constantly to 700 mph after five seconds. The Master Lairalent, which looks like the smaller version but 30 feet in diameter and more opaque, is visible upon the ground caving in, which fades away in a half second upon caving in.

Knuckles casts "wind barrier 81" on Ivan, Tu, Tyler, and the platform, but not on himself. A gray "81 blocking wind" pops out. The effects of the wind vanish.

The Master Lairalent rises at 400 mph. When it reaches the platform's height, going 50 mph at that moment, Knuckles casts "possession blocker 82" on the Master Lairalent with the same effects and popup as before. The Master Lairalent disappears.

Master Lairalent
Thank you Knuckles. I knew I could trust you.

Evil force
Oh, so you're brave enough to go into my anti-teleportation barrier, huh?

The evil force casts "energy barrier 52" on Knuckles. A thin, red (10FF0000) sphere ten inches in diameter surrounds Knuckles. It fades in in a half second, fades away in one second, and remains for two seconds. A red "immune" pops out.

Knuckles
Go ahead, waste all the spell power you want!

Evil force
(one-second pause) Wanna play a game?

Knuckles
It's a near-certainty that I'll win, but, whatever.

Evil force
Being sneaky again eh? Okay, I dare to you to use your ultimara6 spell on me. Go ahead!

Knuckles
I will when I see you, and then some! He's gone now so, (hollering) lairalent land to normal!

The ground returns to normal but already cracking apart.

Master Lairalent
How did you guess that phrase?

Knuckles
Patterns from the other masters.

The ground caves in. An endless sheet of clear ice resembling Jupiter's Europa replaces it. Crevices are visible at the surface, from 3 to 1500 feet deep and 0.1 to 300 feet wide. The Master Lachalent rises at 400 mph through the ice bursting through.

Ivan
Brr! It's cold!

Knuckles casts "ice shield 87" on Ivan, Tu, Tyler, and the platform. The effects are the same as that of "fire shield" except that the sphere looks like clear ice instead. A gray "87 ice shield" pops out at the same time the spell's effects start.

Ivan

Thank you.

Tyler

What's with all these huge elemental monsters?

Knuckles

Ask you know who.

The Master Lachalent appears.

Evil force

Turn them into ice cubes, now!

Knuckles casts "possession blocker 82" on the Master Lachalent with the expected popup.

Evil force

Not again!

A green "blocking possession" pops out of the Master Lachalent and Knuckles immediately recasts the "possession blocker 82" spell. The Master Lachalent disappears 100 milliseconds later.

Knuckles

Removing that status effect isn't going to help you. You cast far too slowly!

Evil force

Fine, if you want it that way, you'll meet me in Amazonia. Bye!

Knuckles

Amazonia? (two-second pause) Something about that name doesn't make sense. There's nothing.... Oh, yeah, obviously I won't find it in the elemental worlds. (hollering) Lachalent land to normal!

The ground returns to normal and the dark gray cloud above the mountain is no longer present, as if it didn't exist.

Knuckles

Now, let's try again. (two-second pause) Still nothing? Something about the name "Amazonia" isn't making sense. Nothing with my sensing checks out with anything around. (one-second pause) Even that house on that continent doesn't check out. I'm in need of a time out to figure out the clues I have. It's just one emergency after another!

Knuckles casts teleport but nothing happens.

Knuckles

Oh, yeah, the teleport barrier.

Knuckles casts, in order, "barrier removal", "barrier removal 76", "cancel teleport barrier 72", then "cancel teleport blocker 70". These spells have no effects. Knuckles speaks after casting.

Knuckles

(on the first cast) Spell failed. That I haven't gotten in centuries! This must be one tough barrier then. Oh, yeah. (on the second cast) Still nothing, even with level 76? (on the third cast) No effect? There's something strange about this teleport barrier. Maybe it's a teleport blocker? (on the fourth cast) That seemed to have worked and the ability leveled up too!

Knuckles casts teleport and appears inside his dark house. He casts "lighten" in the center of the ceiling. This lightens the house in the same way as before. Tyler looks around.

Knuckles

Good, got rid of it.

Master Larockalent

You're smart with spells and a level up is a nice treat. What level is it at now?

Knuckles

It's at level sixty-nine-sixty-two. I rarely use it.

Tyler

Two beds? What about me and you?

Knuckles

I'll just add another. I don't need sleep; I'm
immune to it.

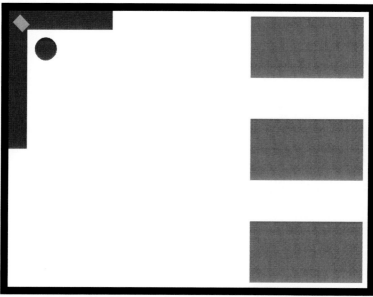

Map 5: Knuckles' house after the new changes (Scale: 1:75)

Knuckles casts edit. The house resizes to 24x18 feet. A third
bed with a brown (FF804020) quilt and a photo of the Grand
Canyon's banded rocks is added in the southeast corner and the
beds are spaced more apart. Everything else is unchanged.

Knuckles

You get that one (points to the southeast corner). I
made it of your favorite design.

Act 5: Flashback
Scene 13: Studying the clues

May 28, 1999 at 9:28 PM UTC – 25 hours, 31 minutes remaining

The humans run to their beds and lie down. Knuckles hops onto his stool and draws a waveform for the main event. Its shape, except amplitude being scaled to 29.9 dB, is unchanged.

<u>Knuckles narrator</u>
Four down, six to go, but a day-long break finally came. I could finally begin studying the clues from recent events in great detail. However, just as I was getting started, I sensed something that I urgently had to report. Atlantis was unsafe due to monsters and I had to warn everyone about it.

<u>Knuckles</u>
I'll be studying the various clues I have.

<u>Tyler</u>
Could I help?

<u>Knuckles</u>
There really isn't much you humans can do as your abilities are far, far below mine. You can, however, suggest ideas as this is something completely new to me. Normally, I'd have Speed, my friend, at it, but he needs to watch over Korona.

<u>Tyler</u>
Okay, suggestions still count.

<u>Ivan</u>
What clues do you have?

<u>Knuckles</u>
I have a few direct clues, thanks to sensing and direct experience. The evil force appears to be involved with trying to get the ten masters of the

110

elements. The evil force, from sensing, has a direct relationship to that of the main event. The house on Atlantis is the focus of the main event. (one-second pause) Yikes! I need to warn the public!

Knuckles casts teleport and the team appears inside the CNN news room. Several cameras are focused on the news desk with Jimmy Wilson behind them speaking with the manager.

Jimmy Wilson

Hey, it's Knuckles! It must be important!

Knuckles

I need to warn everyone about the newly risen piece of land as it's very dangerous to be on or even near it, due to monsters and traps.

CNN Manager

More monsters? Isn't doomsday nearby? You're on in five seconds.

Knuckles runs to and jumps on the counter between the two reporters behind the desk. The TV, like at the airport in Puerto Rico earlier, shows "Knuckles news update".

Knuckles

(the moment the TV shows Knuckles; with emphasis) I have an urgent warning! (normal) With the earlier earthquakes in Puerto Rico, a new Texas-sized floating island rose out of the ocean. (with great emphasis) Do not approach that island! (normal) There are several very powerful monsters moving around it. (with emphasis) These monsters can destroy anything with ease and are very fast.

Knuckles moves to the left of the TV screen and casts "mind thoughts to visual". The lavalent's stats show in the window with the speed stat highlighted in the same way as before.

Knuckles

These monsters move at up to 179 meters per second, or 400 miles per hour. If any airplanes, ships, or otherwise are within 100 miles from the island, (with emphasis) redirect them around it!

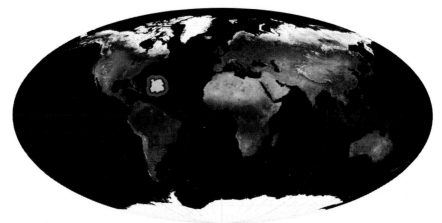

Map 6: World map with Atlantis warning area (Scale: ≈1:350,319,073)

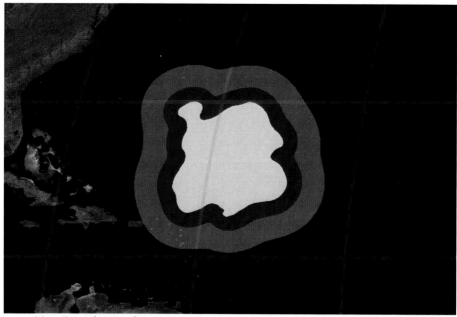

Map 7: Atlantis close-up with warning areas (Scale: ≈1:43,789,884)

An ellipse-shaped true-color map of the world shows in the window with the outside of it fully transparent. These images explain a lot. A red (50FF0000) zone extends 100 miles from Atlantis and a yellow (50FFFF00) zone 150 miles further out. Gray (30808080; 60808080 for multiples of 90°) lines of latitude and longitude are marked, spaced every 15°.

After five seconds, the map zooms in showing a close-up of Atlantis and the warning zones.

Knuckles

I've marked on this map where the three zones are. On Atlantis and within 100 miles of it, the red zone is the danger zone. (with emphasis) Do not go into this area! (normal) The yellow zone, 250 miles out, is a caution zone. It is generally safe outside the yellow zone but this evil force I've been fighting could strike anywhere at any time. Both the public and the military must avoid the red zone and likely the yellow zone areas at any cost. The monsters seem to be limited to 120,000-foot elevations so any satellites or high-flying airplanes that can get to 150,000 feet high or higher are safe, even if directly over the floating continent. This is all I need to say.

The window disappears and Knuckles runs to where the team waits, near Jimmy Wilson and the manager. A second later, CNN does a sports report on the race in Australia mentioning of the monster outbreak and that Knuckles came to the rescue.

CNN Manager

Thank you for the warning.

Knuckles

No problem. While studying clues, I sensed danger at Atlantis and knew I needed to warn everyone.

CNN Manager

Whenever I see you coming in here like that, I know you have something very important.

                              Knuckles
I gotta go though. Bye!

                            CNN Manager
Thanks, bye!

    Knuckles casts teleport. The team appears back in Knuckles'
house, still lit from the spell. The humans return to their beds.

                              Knuckles
Let's recap the clues. The evil force is involved with
getting the elemental masters to do stuff for him
and it is directly related to the main event. The
house on Atlantis is involved with the main event. I
also cannot see him, although I can sense his
presence, appearing as a black dot on my radar.

                               Ivan
What does this evil force intend on doing with these
master monsters?

                              Knuckles
That I don't know. He seems to want them to get
rid of me as I'm preventing him from apparently
accomplishing something that he needs.

                               Tyler
What other clues do you have?

                              Knuckles
The not-so-trustworthy ones, those he said, involve
him being eighteen hundred years in the future,
Amazonia, and his house being on Atlantis.

                                Tu
If your supposed main event is a day away, then
how is he eighteen hundred years in the future?

                              Knuckles
That bothers me too. Though there is the vanish
spell and status effect, which can hinder things, I
just don't know what to make of that. Vanish

114

makes you invisible, but still vulnerable, outside sensing. Eighteen hundred years from now would be the year thirty-seven ninety-nine. Rounding has likely been done so there's likely a 50-year span.

Tyler
What about that Amazonia thing?

Knuckles
That also doesn't check out. While I've found a few potential targets that may relate to Amazonia or the Amazon area in general, no upcoming events even hint at a relationship between the evil force or the main event, and anything with Amazonia.

Tyler
Hmm. Have you checked phone books, atlases, or other references?

Knuckles
I've sensed that and nothing checks out.

Tu
What about the house on that newly risen continent? Why did it rise?

Knuckles
That I find suspicious, but the house is vacant. I have no idea why that continent appeared, but I know the evil force caused it.

Tu
What is inside of that house?

Knuckles
It appears to be some sort of maze riddled with very well-hidden traps from what I'm sensing.

Tyler
Here's a question. If the main event is to occur in about a day, and if the evil force really was eighteen hundred years into the future, then, how are you supposed to get that far into the future?

Knuckles
Time travel is done with the "time warp" spell.

Ivan
Cool! You can time travel!? I never knew that!

Knuckles
What I'm getting with sensing and the clues I have aren't adding up properly. For some odd reason, I can't sense anything beyond that of the main event. I'm unable to sense any millennium celebrations and festivals, the technological improvements, or anything else. That I find rather strange though.

Ivan
Can't sense beyond the main event... is that a clue?

Knuckles
I wouldn't know, but I would think it may belong in the bin of clues. I'm not sensing anything major for almost a full day now. I can sense the occasional earthquake, crime, and traffic collision, but the next major event is just under 24 hours away.

Ivan
What is that next event a day away?

Knuckles
It seems to be something very related to the other elemental master encounters. I can't tell which ones though, though I can sense where they are.

Tu
I just thought of something. Suppose that he's eighteen hundred years into the future. Wouldn't Amazonia, then be his home, in our future? Then, what about the house on Atlantis?

Knuckles
Good idea, but I can't sense for that.

Tyler
So, what now?

Knuckles
I apparently need more information, probably checking out that house on Atlantis would be the best bet, but I'm not sensing anything there that would hint at being a clue.

Tyler
Well, someone will think of something.

Scene 14: Knuckles' long history

May 28, 1999 at 9:46 PM UTC – 25 hours, 13 minutes remaining

Knuckles jumps onto the stool and draws another waveform of the main event. The humans lay on their backs in bed.

Knuckles narrator
With only a few bits of progress in studying the clues, I was about to return to working on studying sense waveforms for more clues and combining the several that I had with this. It was like putting a ten-thousand-piece jigsaw puzzle together with half the pieces missing fitting closely together. I got sidetracked, however, by Ivan's curiosity.

Ivan
(two-second pause) Ya know, I've been wondering. How did you get so powerful? Why are you able to cast spells? What happened when you first came to Earth? Ya know, what is your history?

Knuckles
I was born on June 13, 1684, but not on Earth. I was born on a planet called "Korona" in an area called "Ramusi" in a state called "Uametik".

"Korona" is pronounced as "corona", the Sun's atmosphere seen during a solar eclipse. "Ramusi" is pronounced as "RAM oo see" and "Uametik" is pronounced as "YOU Am eh Tick".

Ivan

What is Korona like? How does it compare to Earth?

Knuckles

Korona, to astronomers, orbits an F8 star twenty-six hundred light-years from Earth called "Criscoma". It's about a hundred nine million miles from its star, a bit closer to the star based on light received.

"Criscoma" is pronounced "Chris CO muh".

Ivan

What is an F8 star? What is the Sun?

Knuckles

Sol, Earth's star, is a G2 star. F8 is four "notches" higher on the scale. F8 is a little hotter and brighter than the Sun with a somewhat shorter lifespan, but very close. Due to being brighter, Korona needs to be further from its star to receive equal lighting, and thus energy, than that of Earth, but Korona gets slightly more light. Its orbit is also a bit more elliptical as well and there's a smaller axial tilt.

Ivan

What is life like on Korona?

Knuckles

It's the same as Earth in many ways, though it has more water coverage, 85%, and is a little smaller and less dense than Earth. From space, they look about the same, only no ice caps, more forests, and significantly less pollution than Earth since we don't cut down trees or be careless. While some spells wreak havoc, other spells undo and/or restore this.

We live like animals do on Earth, but without hunting or gathering. Spells take this role.

Ivan
Where did you learn how to cast spells? How do they work?

Knuckles
Spells were around well before I was born. Spells work by using a special form of energy, lots of it. Have you heard of hauntings? The same energy ghosts use is also what I use. It's not necessarily matter turning into energy, knowing Einstein's formula, though this does play a role. Spells use one form of what scientists call "dark energy". Weak spells like low levels of the fire or blaster series use very little energy, but extreme spells at high spell levels like plasma ball or hypernova, use a tremendous amount. Ultimara6 is the most extreme of all, though create, edit, and delete can be if used to change or form a lot of matter.

Ivan
But, how do they work?

Knuckles
Spells involve shockwaves. In school, you learned about constructive interference where two sounds meeting crest to crest amplify each other. Spells use the same thing. By themselves, they don't do much, but when they combine, the effects are very extreme. The frequencies control the spell itself, such as fire, flare, or ultimara, and the amplitude controls the intensity, the spell level. Spells modify matter – the first law of thermodynamics doesn't allow for creating matter. Fire is the basic spell while flare is the upgrade followed by fire storm and plasma ball. I don't know what lies beyond plasma ball though, if anything. Upgrading the series improves efficiency and attacking power.

Ivan

That's interesting! What happened while you were on Korona? What's this war you keep mentioning?

Knuckles

For several years after I was born, all was peaceful. By Earth year 1724, The Great War occurred due to a dispute between territories after a supervolcanic eruption. The war lasted 253 Earth years. After 7 years into the war, peace talks finally began making progress. After the 8th year into the war came, the peace agreements were nearly finished, but then, disaster. A group of powerful invaders from a nearby star came and raged war. This caused The Great War to last for well over 200 years. Speed, at first, was involved with most of the fighting, but the invaders just kept on coming. Since I was very skilled with battle, spell-casting, and abilities in general, though not statistically skilled, Speed saw me as his magic-based sidekick. I was on level 542 at the time this happened, if I recall. Speed was just over ten thousand at the time, far, far above me. He transferred a few abilities to me and I got involved with many more battles. I focused heavily toward support and resistance rather than being on the offensive side. Within just a day after getting the abilities transferred, I passed the one-thousand mark for the level and continued to battle ever more powerful enemies. Speed and I were both going crazy with defending our only home planet. Days turned into months. I began learning the "ultimara" spell, taking a week to learn it. I also began learning the slot-expensive "max defense" ability. Months turned into years. Six years into battle, I passed the eight thousand mark for the level, and, with so much experience needed for a level up, I was slowing down. Years turned into decades. 89 years after the invasion, I finally learned the "max defense" ability which made me immune to everything so Speed or the natives didn't have to keep reviving me. Decades turned into centuries. After a long 245 Earth years since the invasion, all of the invaders were defeated and no more came. I was finally relieved of battle. I was at the level I'm currently at at the time. Speed only gained 900 levels. Then, having obtained such a massive level for numerous abilities, I was aware of many things going on I never knew about. I sensed something strange going on around another very distant star I later knew was the Sun, Sol. Wanting to gain more levels, I figured I'd attempt to look into that. I got Speed to take me there.

Ivan
Man! That is one long war you had. Alien invasion.... Could I get powerful like you?

Knuckles
With what you humans basically do, you won't live long enough to get to even level 500, let alone into the thousands. It can happen though. Four-thirty-eight is the highest I've seen so far.

Ivan
I forgot to ask you something. What is the difference between standard level and spell level?

Knuckles
Spells have a standard level as well; it determines the max spell level. The max spell level increases every 100 standard levels. Each higher spell level uses 30% more spell power, a 28% higher magic potency, but do 25% more damage or cure. Fire60 is 70,000 times as powerful as fire10. Upgrades raise this several notches. Flare10 is twice as powerful and efficient as fire10, but takes three times longer to cast. Not all spells, like ultimara,

use this system. Ultimara6 is available when the spell's standard level is level 8001. Speed has 8.

Ivan
What is magic potency?

Knuckles
Magic potential. It affects both the speed of charging for casting spells and the success rate.

Tyler
Question. Why can't we see those popup numbers?

Knuckles
It's an ability called "view damage", very useful if you're into battles. Red, blue, and white numbers are for H-P damage, green for restoration, gray for status effect addition or intensification, and gold and black for the gain and loss of spell power.

Ivan
What were things like when you first came to Earth?

Knuckles
When I first came to Earth, on my 312th birthday of all things, I landed in what I now know were wheat fields in southern Kansas. There was an empty two-laned roadway nearby, a county road. At first, I checked my radar, of which I always did when entering new areas, just in case I needed to fight.

Tu
Question. What is this radar? How does it work?

Knuckles
I detect auras, energy stored within living things, and I can tell, with extreme precision, if they are good or evil by the color of their dot. A yellow dot means neutral, one neither good nor evil. A fade from yellow to red then to black is more evil. The evil force is practically the darkest black. From yellow fading to green then white is more good.

The scale is logarithmic. That is, it's sensitive in the middle but not at the edges. Most humans are a third to two-thirds of the way to green from yellow. Hardcore criminals get into the reds.

Tyler
What happened when you first saw some Earthling?

Knuckles
The first Earthling I saw, assuming you're referring to humans, was that of a car coming at me at 65 m-p-h. It was a yellow-green dot; I didn't think much about it. I soon saw it and the driver freaked out.

Ivan
Why do military guards and TV stations allow you to get into these areas or break into their broadcasts?

Knuckles
For the military, this occurred after the car event. I began to glide around closely watching my radar and soon came across a fairly large city, Omaha, Nebraska. I got a ticket for jaywalking. At first, the policeman had a hard time communicating with me so I began to sense to figure out how to speak with humans, taking ten seconds. I finally answered and mentioned that I wasn't from this planet. The cop didn't believe it; I took about a minute to convince him. I was taken to the police station and the military got involved at that point. They were about to take me to a secret area that I cannot mention to you due to my contracts with them. They tried to tranquilize me and otherwise knock me out, but couldn't due to my maxed defense and immunity to sleep. Blindfolds were useless as I could sense my surroundings and still see through the inch-thick fuzzy cloth very well. I mentioned that I could sense their top secret info and they got wild about that. They told me that I was not supposed to. I told them that there was no way they could block it

as they're too weak. Level one-eighty humans versus myself at over nine thousand is an obvious unfair match. I was forced to sign a contract about the top secret info and other military secrets, which applied to that of the world, but I had a problem – I couldn't read. I sensed for five seconds to learn how to read. The signature was made with the edit spell, since I could not write either. Keep in mind that I process things at four million times faster than humans can. I cast teleport to return to where I was but news reports came in mentioning of an alien visitor and that life outside the Solar System does indeed exist. I saw a photo of me on what I thought were terrible-looking TV's.

Ivan

Why did you think they were terrible-looking?

Knuckles

When you can see in the 200-nanometer range, half-millimeter pixels are gigantic. I see at 500,000 frames per second so the flashing is easy to see. It's a consequence of learning related abilities and being at such a high level.

Ivan

You mentioned of spells taking nanoseconds to cast. How do know how long they take?

Knuckles

My stats and patterns with spells. It takes thirteen-dot-one percent longer to cast a spell a spell level higher. Fire70 takes 5000 times longer to cast than fire. My "actions per second" stat and the "fast cast" ability limit the maximum possible. Four nanoseconds is the fastest possible given this.

Tu

What is your IQ? Did you ever go to school?

Knuckles

Korona doesn't have schools. From sensing books on Earth, I was able to more than max out every IQ test known. Without spells and time-altering status effects, I'm too fast even for high-speed cameras, since they can't approach 13 million frames per second, let alone get that many actions per second. I could add more plus abilities to boost that further.

Ivan

How did you get money, like you had at that party?

Knuckles

I studied how the economy system works on Earth, which is slightly different from Korona's. Since laws forbid duplicating money, creating and duplicating items was the next best method. My first sale was a ruby-lined desk that I sold for fifty dollars when it would've gone for a half million. It took two weeks to sell it, but upon seeing the quality and complete lack of defective items, my items sold at an extreme rate. Since the create and duplicate spells take a lot of spell power, I stopped after a month, already a multi-millionaire in every country. I'm still trying to recover the spell power used from that! Freelance police and military jobs provided extra, as you saw at the race earlier, taking care of the riot.

Tyler

How come you're so well-known on TV? What got CNN into breaking into their normal broadcasting at any time for you to make comments?

Knuckles

To news agencies, I was the first known alien and they had constant attention on me. I soon began to warn others about impending disasters and with my 100% success rate, all news agencies found me a very dependable source. A level 9000 sense ability helps significantly with that. I warn of earthquakes, volcanic eruptions, solar flares, and many other hazards. I keep the notices as short as possible though the more important details I have for the event, the longer I may go. The "mind thoughts to visual" spell is very handy for them.

Ivan

So, (two-second pause) what are we going to do?

Knuckles

With nothing happening for nearly 23 hours, there's not much to do. I intend to study sense waveforms in detail to see if I can pick out more clues.

Ivan

How do you sense things, especially the future?

Knuckles

I use both auras and dark energy. I also have an ability called "time manipulation" where I can sense things past, present, and future and bring them into the present. My brain processes the information I get. Future things are prone to change. The amplitude on the main event, for example, is ever-so-slightly getting higher in amplitude.

Ivan

You sure have an interesting past and set of skills!

Tyler

I agree.

Act 6: Answers revealed
Scene 15: A sense-proof barrier

May 29, 1999 at 9:17 PM UTC – 1 hour, 42 minutes remaining

A minute-long time lapse occurs where each second is 24 minutes. Knuckles remains inside his house at all times. The humans eat for a half second in bed then play Parcheesi and Uno on a table appearing in the house's center. Three small, fancy, cushioned, yellow (FFF0D020) chairs are around the table 120° apart. Ivan takes the northwest chair, Tu the east, and Tyler the southwest. The two-feet-in-diameter table has a fancy frosted glass top. Parcheesi lasts for three seconds. Uno lasts five seconds where Tyler is once seen with almost 20 cards.

The humans read a book for 1.5 seconds and go to sleep. The light dims to 25 lumens, moving to the northwest corner and remains for 22 seconds. It returns to the center position and brightens to the original 1200 lumens. Breakfast is served, taking a half second, then the humans play Yahtzee for two seconds.

Tyler plays a pinball game until lunch in the north center area using a pinball machine involving a cross-country driving theme. Ivan and Tu play checkers for one second and four chess games for three. They watch TV for six seconds then eat lunch for a half second. Tyler returns to his pinball game for four seconds. His last game takes two seconds where he gets an extreme score.

Ivan and Tu read their books for two seconds. They build a clone of the Eiffel Tower eight feet tall in seven seconds using the table as a stepping stool and small Legos only of the rectangular type. Odd sizes like 3x1 or 5x2 are used. When Tyler finishes his big game, scoring 17 billion points, he helps build. They watch three movies in 4.5 seconds, the second in grayscale (an old movie). Another game of Uno uses up the last 1.5 seconds.

Throughout this, Knuckles draws a main-event waveform once every two seconds and doesn't move from his spot. They reach 31.8 dB for the amplitude slowly increasing linearly (by the number) and the scale extends to 35 at the edge of the page at the start. The time is based on that at the end of the time lapse.

Knuckles narrator

(during the time lapse) With my lengthy, battle-prone history now known to them, they ate and began to have almost a full day's worth of fun. If they wanted something, I just used the create spell to get it. Because of my abilities, particularly sensing, I didn't join them nor help them outside simply creating the materials. When they didn't need anything, I was studying sense waveforms in intense detail using the numerous clues that I had. I didn't really get far, but all I knew was that that house on Atlantis needed a closer inspection as strange energies were coming from it and soon a very strong relationship between it and the main event. I was still stumped about the Amazonia and eighteen hundred years parts though. After nearly a whole day went by, something caught my attention. I struggled to figure out what it was, as, for some strange reason, I couldn't sense beyond it. I thought it was another prank by the evil force.

Ivan

Draw two, Tu.

Tu

You just had to do that, didn't you?

Knuckles

(to self) That's strange! All of a sudden, I'm not able to sense past where Brazil is. (one-second pause) There seems to be some dome-shaped boundary around it, a huge dome-shaped boundary.

Tyler plays a wild card and has a green four left in his hand.

Tyler

Green! Uno!

Tu

Uh oh! Quick, change the color!

Knuckles
(to self) I can sense a position just a millimeter from it just fine, but for some reason, a millimeter closer or 300 miles behind and I can't!

Tyler lays his green four on the green seven.

Tyler
I win!

Ivan and Tu lay down their extra cards. Ivan has a red three and a blue two, and Tu has a green five and one, a yellow zero, and a blue skip. Tyler begins working out the math for scoring.

Ivan
Rats! Five points though.

Tu
What, no fours? I have 26 points.

Tyler
The score is now three-twenty-six for me, two-ninety-four for Ivan and three-seventy-seven for Tu. This is a pretty close game.

Tyler shuffles the cards, splitting the stack in half, and takes 30 seconds. Afterwards, he deals seven cards out and lays down a red four as the starting card.

Knuckles
(to self) Either there's a sensing barrier there, or something has gone haywire with my sensing. It's not the latter case so it's got to be a sensing barrier, but why only that area? I can sense an area in San Francisco and Tokyo just fine, but not that area in Brazil. What spell was that for removing sensing barriers? I think that the evil force is behind it.

Knuckles casts "cancel sense blocker 64" twice followed by "fire", "cancel sense barrier 66", and "full normalize" in this order, each a half second apart. The spell effects cannot be seen.

Knuckles
Oh boy, here we go with this again.

Ivan
Now what?

Knuckles
A sensing barrier around a certain spot. Spells are not removing it and I even cast a fire spell there to make sure I'm targeting the right area.

Tyler
First a teleport barrier, now a sensing barrier? I think that evil force is back again!

Knuckles
Yeah, it's about that time, though there's still 15 minutes which makes it even stranger. Then again, if there is a sense barrier or sense blocker, I may have missed the other elemental masters as well. That sense barrier just appeared out of nowhere though. I find that strange.

Ivan
I would say that that would raise some warning signs. Should we investigate?

Knuckles
Yeah, I think we should.

Knuckles casts teleport and the team appears in a rainforest in an isolated area quite far from the Amazon River.

Knuckles
Oh sure, a teleport barrier around it as well. Well, since it worked before....

Knuckles casts "cancel teleport blocker 70".

Knuckles
That didn't work? Something is odd here.

A dome-shaped object fades in within two seconds. It glitters in the light with ten specs, of all hues, per cubic inch going three inches into it. The glitter does not fade away but does move around randomly as if it was in a liquid at a half inch per second on average, 1.5 inches per second at the fastest. The dome, 180 miles in diameter and 20 miles high, is so big that the glitter appears like a flat wall. The trees behind it are not affected.

Ivan
(one-second pause) Pretty!

Ivan attempts to walk through it but runs into it as if solid.

Ivan
Ouch! (confused) Solid? What is this?

Knuckles
It doesn't register on my radar so it's not something with a soul. I see a blue outline of a dome 180 miles in diameter and 20 miles high. Beyond that, I don't know what it is. I can't sense it beyond radar, especially the interior. Well, if radar is working, then it's obviously not a sense barrier, but something else. Alright evil force, where are you!

A three-second pause occurs. A small "doorway" forms in the dome four feet wide, ten feet tall, and five feet deep. It forms in one second by "sliding" inward. The rules for the glitter still apply – the ceiling and walls have it and it behaves in the same way.

Tu
A doorway? I have a bad feeling about this.

Knuckles
Strangely enough, the evil force isn't around.

Knuckles punches the side of the dome, a red "0" pops out.

                    Knuckles
Normally, glass would've easily broke with that, but
no damage is odd.

                      Ivan
I'll throw a rock at it.

                    Knuckles
My punch was much harder than your thrown rocks.

Knuckles punches the same spot far harder, but another red
"0" pops out. A visible shockwave spreads out in all directions to
the sides, but focused upwards, making a small explosion sound.

                    Knuckles
That's with the force of ten megatons of TNT an
inch away from it and it still did no damage.

                      Ivan
Cast a spell on it instead.

Knuckles casts hypernova90 on it. A red "0" pops out.

                    Knuckles
Alright, full scan.

Knuckles casts "full scan" on it, but a red "no effect" pops out
instead of the window appearing.

                    Knuckles
No effect? That's the first time I saw that happen!

                Mysterious voice
(somewhat faintly but yelling) Knuckles!

                    Knuckles
Someone is around here, but I'm not sensing
anyone for miles. Humans can't yell loud enough.

                Mysterious voice
Enter the doorway. This is not a trap.

Evil force

Oh, so you found my home now! Good job! Now for a teleport barrier so you're stuck here!

Knuckles

Not you again!

Mysterious voice

(mad) Get outta here Seth! This is not for you!

Knuckles

Seth? That's its name? Apparently it's not a trap.

Mysterious voice

Please enter Knuckles, but not you Seth.

Seth

(very upset) Why? I've got a plan that'll take you out for good!

Knuckles and the three others enter the doorway. Seth casts "defenseless42" on Knuckles. A medieval-style shield fades in in a quarter second and appears to "fall" toward Knuckles. Upon landing, and a half-second pause, the shield shatters, bounces, and "falls" away, fading away in one second while "falling". A red "immune" pops out of Knuckles. A second later, the edge that was "moved inward" closes forming a box around the team.

Knuckles

Are you sure that this is not a trap?

Mysterious voice

This is not a trap.

Suddenly, a loud, buzzing alarm sound occurs where the buzzes repeat every second and last for a half second each.

Mysterious voice

(annoyed; yelling) Seth, I told you to stay out of here! Now get!

134

Seth

(upset) But why can they get in?

Mysterious voice

(annoyed; yelling loudly) You've been permanently kicked out! Now go!

Seth

(very mad) Fine! I'll go get the very things I want before that short nuisance can stop me! I'll then take my plan to the next level and take you on for good! Ha, ha, ha!

A second later, the alarm stops. Three seconds later, the area that was the dome fades to a futuristic city in five seconds.

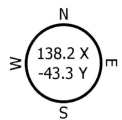

Figure 7: The design of the street markings (Scale: ≈1:16.8729)

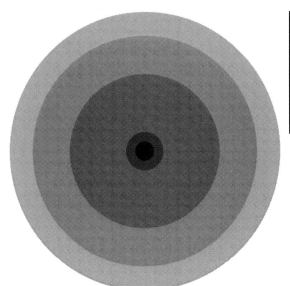

Color	Type	Floors
	Government	200-1200
	Offices	80-400
	Industrial	10-100
	Commercial	1-20
	Apartments	1-15
	Houses	1-5

Map 8: Basic, general layout of Amazonia's buildings (Scale: ≈1:1,968,323)

The city uses the metric system for all its measurements. The city's layout uses a grid spaced 100 meters apart. Each 100x100-meter section is a "block". The dark gray (FF404040), ten-meter-wide roads form the boundaries of blocks. Each intersection has a circle a half meter in diameter with compass directions outside and a coordinate inside. X positive is east and Y positive is north. The coordinate is how far that point is from city center, in kilometers. Buildings, with three meters per floor, large windows, and with eight entrance doors, two per side, use the 90-meter center part; large ones occupy more than one block.

The city's radius is 144.82 kilometers. Generally, buildings get taller the closer one is to the city's center. There are six zones. From the innermost to the outermost, there are 5 kilometers of very tall government buildings, 5 of offices, 10 of industrial, 60 of commercial, 40 of apartments, and the rest in houses. There are four houses in a 2x2 grid in each block nearer to the center and 16 small ones in a 4x4 grid at the edge. Amazonia is known as a hypercity, a city with at least 10,000 square kilometers of area.

The city uses white (FFFFFFFF) cylindrical teleporters 2 1/2 meters tall, two meters in diameter, with 1.5 meters of interior space. Two 10-centimeter-in-diameter pipes in the back, a dome "cap", and many buttons inside resembling a keyboard are also present. The floor is sky blue (FF4090F0) and the walls and buttons are light gray (FFC0C0C0). Four of these are at each block, two at each buildings' corners nearest to the intersection.

Very few walk on the vehicle-free, light gray (FFA0A0A0) roads. The team appears in the west-southwest edge of the city at "138.2X, -43.3Y" where someone stands four meters in front.

Steve, a cute-looking, 170-pound, 74-inch-tall, Caucasian male with average muscle mass stands in front. His red (FFFF0000) T-shirt and blue (FF0000FF) shorts, both glittery and made of silk, stick out. He has brown hair three inches long coming to a point at his front right tip. Steve does not wear shoes or socks. A silver badge, like what policemen wear, is on his shirt's left side. It has a large "2", identifying rank, and a half-sized "Steve" on it.

Steve
(a second into the fade) I'm Steve, second in command of Amazonia.

Knuckles
(shocked) Amazonia!? I was wondering about that as my sensing wasn't checking out. Now I see why.

Steve
Who are those others with you?

Knuckles
They're mostly just tag-alongs, helping me. What is this Seth trying to do here?

Steve
We'll explain in the library. I'll stop time on the outside so you can stay for a while.

Knuckles
What was with the sense barrier though?

Steve
To prevent Seth from finding us, provided it works.

Knuckles
Let's see here.... (one-second pause; shocked) Man, how big is this city!? At least I can sense again! 180 miles in diameter....

Steve
Miles? What's that? In case you're wondering about its size, the actual diameter is two-eighty-nine point six-four kilometers.

Knuckles
Oh, I see, you use metrics. A mile is one-dot-six-oh-nine-three-four-four kilometers.

Steve
Let's go to a teleporter to get to a library.

Knuckles

Why not use the teleport spell instead? I cast it in
114 nanoseconds and I found over 600 libraries.

Steve

Man are you fast! How can you find almost all the
libraries in nanoseconds!? What level are you on!?

Knuckles

Nine thousand two hundred....

Steve

(interrupting; shocked) Wow! No wonder why!

Knuckles

Let's just go to the library.

Knuckles casts teleport. The team, including Steve, appears
on the library's floor 62 in the southwest corner. The library's six
rows of 35 half-meter-wide shelves spaced ten meters apart
north to south and 2.5 meters apart from east to west are in the
northern area of the library. A walking space of two meters
separates the shelves. Each shelf has gold-colored (FFFFC000),
3D text on it like "62-XXX"; "XXX" is a number with three digits
from "001" to "210", increasing from west to east, north to south.

The library's southern area has 129 tables, 8 monitors, and 4
teleporters. The tables, forming equilateral triangles spaced four
meters apart, are two meters in diameter with ten chairs around
each, all painted with a dragon skin texture, have a 1.5-meter
walking space between them. The monitors, three by five meters
and three meters tall, with "4D hologram research station" on the
front in a fancy red (FFFF0000) font four centimeters high, are
spaced 11 meters apart. They have a black (FF000000) awning
and curtains to filter out light. Teleporters line the southern walls
between every other monitor. The library is somewhat crowded
– about 150, most reading, few scattered around on this floor.

Steve

You are indeed fast, much faster than I thought!

<u>Knuckles</u>
Like I said, sensing and teleport, especially at my level, are faster. Yet, it's not my fastest possible!

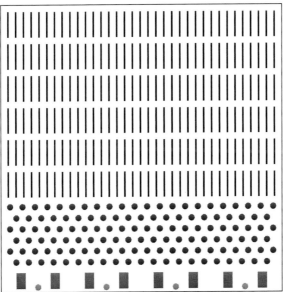

Map 9: The library's layout (Scale: ≈1:1181.1)

<u>Scene 16: The library</u>

May 29, 1999 at 9:25 PM UTC – 1 hour, 34 minutes remaining

The timer does not change while in Amazonia. The group slowly walks toward the southwest monitor. They show animated text in 3D, complete with lighting effects. The four-centimeter-tall text, of the Arial font, is "state search query". It slowly shifts through the continuous spectrum at 30° per second.

<u>Knuckles narrator</u>
After the surprise encounter and finally knowing more about what I used to call "the evil force", I went to the library and began getting a lot of answers for almost every unanswered question I had, and everything made sense, a lot of sense.

                          Steve
             (one-second pause) Seth King.

    The monitor displays something resembling Wikipedia's
format, only more futuristic. There is a white, flat background
with black text scattered around giving details about Seth King
such as his stats, where everything has "???" for them, age,
gender, history, and other things. The top right corner has an
image area with a black background extending into the back 24
inches from top to bottom by 8 inches wide with a 3D image of
what he looks like. It rotates in full every four seconds as if
running around him in circles while he stands perfectly still.
    Seth King wears everything in black (FF000000). He wears a
half-inch-thick black cape going down to a foot above the ground
a bit big for his size, black boots, a black straw hat a foot tall, a
black cotton T-shirt, and black-dyed denim jeans. Seth King is a
white male standing 74 inches tall with short black hair.
    The text and white background are 2D. Tables have edges
sticking 1/8 inch outward. Perspective effects are easily seen
when one moves. The monitor has everything in true color.
    The left side shows links to related content: "Knuckles",
"Amazonia", "statistics", and "Elemental Masters". The top shows
the title of the article, "Seth King (Amazonia mastermind)". The
bottom right contains the main content. Unlike Wikipedia, there
aren't any banners (such as cleanup or login).

                          Ivan
        That's an awesome display thing you've got.

                        Knuckles
        Oh, I see how it works. It's a bunch of 50-
        micrometer cubes updating 50,000 times a second.

                          Steve
        How do you know?

                        Knuckles
        I can see it, though barely.

140

Steve

You must have extreme vision then because I can't. (reading from the monitor) Seth King is a master criminal of Amazonia. He, sentenced to death, was recently kicked out for his crimes. It is believed that he is looking for a way to get back into Amazonia, but this is unconfirmed. (skips reading the "history" header) Seth King was born on October 25, thirty-seven fifty-eight making him 39 years old. He was born with unusual skills, particularly being very intelligent with problem-solving skills. In-depth brain scans reveal a problem-solving intelligence rating of 652, 320 units beyond that of the norm. Although weak in physical development, based on data eight years old, his unusually high problem-solving intelligence rating amazed scientists. Despite being physically weak, he joined fighting arenas for decades and continuously got more powerful. (skips reading the "Seth's mayhem" header) He soon found a way to prevent the anticrime device from working which worried Amazonia's highest level of authority. By age 35, both his immunity to the anticrime device and his high power gained in the fighting arenas were used for criminal acts. Over the next four years, his bad acts escalated to an extreme, causing terror and fear among Amazonia's residents. He sometimes was seen in the library, but everywhere he went, he caused destruction and mayhem. In addition to property damage, he created a dragon-like monster that was thankfully captured before it caused further destruction. He also committed several murders and created a very devastating computer virus that took five days to recover from. Two days ago, Seth was forced out of Amazonia and a special barrier was erected to prevent him from entering, but we don't know how long it'd last before he finds a weak point. Amazingly, 99.94% of all residents in Amazonia voted to sentence him to death.

Some parts, in blue (FF0000FF), are double-underlined. They are, in order: "born", "intelligence rating", "3758" (Steve spelled it out), "physical", "statistical development", "fighting arenas", "anticrime device", "Amazonia's", "authority", "library", "dragon-like monster", "computer virus", "special barrier", "voted", "sentence", and "death".

The monitor jumps to the next page. It looks exactly the same as the previous page only different text is shown.

Steve

(reading; one-second pause; skipping the "his grand plan" header) After getting ejected from Amazonia, some say that he began to execute one of his grand plans, that of using legendary masters of the elements, as a way to get back inside the city. He continued causing problems to our city and we thought of going back into the past to take another route of events, but strangely, he followed us everywhere we went. (skips the "Amazonia's hope" header) We soon heard of an alien on Earth from Korona that seemed to be the right stuff, but he was around May 29, 1999. The city agreed to go to that time and wait for Knuckles, but attempted to hide from Seth as much as possible. As of today, we do not know what his plans are, but they most likely involve using legendary masters of the elements as a way to get in, or to destroy another hypercity like Amazonia.

Here, the phrases "legendary masters", "elements", "back into the past", "alien", "Earth", "Korona", "May 29", "1999" (these are separate), "city", "another city", and "hypercity" are the "links".

Steve finishes reading the text, skipping headers. Knuckles looks carefully at the rotating image of Seth King.

Knuckles

Question. How come I can sense his location very well, but not actually see him?

Computer

Sorry, I do not know the answer to that question.

Knuckles

While I do have the vanish spell and billions of others, none of them provide the exact effect I'm getting, even in combination, mostly as status effects. I was just wondering. Also, how did he figure out details about the elemental masters? How does he access their worlds and face the level fifty-six-hundred monsters?

A low-detail report about the elemental masters appears. The design is unchanged. Every element, except the main area, has "???" showing. A 3D question mark is shown for the image.

Computer

How do you know their levels?

Knuckles

Seth King entered their worlds and I went in with him unexpectedly. A quick "full scan" spell revealed the monsters' levels and stats.

Computer

If you've seen them and have their stats, could you provide the details about them?

Knuckles

Although I'll need to study the design of the computer systems, which takes a few seconds, I can easily provide them, at least, for those that I've seen anyway, which are strikingly similar.

Computer

Thank you for providing new information on something that little is known about.

Knuckles remains still for five seconds then casts "mind thoughts to storage device", a spell with no spell effects. The page instantly updates with new text, the stats filled in (age at "4,526,898,074 years"), and the Master Lavalent's image.

Knuckles
It's done.

Computer
You are very fast and thanks for the info.

Steve
(reading; skips the "the discovery of the legend" header) The legend of the 10 elemental masters was first discovered in Ancient Mesopotamia in a very well-hidden underground cavern in twenty-seven thirty-nine. Scientists took 23 years to decode the messages inscribed throughout the tomb and after a half of a year into reading the messages, it was discovered that special elemental masters existed in a version of Earth entirely of their element. Each element – fire, ice, electric, earth, chemical, wind, water, light, gravity, and dark – has their own master. It is believed that Seth King, our city's recently evicted criminal, is using these elemental masters to break back into the city to continue his destruction. (skips the "about the elemental masters" header) Until about a minute ago, little was known about them. Knuckles, the alien from Korona visiting Earth, had encountered some of the elemental masters due to Seth King trying to kidnap them. Having unexpectedly visited their elemental worlds, a "full scan" spell cast on them while there revealed in-depth stats for five of them – that for fire, water, earth, wind, then ice – that were very similar. It is not yet known how these elemental worlds are accessed.

These phrases are made as "links": "Ancient Mesopotamia", "cavern", "2739" (Steve spells this out), "decode", "tomb", "Earth entirely of their element", "element" (the second), "fire", "ice", "electric", "earth", "chemical", "wind", "water", "light", "gravity", "dark", "Seth King", "our city's", "criminal", "Knuckles", "alien", "Korona", "Earth", "full scan", "spell", and "stats".

Knuckles
So, if he has a house on a newly risen piece of land he calls Atlantis, what is the significance of that?

Computer
I'm sorry, but I cannot find any details about this.

Knuckles
Rats. I guess I'll probably have to go to it to investigate. I sense many traps there. Oh, and what about this dragon-like thing?

Computer
Seth King created it in one of the 15 fighting arenas, the one at location 38 dot 3 X, 61 dot 9 Y.

Knuckles
Oh yes, I can sense it.

Computer
Even a group of our 20 best fighters haven't been able to defeat it or even scratch it, so be warned.

Knuckles
I should give it a go. At a level over 9000, I should easily take care of it.

Computer
Nine thousand sounds like the perfect candidate to getting rid of this visitor-reducing menace.

Ivan
What sports games do you have here?

Computer
I see that you're a time traveler or a visitor. We can certainly go by the rules from what your sports games were like, but with numerous, optional twists. Visit a sports game center once.

Tyler
What about adventuring and exploring?

Computer
There are parks and underwater cities you can visit, or you can try out our exploration simulator, which works with any place, time, and skill level. You don't die, get injured, or get into trouble in these. Most sports games use them.

Steve
"If you can dream it, you can do it" – that's Amazonia's motto.

Tu
I'm more of the travel and science type.

Knuckles
I guess I'll be doing what I like best, battles. I'll take care of that dragon with ultimara6.

Computer
What is ultimara6?

Knuckles
It is the most powerful spell series, obliterating practically anything with ease. It's not available until all extreme spells are at level 5001.

Ivan
I would like to play volleyball. It's my favorite sports game. Matball follows along with Soccer.

Scene 17: Fun time

May 29, 1999 at 9:25 PM UTC − 1 hour, 34 minutes remaining

Knuckles casts teleport. He appears alone by a doorway a meter wide by two meters tall in the southeast corner of the gray (FFA0A0A0) brick building with an ID-scanning machine a meter tall near it. The ID-scanning machine resembles an ATM but has a display identical to the monitor in the library. It has 3D text on it with "Fighter's entrance." at the top, centered, "Please provide three of the following to enter:" below it, and "member's card (counts as 3), fingerprint, iris, voice, brain scan, ID card, anti-crime chip ID number" at the left side with new lines instead of commas. The top is size 96, the rest is size 24, all Verdana.

Map 10: Amazonia's fighting arena (Scale: ≈1:2362.2)

<u>Knuckles narrator</u>
With most questions now answered, I had a side task. I did some cleanup by getting rid of the dragon. The others went at playing volleyball and exploring the city's underside.

Computer
Attention! It will rain here in about five minutes. Please prepare.

Knuckles looks at the ID-scanning machine.

Knuckles
This presents a problem, but it's a simple design. I don't have a brain scan, an ID card, nor an anti-crime chip, but these are useless for me anyway.

Knuckles casts teleport. An empty golden-yellow (FFFFC030) ticket 6 inches long by 3 1/4 inches wide appears on the ground showing empty stats and "06-00078020187-14" as the ID number on the top side. The layout is the same as that of the "full scan" stats, only without the top two sections and black (FF000000) text. Knuckles casts edit and his stats appear on it accordingly.

06-00078020187-14

?	5.4 ★		24.8 ★		13 ★		15.6 ★		12.1 ★
	15.3 ★		10.4 ★		9.9 ★		4.8 ★		9.5 ★
	12.1 ★		12.2 ★		11.6 ★		10.7 ★		12.4 ★
	7.6 ★		8.5 ★		11.3 ★		13.3 ★		10.8 ★
	7.2 ★		10.3 ★		9.7 ★		14.6 ★		8.8 ★
	18.4 ★		17.9 ★		21.7 ★		13.5 ★		6 ★

Physical attack	870,106,894	Magic attack	19,726,182	Strength	683,498
Melee accuracy	294	Magic efficiency	4.02724E35	Speed	378
Ranged accuracy	291	Magic accuracy	467	Hit points	1.00084E19
Physical defense	∞	Magic defense	∞	Spell power	1.2996E28
Physical evasion	212	Magic evasion	248	Level	9218
Actions/second	13,544,252	Magic potency	1.5904E21	Experience	2.94627E22

Figure 8: The fighting arena's ticket for Knuckles (Scale: 1:1.25)

Knuckles
That was easy. The zero-six identifies the arena number, the 14 the fighter number, and the long one the tournament ID number.

Suddenly, the machine makes a buzzing sound.

Knuckles casts "mute" on the ID scanner. A two-foot-long megaphone fades over it in a quarter second and emits sound as three spreading 60° arcs for two seconds at five feet per second abruptly vanishing when five feet away. All arcs suddenly vanish as a red "X" instantly appears over the icon. A second later, the effects fade away. At the moment the effects start, a gray "1 muted" pops out and the buzzing and speaking abruptly stop.

Knuckles
Simple machines prone to simple status effects. Oh well. I'm Knuckles, Seth King's biggest adversary.

The door opens, lifting up into the ceiling, and Knuckles enters through a small alley. The map explains the layout.
The floor has 40-millimeter, dark blue (C02000C0) stained glass tiles with a five-millimeter spacing. The underlying floor, three-meter-high walls, and ceiling are white (FFFFFFFF).
Benches 40 centimeters wide are all around the waiting area of the fighter's den where 15 other fighters wait. They are at least 3/4 meter from the battlefield entrance in the northwest, bathroom in the east, or ticket stand to the west. An invisible wall blocks anyone from entering the battlefield while battles go on. The 3/4-meter-wide by 2-meter-long ticket stand has a female clerk behind it, who gets to it by a door on the north side.
The fighter's den is in the southeast. The monsters come out of the monster's den in the northwest. The announcer's watch tower, with windows bowing a meter outward for best viewing, is 20 meters above the east central area. The stands (for audience) extend ten meters into the battlefield five meters above it with seats a half meter apart rising a half meter each step higher away from the battlefield. A ten-meter safety zone surrounds the two dens and the announcer's tower.
A 3D display 24 meters wide by 16 meters tall 100 meters above the center of the battlefield shows other angles of the battle or replays. It tilts toward the audience for best viewing.

The battlefield covers an area of 170x170 meters. The center 160x160 area has green (FF00C000) and green-cyan (FF00D060) fake, retractable grass seven centimeters tall in a checkerboard pattern using one-meter squares. Five meters around the edges where water comes from uses only the green color without squares. The ceiling is 125 meters high here.

As Knuckles enters, he runs to the ticket stand at 20 mph and jumps up onto it handing his self-created ticket over.

Arena ticket clerk

A short one huh? Are you playing mode 1, survival?

Knuckles

I'm new here but sensing tells me mode 1 is right.

Arena ticket clerk

Okay. You are fighter number 14. Good luck.
Here's the rules.

The arena ticket clerk takes a pamphlet.

Knuckles

I already know the rules, I sensed them.

The arena ticket clerk puts the pamphlet back.

Arena ticket clerk

You'd better be sure on that as disobeying the rules means disqualification and spending 50 hours doing hard labor and sewer cleanup before you return.

Knuckles

That's no big deal.

Josh, a male with 20-inch-long blonde hair, is on the east bench furthest to the north. Knuckles jumps a foot high off the desk and runs at 15 mph to the entrance stopping on the south side before it in a location where he can easily see what goes on.

Josh

He must be confident with himself, though suspicious. He doesn't look or act like Seth King though, thankfully.

Knuckles

I'll put on another actions per second plus, for good measure. I don't need magic attack, as it's already high enough as it is. I don't need another magic potency as I cast the fastest anyway.

Josh

You shouldn't underestimate the monsters you face here ya know.

Knuckles

You've apparently underestimated me, a lot. I've already got a bunch of plus abilities equipped as it is and my equip slots are very disorganized.

Announcer

The computer seems to have malfunctioned apparently as its not emitting any sound so I'll take over. This is a survival battle tournament. You are put against strong monsters and you have a ten-minute time limit. The half that deal the greatest damage in one action and survive will proceed to the next round. First, we'll be receiving word from our fighters so you get to know them.

The scene switches to that of where Ivan, Tu, Tyler, and Steve are, walking outdoors to a teleporter 50 meters away by a sports stadium. When 30 meters away, it starts to rain. The rain slowly increases to 42 dBZ (on Doppler radar) in five minutes. There isn't any lightning or thunder, just rain and mist.

Steve

While Knuckles is doing the battle arena stuff, what do you three want to do?

Ivan

Volleyball!

Tu

Sports, yuck! Leave me out of it!

Tyler

Sports of my type aren't bad – exploring. That's what I want to do.

Tu

Exploring? What about getting lost in a place like this?

Steve

The computer can help. Just ask it.

Ivan

Remember that Knuckles can sense? With him here, it's impossible to get lost! Remember how he found me very high and far during the Hawaii visit?

Steve

Since I already know this place, perhaps I could suggest the underside. There's a huge theme park, underwater cities, and most of the farming stuff down there. Another option is the adventure simulator which extends this almost indefinitely. Pick any place, time, and skill level, and go at it. I'll go with Ivan though. I haven't played volleyball in a long time, seven years if I recall.

Ivan

Wow! Alrighty then, volleyball it is! But, how do you enter? Where's the stadiums at?

Steve

To use the teleporters, tell the computer where to go. The rain's getting a bit heavy so we'd better go.

   Ivan and Steve go into the teleporter on the left while Tu and Tyler go into the teleporter on the right.

Steve
Take us to a volleyball court.

Ivan and Steve are teleported to an area that is all white all over, without any shading effects. The effects of teleportation using the teleporters take five times longer than the spell.

Ivan
What is this!? Where is everything at?

A volleyball court appears below, but with differences. The whole course looks like it would rotate on something. The net's posts, but not the net itself, are the rotation source. One meter around the court is for the out of bounds area. The edge of the court, 20 centimeters thick, is seen when looking over the edge.

Ivan
Hey, that was strange! The whole court just appeared outta nowhere!

Steve
This is an adventure simulator where pretty much anything is possible. You could even have a floating court or reduced gravity or ball mass if you wanted. It adds so much more flexibility. The swinging platform is a hit feature for extra challenge.

Ivan
That's awesome! What about the white scene?

Computer
Choose the setting in which the game is played.

Ivan
Do you have anything of San Francisco's Golden Gate Bridge on May 29, 1999? That's the time I'm from. Obviously, use year 1999 rules.

Computer
Would you like the court suspended above the bridge or by it?

Ivan
Centered but about 150 feet above it.

Computer
Do you mean 50 meters? We only use metrics.

Ivan
A yard, three feet, is about a meter so I guess so.

The white background suddenly changes to that of a scene 50 meters above the Golden Gate Bridge. Cars are seen on the road with the rather frequent 18-wheeler. The water below has a few small boats like sailboats and canoes. A ferry goes up and down the canal. Ten miles west, barely visible, is a large ship hauling several containers heading toward the bridge for docking. The scenery is in true 3D. A 20 mph wind blows with cumulus humilis clouds 1/4 scattered above.

A one-second pause occurs then Ivan jumps 14 feet high twice watching the 3D effects, first straight across, then down.

Steve
(when Ivan jumps) San Francisco, back then, looks pretty nice, but too bad it's underwater now.

Ivan
Underwater? Maybe in your time. What, global glacier melting rose sea levels?

Steve
Unfortunately, I don't recall. It occurred over 1700 years ago as far as I know.

Ivan
Just curious. If I deliberately cause a car crash or sink a ship, would I be arrested?

Steve
That's the neat thing about adventure simulators! You can cause all the destruction and mayhem you want and never face the penalties. You can only do it in these though and not outside. Seth King did it on the outside and he got evicted.

Ivan

What about causing a volcano to erupt or sending an asteroid or even Jupiter toward Earth?

Steve

You can do that too! Remember Amazonia's motto, "if you can dream it, you can do it"?

Ivan

I'd love to live here, but too bad I'm from a time long, long ago. Playing all the sports games would be so much fun. I wonder what matball is like.

Steve

Yikes! I forgot to tell Knuckles about the ID-scanning thing that they have. Then again, knowing him, I'm expecting he found a solution.

Computer

You can set some options if you'd like. How many points should a team get to win?

Ivan

The standard, 15.

Computer

At what score should the platform begin to swing?

Ivan

(confused) Swing?

Computer

This platform you're standing on, if used, will begin to swing, as a whole, when one team gets at least a certain amount of points.

Ivan

I guess I'll try it. Start it when 11 points are scored.

Computer

What skill level for the opposing team do you want?

Ivan

Something between beginner and advanced.

Computer
Do you know what your numerical level is? Beginner and advanced has a very wide range of possibilities, from thirty to one-fifty. The highest used and still win is just over nine hundred.

Ivan
I'm completely unfamiliar to level in that sense. Perhaps an average of me and Steve? It's all I can say in that case. I don't know squat about levels. I don't even know how to find out what my level is!

Computer
You're level 64, almost 65. Steve is one-twelve so skill is 88. I'll set skill deviation, affecting other players for a balance, to 10%, the default.

Ivan
Oh, and randomize who goes and serves first.

Computer
What would you like the mass of the ball to be for this game or the strength of gravity?

Ivan
Standard mass and standard gravity.

Computer
Would you like to configure time of day, weather, or any other settings?

Ivan
I just want to get playing. Use a five m-p-h wind instead. Pick a direction.

Computer
Five m-p-h? I'm assuming you mean two meters per second. Will you both be playing?

Ivan
I am for sure!

Steve
I am too; I haven't played in a while, a long while.

Ivan

I'm eager to get going!

Steve

Did you know that you can cause mayhem and
chaos from balls going out of bounds? It's rare for
volleyball, but it does happen. It's fun too!

The ball used in volleyball appears in the middle of the court.
Ten other players fade in in one second lined side by side next to
the net. They look and behave exactly like humans naturally do.

Computer

Ivan is player one and Steve is player two, both on
the home team. Extra players have been added to
get six on both teams. The opposing team goes
first and player four serves first. Get into position.

Everyone, including the extras, get into position.
The scene, a second later, goes to where Tu and Tyler are, in
the weakly-lit (2.5 lux) underside. All lights are two kilometers
straight above. Glittering effects from light on water can be seen.
The layout resembles an open maze, where multiple routes can
be taken to reach a point. Small buildings typical of a small
village are scattered around the area.
Tyler looks around and walks to where the glitter is.

Tyler

This area is weird, dark, and sort of a maze. I've
been in worse conditions than this. I'll head toward
where that glitter is. It seems a lot like water.

Tu

I wonder what an underwater city looks like, if they
are here.

A few seconds later, the two see the clear, greenish-colored
(1000FFA0 at 10 meters) water with five-millimeter waves. Five
meters underneath is the top of a glass dome 200 meters tall by
2000 meters wide. The city is much brighter, at 250 lux. There's

a sudden vertical drop of ten centimeters at the cliff's edge. A sign just over the edge has "Janet" on it, the name of the city. A few residents are swimming underwater near the surface but don't surface. Two are speaking with each other underwater and one is at the surface treading water. Residents in Amazonia have the ability to breathe underwater like one breathes air.

Tyler approaches the edge and stops. He looks down and sees the glass dome. He looks at the sign next.

Tyler

So there really are underwater cities! Amazing! It seems like a few swimming around, but oddly, they aren't surfacing. Must be a new form of scuba gear.... (sees the sign) Janet? Maybe it should be called "Hydrocity" or "Watercity" instead.

Tu

You do have a point there. Let's just glide across and see what else there is.

Both Tyler and Tu run at 10 mph, jump 14 feet high, and start gliding across picking up speed. They pitch up to climb just as they are about to hit the one treading water at nearly 45 mph. They climb to 40 feet high, learning off of Ivan's trick, then level.

Janet resident

(as the others pitch up) Watch where you're going!

Tyler

I didn't see him. Oh well. We can get almost anywhere thanks to Ivan's discovery! Climb again.

Tu and Tyler pitch up, now climbing to 100 feet high. They cross over the entire area passing over 100 mph.

The scene returns to where Knuckles is, in the fighting arena. Knuckles is in the same spot.

Announcer

Knuckles, it's your turn.

Knuckles
My history dates back over 300 Earth years ago,
born on Korona rather than Earth. For centuries,
I've been involved with intense battles, first a
dispute then alien invaders. I've since become very
powerful and wanted to get more powerful and I
came to Earth sensing trouble. Years passed until I
encountered Seth King attempting to get legendary
masters of the elements. I've since been after him.

Announcer
(surprised) Seth King!? Good luck but great intro!
Most of our fighters have been involved with battles
for a long time, especially our masters. Anyway, let
the games begin! First up is fighter one, Sandy.

Sandy, an average-height female near the center of the west
bench, gets up and walks into the battlefield. One second later,
the door for the monster's den opens up by lifting up and a
leopard-like monster with one-foot-long horns comes out. The
computer-generated monster runs out.

Sandy casts fire on it, a spell, for her, with a half-second cast
time. She, and others here, cast spells using the diagram in
scene 1, but until now, without skipping the middle two steps.

A small flame bursts over the monster. A red "298" pops out.
Sandy runs to it at 15 mph, drawing her sword. Upon reaching it,
she slices through it before it strikes. A red "506" pops out. The
monster fades away in a half second when the number appears.

Knuckles
That's stronger than most humans I've seen!

Announcer
Sandy wins with five-oh-six for the score.

Sandy runs back into the fighter's den.

Knuckles
You're pretty good, better than I thought!

Sandy

Thank you. You should watch the true masters going at it, doing over 20,000 damage and facing real powerhouses I wouldn't want to mess with.

Announcer

Number two, William, is next.

Fifteen minutes pass. Josh is returning from the battlefield.

Announcer

Josh scores five-eleven. This is shaping up to be a close game already. I like close games; they add suspense. Number 14, Knuckles, you're next.

Knuckles

Alright. I'll show you something unique.

Knuckles runs into the battlefield going 40 mph then stops by sliding on the ground stirring up dust. A python-like monster 11 feet long comes charging out of the monster's den.

Knuckles

Snake: weak against fire, ice, and wind. Testing....

Knuckles casts "stop" on the snake. A gray "1 stop" pops out.

Knuckles

(when the effects start) Good, that works.

Announcer

That's a spell I haven't seen. It's apparently "stop", given the gray popup.

Knuckles casts ice6 on the snake. A large chunk of ice forms over it completely encasing it in ice. The ice remains for a second then shatters with little force at ten mph. When the effects start, a red "121,893,149" pops out. The snake fades away.

Announcer
(shocked) What the! Over a hundred twenty
million damage!? No way! What spell was that!?
You're casting unusually fast too, much faster than
I've seen with the masters using their lowest levels!

Knuckles
That was stop and ice6. I could do a lot more
damage if you want.

Announcer
Well, anyway, it's time for fighter number 15,
Hector, to play.

Knuckles runs back to the fighter's den at 50 mph stopping
right in the entrance and returns to his original standing location.
Hector, a somewhat short male with almost no hair near the
entrance on the north bench, walks into the battlefield.

Josh
A hundred twenty million damage is incredible! I
did underestimate you!

Knuckles
You haven't seen anything yet. Wait until I use
ultimara6 on that dragon.

Josh
You mean the super dragon? Good luck with that
thing! The masters can't even scratch it!

The scene changes to the volleyball game. Ivan is up to
serve. During the game, the "home team" refers to the team
Ivan and Steve are on. The "opposing team" is the other team.

Ivan
10 to 8, serving.

Ivan serves the ball barely making it over the net and three
more swaps are made. The opposing team hits the net.

A second after the ball hits the net, the court starts rocking back and forth reaching 10° for the maximum tilt completing a full cycle every five seconds. The net does not rock with it.

Two seconds later, the opposing team rolls the ball to Ivan, still in the serving position. Ivan, disoriented from the swinging, misses the ball and it rolls off the platform falling, hitting the sides of the bridge. The camera (not the scenery) follows the ball always pointing in the direction it travels and five feet away from it. Five seconds after falling out, the ball instantly disappears and instantly appears by Ivan at the same time. Ivan grabs it.

<u>Ivan</u>
Wow! That was so sudden! That falling ball was neat though. It hit the sides of the bridge! I think I'm going to like it here! 11 to 8, serving.

Ivan serves the ball straight up at 45 mph, affected by drag. It goes out of bounds behind him slipping past the platform, from which the camera chases it. Four seconds after falling out of bounds, the ball hits the bridge's roadway, but doesn't cause any damage to traffic. The ball reappears where the opposing team's next server is 3/4 of a second later rotating as needed.

<u>Ivan</u>
That was a high one; it even hit the road below!

The opposing team serves the ball, swapping twice. The ball goes under the net when attempting to return it. Ivan barely catches it. The home team rotates. Ivan hands the ball to Steve.

<u>Steve</u>
The score is still 11 to 8.

Steve serves the ball but hits the net near the top.

<u>Steve</u>
Rats! Missed!

One of the home team's extras rolls the ball to the opposing team, rotating again. The receiver grabs the ball, falling over due to loss of balance. He gets up serving two seconds later. Three swaps are made. When the home team is receiving the ball, Ivan walks backwards away from the net beyond the out-of-bounds line, returns it, but, due to the swinging, slips and falls off the edge. He glides going under the platform a half second into the fall, but instantly appears back in the court 4.5 seconds later.

Ivan

I slipped on that one, though I could've returned by gliding. Eleven to nine is the score, still winning.

The scene changes to where Tu and Tyler are, near a river 50 feet wide, eight feet deep, and the same color (1000FFA0) as before. The river has a five mph current, a six-foot waterfall, and appears very smooth on the surface. To the far left, a kilometer away, a theme park is visible with dazzling, colorful lights. A Ferris wheel 400 meters high stands out against the rest of the rides. A sign next to the river on the other side has "haunted river" on it in a dark-blue-colored (FF000080) dripping type of font. Below it, at half the size, is "0 tickets".

Tyler

Hey, lookie there! How can a river be so clean like that? It's almost crystal clear! I've only seen this in deserts and some areas in the mountains. Oh yeah, and glaciers. If I had my equipment, I could test it.

Tu

You must be well-traveled. (sees the theme park) Oh, look to your left and tell me what you see.

Tyler

(looks left) Hey! A theme park! I wonder what this river ride thing is then. I don't see anything special here, other than being artificial. No one is in it that I can see.

Tyler walks up to the water's edge and looks more closely. He then sees the sign at the other side and glides over to it.

Tyler
(seeing the sign) A sign. I wonder what it says.

Upon landing, pitching up then falling to land more accurately, Tyler reads the sign. Tu follows after Tyler a second later.

Tyler
(confused) Haunted river? Uh, what kinds of spirits are here and where are they?

Tu
It's probably just a bunch of cloths on wires, nothing special. Then again, it could be more advanced than that, knowing this place. Nothing has happened in a while though.

Tyler walks over to the waterfall's highest part and tries to touch it but finds he can't due to something completely invisible.

Tyler
Huh? There's something covering the water, and it's not wet either. That's probably why it's called the haunted river.

Tyler steps on it then walks across as if it was solid.

Tyler
Yep, solid.

Tu steps on without falling in. Tyler walks to the theme park over it but slips through an open space falling in making a splash. Tyler is carried underwater until the waterfall where he hits something and surfaces gasping for air. He "walks" against the invisible wall neck deep in the water back to shore where it suddenly gets shallower, a foot every two feet. Tu runs back to land and goes to the waterfall where Tyler gets out.

Tyler

That was scary! The water's quite warm though.
Let's just skip over to those hills I'm seeing over
there (points straight ahead).

The scene changes to the fighting arena where Knuckles is.

Announcer

Number 13, Josh, you're next.

Josh

Alright, round two!

Josh runs into the battlefield. A small alligator-like monster
comes out of the monster's den. A three-second pause occurs
then the alligator charges after Josh.

Josh

That's going to be a little tough. What were
alligators weak against again?

Josh casts "spell power draw" on the alligator. This spell, for
Josh, has a 400-millisecond cast time. A ray of sky-blue-colored
(A04080FF) light comes from Josh to the alligator. A magenta-
colored (A0FF00FF) ray comes back a second later. Both lights
disappear a second later. A black "4" pops out of the alligator
and a gold "4" pops out of Josh at the same time the moment the
spell's effects start. The black popup, indicating sudden SP loss,
behaves the same way as red numbers; the gold one, indicating
sudden SP recovery, behaves the same way as a green number.
Josh casts ice on the alligator taking 400 milliseconds to cast
it. A red "308" pops out of it. The alligator barely moves.

Josh

It hasn't disappeared yet, so I guess I'll take the
opportunity.

Josh casts "spell power draw" but a red "missed!" pops out of
the alligator without spell effects. He tries again and the spell

works causing a black and gold "5" to appear in the same way as before. Josh runs to the alligator at eight mph and stomps on it hard. A red "238" pops out and the alligator disappears.

Josh

That close! Wow! Full spell power too! Sixteen isn't much to work with.

Announcer

Great, three-oh-eight is the current highest for the round. Knuckles, you're next.

Josh runs back at six mph while Knuckles runs out at 50 mph. Two seconds after Josh returns, a medium-sized bear with antlers on the head appears. It immediately runs to Knuckles.

Knuckles

Bear: weak against fire, earth, and gravity.

Knuckles casts lightning4 on the bear. A small lightning bolt appears striking the bear. A blue "126,696,165" pops out and the bear disappears. Knuckles runs back at 50 mph.

Announcer

A hundred twenty million damage again!? He must be very powerful if he can consistently do that! Then again, that was a critical hit. He should belong in the master level rather than the advanced level, unless he's after the super dragon. We'll see though. Number 15, Hector, you're up.

Hector runs into the battlefield, drawing his sword.

Josh

You're pretty good Knuckles!

Knuckles

So what, luck of the draw due to a critical. You still haven't seen anything yet.

The scene returns to the volleyball game. Ivan serves.

Ivan
Two more points on any side and the game is
finished. This is a close game! 13 to 13, serving.

Ivan serves the ball. It lands right on the boundary line and
bounces out of bounds, returning to Ivan five seconds later.

Computer
(two seconds after falling out) The ball impacted
right on the boundary line. No score is made and
the serve is repeated.

Steve
That's rare!

Ivan serves, swapping seven times. The opposing team
doesn't save the ball before it lands.

Ivan
Yay! One more point and our team wins!

The opposing team returns the ball to Ivan by rolling it when
the bridge is at its best tilt. Ivan grabs the ball.

Ivan
14 to 13.

Ivan serves the ball; two swaps are made. Steve, attempting
a rescue, causes the ball to go under the net. It hits the knee of
someone in the opposing team and a red "0" pops out. The
opposing team rotates and the ball is thrown gently to the server.
The opposing team serves the ball three seconds later and
five swaps are made. On the fifth swap, Ivan hits the ball off to
right and goes out of bounds without hitting anything. The ball
reappears by the opposing team's server.

Ivan

(a second after the awkward hit) Oops. Whoever scores the next point wins the game.

The opposing team serves the ball but hits it very awkwardly causing it to continue dropping with little forward movement.

Steve

(laughs a bit) That's a strange serve!

The home team rotates while the ball is rolled back to the home team with Steve grabbing the ball.

Ivan

The score is 14 to 14. Who scores next wins.

Steve serves the ball. After a swap, it lands an inch inside the boundary lines. Ivan dives after it to get it but misses. The ball rolls over the edge and falls off. It bounces off the wires holding the bridge up. The ball reappears on the opposing team's side.

Computer

The ball was in bounds so the opposing team has the ball.

The opposing team rotates. Their server picks up the ball.

Ivan

Rats! I was very close! It's still anyone's game.

Steve

This is a good game you've got going here.

The opposing team serves the ball and 11 swaps are made. Upon getting into the home team, one of the extras hits the ball awkwardly causing it to go to the left at 50 mph out of bounds.

Ivan

That was a long one, but unfortunately, we lost the game. It's just a for-fun game though.

Computer
Would you like to play again?

Ivan
I'd like to watch the battle arena that Knuckles is at.

Steve
I do too! I guess we'll not play again. We'll go to fighting arena number six.

The scene switches to where Tyler and Tu are. They see a building with Amazonia's layout map on it. A red "X" is found on the north side on the boundary between the government and office sections. A gate has a sign on it stating, "Government property: do not cross without permission". A tall, thin female security guard in a medium-dark green (FF00A000) uniform and a bronze badge like Steve's with a "4" and "Elizabeth" on it is behind the gate.

Tyler
What's this?

Elizabeth
This is government property. Do you have a pass?

Tyler
(a bit scared) Uh, no. We're just looking around.

Elizabeth
That's all right.

Tu
We're looking for small hills we saw, but ran into a small maze and got lost.

Tyler
Hopefully, they're not guarded....

Elizabeth
The Sentus Hills? They're not guarded, and you'll find them to your right, across Lake Sentus.

Tu
We were closer than we thought! Thanks miss!

Tu and Tyler get a running jump at 10 mph to the right of the gate then glide over, pitching up when about to hit.

Elizabeth
(as the two leave) You don't see visitors that often, not since Seth King wreaked havoc here. Thank goodness he's gone! And I've never seen anyone glide like that! Must be from the fighting arenas....

Lake Sentus is a small lake only 100 meters across by 120 meters wide. A teleporter is found on three sides of the lake. A series of gentle, rolling hills around 180 meters high are ahead of this. One of the hills nearby reaches 500 meters high.

Tu and Tyler continue gliding across the empty lake and reach the hills. At the hills, they pitch up to follow them, but land on the top by pitching down. Upon turning around, the theme park, now five kilometers away, is very clearly visible since there aren't any obstructions, but the rides cannot be made out.

Tyler
(upon turning around) What a view! That theme park couldn't be any prettier!

Tu
And we've got a clear view of it too!

Tyler
I wonder how I managed to pick this spot.

Computer
This is a popular location of Amazonia where tourists frequent due to the wonderful scenery, skiing, and swimming. Seth King caused a lot of destruction. Tourism has been zero ever since. This is also the third-highest area in Amazonia's underside. The highest, 160 kilometers south of here, has a height of seventeen hundred meters.

Tyler
I like mountains, but seventeen hundred meters
seems a bit short for me.

Suddenly, a strange cracking sound like that of glass breaking occurs that is fairly loud (about 60 dB where Tu and Tyler are).

Tu
What was that sound?

Computer
A cracking sound by Janet.

Tyler
Janet? Oh, that underwater city we saw!

The scene switches to the fighting arena. A second later, Ivan and Steve appear together in the audience near the fighter's den.

Announcer
Just five more battles to go! Number 10, Chris.

Chris, a short male on the east bench, enters the battlefield.

Steve
(right after the announcer) Why is the announcer
doing what the computer is supposed to do? That's
strange and I don't recall Seth King doing that.

Scene 18: The fighting arena rescue

May 29, 1999 at 9:25 PM UTC – 1 hour, 34 minutes remaining

The battlefield fills with a half meter of crystal clear water five centimeters per second. The water doesn't get into either of the two dens. A five-foot-long, red-orange (FFF06030), octopus-like monster comes out using its legs to slide along the ground.

A second later, Chris casts "blind" on the octopus, which has a 600-millisecond cast time for him. A very dark gray (FF202020) cloud fades in forming around its head in a quarter second. A second later, it shrinks, moving to its eyes in a second. It fades away in a half second. A gray "1 blind" pops out when the spell's effects start, and it begins wondering around randomly, blind.

Chris runs to the octopus with a medium-sized ax taking high steps to move through the water quickly. He trips while doing so, falls over, and makes a big splash still holding his ax. The audience laughs. Chris, wet, gets up, reaches the octopus, and swings the ax down to it causing a small splash. A red "218" pops out and the octopus fades away. The water drains away at the same rate it filled. Chris runs back, on dry land.

Knuckles narrator

(as Chris fights the octopus) As the volleyball game finished, the others were still in the underside and I continued getting through the tournament to take on the super dragon, as I now knew it as. I kept my true power hidden for a while, until now. I began sensing problems.

Announcer

(after the battle) Chris got two-eighteen points, plus humor. Number 13, Josh, you're next.

Chris

I hate those water ones! I'm all wet thanks to it!

Josh walks out into the battlefield.

Knuckles

I'm sensing something going on below.

Sandy

What do you mean?

Knuckles

I'm sensing something bad going on below. It's going on in the city's underside where a town called

Janet is. Tu and Tyler are fairly close, though protected by walls and lots of distance.

Sandy
Janet? The underwater city? What about it?

Knuckles
I don't know, but the pressure inside the glass dome is reaching a breaking point. (shocked) Yikes! Janet's going to blow in four seconds!

Announcer
(shocked) Janet's going to blow!? What do you mean?

Knuckles
Well, it just blew. Three seconds and you'll feel it.

Two seconds pass and the battlefield rumbles for a bit from a massive explosion, about 3.8 on the Richter scale. After another second, a bigger rumble occurs, twice as powerful, at 4.1.
The scene changes to where Tu and Tyler are. A lot of water comes raining down hard, like 65 dBZ on Doppler radar.

Tu
What was that big explosion!? Wait! Wouldn't that be where Janet is or something near it?

Tyler
We should get outta here. If it's that dangerous down here, we might as well go where it's safe.

Tu and Tyler head to the teleporter in the now-flooded valley by gliding to it. They enter it.

Tyler
I agree. Let's watch Knuckles take on that dragon.

Tu and Tyler disappear. The scene changes to the fighting arena where they appear where Ivan and Steve are.

Announcer
(as Tu and Tyler appear; amazed) Oh no! How did you know it was going to blow?

Knuckles
I sensed it. The pressure inside reached the critical threshold and it went.

Announcer
I'll inform the mayor immediately. Thank you for reporting it.

Five seconds later, a large clam with short legs walks out of the monster's den to Josh waiting by the fighter's den. Josh casts "wind" on the clam in a half-second. A sudden gust of 40 mph wind occurs over the clam. A red "21" pops out.

Josh
Weak hit apparently.

Josh casts lightning on the clam, also with a half-second cast time. A red "218" pops out of the clam. He casts "spell power draw" on the clam and black and gold 5's appear. Josh runs to the clam, with his ax, and cuts through its shell. A red "102" pops out and the clam fades away. Josh returns.

Josh
A few weak ones.... Hopefully I can move on.

Announcer
This is the last battle of round three. Knuckles, number 14, get ready.

Knuckles runs to the battlefield at 60 mph. Water five feet deep fills the battlefield but Knuckles stands on it as if solid.

Josh
(shocked) Huh!? Standing on water!? That's something I haven't seen, even with watching the

master-level fighters going at it! It's neat watching underwater battles, but this is a bit weird!

A shark-like monster comes out of the monster's den.

Chris
You can definitely say so! Good thing I didn't get that one! I hate fighting in any water.

Knuckles casts shock12 on the shark. A pair of lightning bolts two feet in diameter forming a right angle strike the monster spinning around it twice in one second. A 110-dB-loud thunder clap occurs startling all of the audience. A red "914,783,664" pops out of the shark and a green "470,485,607" pops out of Knuckles at the same time the effects start. The water drains.

Announcer
(shocked; scared) What spell was that!? I've never seen that one before!

Josh
That was scary and loud!

Knuckles
That, my friend, is only a hint to my power.

Announcer
(shocked) No way! Over 900 million damage!? How's that even possible!? (shocked; confused) Huh? 470 million in cure on himself? That doesn't make sense. None of the masters have approached that kind of power!

Steve
That spell frightened me! I've watched the masters, but no master I've seen even has that spell!

Knuckles
It's level 12 of the shock series, the upgrade to the lightning series. If you're curious, I cured myself as I absorb all elements and lightning in water did it.

Knuckles runs back into the fighting arena.

Announcer

(amazed) Level 12!? An upgrade to lightning!? I
never knew there were upgrades! That's really
gotta drain your spell power away! It's even higher
than Seth King had! You seem prime material for
taking on the super dragon, (normal) but the rules
require that the winner is asked to optionally fight it
so we must continue. Only two battles remain.
Sandy and Chris are now out of the game leaving
just Josh and Knuckles, Josh being the first to go.

Josh

(amazed) Man! What else do you have Knuckles?
No wonder why you seemed suspicious!

Josh walks out into battle arena.

Josh

With Knuckles, I don't stand a chance of winning at
all. Still, however, I can gain useful levels.

A giant earthworm 15 feet long comes out of the monster's
den. Josh casts "spell power draw" on the monster; a black and
gold "8" pop out (higher suddenly due to a critical hit).

Josh

That was convenient!

The giant earthworm casts "slow" on Josh. A watch identical
to that of the "stop" spell fades in in a quarter second. It moves
at 60 minutes per second for one second then slows down to 20
minutes per second in one second. It stays for one second then
the watch fades away in a half second. A gray "1 slow" pops out
and Josh's motion is reduced to 90.909% that of normal.

Josh casts ice2 in 700 milliseconds on the giant earthworm
twice. A red "504" then a red "485" pops out of it. "Spell power
draw" follows with a black and gold "5" popping out.

With the earthworm right next to Josh, the earthworm swats him sending him flying across the field at 30 mph. A red "220" pops out at the moment of impact.

Josh

(taking the hit) Ouch!

Due to the slow status effect, Josh's voice is 90.909% as fast and its pitch is 90.909% of what it used to be.

Josh casts ice2 twice more on the giant earthworm and a red "502" then "518" pops out. The earthworm swats Josh again and a red "230" pops out. Josh is now dead but the earthworm continues swatting him around without anything popping out.

Announcer

Josh didn't make it. Quick, get a life potion!

Five seconds pass. The earthworm stops swatting Josh but remains by him, now confused some.

Announcer

(mad) What!? No life potions? Oh how I hate Seth for destroying the only factory that makes them!

Knuckles

I can fix it.

Announcer

Seeing that extreme damage you can do, I would assume you can. Go ahead.

Knuckles runs into the battlefield but crashes into the invisible wall. A red "0" pops out. Knuckles casts teleport and appears in the battlefield. Knuckles casts "ultimate freeze 52" on the giant earthworm. A white "2.53486E14" pops out of the earthworm and it fades away. Immediately upon the number appearing, life-cure follows on Josh with the green "fatal" and "1" appearing during the effects followed by a green "331". Josh gets up as if nothing happened, then looks at Knuckles and no earthworm.

Knuckles casts "hasten" on Josh. The effects are the same as slow, except the clock goes from 60 minutes per second to 180 minutes per second instead. The timings are unchanged. A green "slow" pops out. This is because hasten cancels slow. Josh's voice returns to normal.

<u>Josh</u>
What happened? Where's the earthworm?

<u>Knuckles</u>
The earthworm defeated you. I came to revive you.

<u>Announcer</u>
(confused) I'm having trouble figuring out the damage popup. It makes no sense. What is an "E" doing in the number?

<u>Knuckles</u>
That happens when damage exceeds a billion.

<u>Announcer</u>
A billion? All right, where's that super dragon at? (confused) I didn't see any spell used though.

<u>Knuckles</u>
You can't because the spell, being as powerful as it is, literally stops time. That was "ultimate freeze 52", three upgrades above ice, and it did over 243 trillion damage, more than expected due to it being a supercritical hit.

<u>Announcer</u>
(very shocked) Level 52!? Three upgrades above ice!? What level are you on man!? What are upgrades and how do you get them?

<u>Knuckles</u>
Upgrades allow for more damage, and less spell power consumption, but take longer to cast. They are available when the lowest grade spell has spell level 11 available and for every extra ten higher for the upgraded version, a new upgrade becomes

available. Besides, haven't you checked my ticket
for my stats? I'm surprised you haven't.

Knuckles' stats show up on the monitor in the center of the
battlefield. They show that of the ticket, but with a white
(FFFFFFFF) background instead. A one-second pause occurs. All
audience looks with amazement and start speaking with each
other. Josh walks back to the fighter's den.

Announcer

How on Earth did you get to level... (very shocked;
very loudly) 9000!? No wonder! (shocked) I've
never seen stats that high before! You should go
get rid of that Seth King as well as the super dragon
in one hit! He's such a moron.

Knuckles

That's what I've been up to before I unexpectedly
arrived here. Where's that super dragon? If you
thought 243 trillion was a lot, that's nothing to
ultimara6. You can't get the ultimara series until all
extreme spells are at least level 5001!

Steve

I have a bad feeling about this one.

Suddenly, the audience stands begin filling up very quickly.
Elizabeth, from the underside, appears near Steve. They reach
98% capacity within ten seconds and stop there.

Announcer

(while the audience appear) We'll wait for those
who wanted to see the super dragon battle with a
certain winner to arrive before we release it.

Steve

Well, it's about time for the battle I've been wanting
to see completed for four years now.

Announcer

Ready? (five-second pause) Release the dragon!

A two-second pause occurs. A dragon 80 feet long from head to tail, standing 18 feet tall, and 15 feet wide appears. Its head, two feet wide and three feet long, is that of a snake except it has spikes for ears. From the mouth to the torso, the head and neck are 20 feet. Spikes line its back from head to tail like that of an iguana. The torso is 24 feet long. The 36-foot-long tail, with a devil's tail at the tip, six feet long by four feet wide, narrows toward the tip from 24 to 6 inches in diameter. A green-colored (FF107020) line extends 18 inches from the line of spikes. The rest of the dragon is a bluish-gray color (FF506080). Its feet, with six toes, are 2.5 feet in diameter and 6 feet long.

Super Dragon		Origin: Virgo Supercluster, Local Group, Milky Way, Sol Earth, Brazil, Amazonia
Level:	2855	
HP:	7.42856E09/ 7.42856E09	Strengths: Magic accuracy, physical, magic, attack, hit points, defense, magic evasion, slow, stop, earth, mass
SP:	462,779,068/ 462,779,081	Weaknesses: Stone, gravity, immobilized, intelligence, action rate, speed
Aura:		
Age:	122,207,667	

	1.4		1.8		1.7		1.5		1.9
	1.1		1.2		1.5		0.8		1
	2		1		1.3		1.2		2.1
	1.5		1.4		1.6		0.7		1.3
	1.9		1.5		1.6		2.2		1.1
	1.8		1.2		1		0.8		1.7

Physical attack	42,676,469	Magic attack	25,632,774	Strength	15,806
Melee accuracy	203	Magic efficiency	5.32522E09	Speed	9
Ranged accuracy	165	Magic accuracy	365	Hit points	7.42856E09
Physical defense	17,882,681	Magic defense	16,520,073	Spell power	462,779,081
Physical evasion	115	Magic evasion	237	Level	2855
Actions/second	8	Magic potency	895,671,329	Experience	5.53504E09

Figure 9: The superdragon's stats (Scale: 1:3.75)

When the dragon is first seen, Knuckles casts "full scan" on it while it casts "stop25" on Knuckles in no time. The dragon raises its head to execute the cast. It casts "slow27", "poison23", "energy barrier 18", then "death" on Knuckles, each a second after the effects end and taking no time to cast it. A red "immune" pops out each time when the effects start.

For the "poison23" spell, a green blob of slime forms around Knuckles in a quarter second and randomly morphs shape for one second. It fades away in a half second.

For the "death" spell, a hole five feet in diameter two feet in front forms in a half second. A grim reaper with an eerie black haze moving around it rises out of the hole in a second after a half-second pause. It swings its ax at Knuckles bouncing off of him as if he was a solid wall. The grim reaper returns to the hole in one second and the hole fades away in a half second.

Knuckles

(when the window appears; amazed) Wow! No wonder why the masters can't defeat it! Even level 3000 isn't close enough! Don't bother with status effects, dragon, they won't help.

The window disappears. Knuckles casts "blind85" on the dragon. A gray "85 blind" pops out. He casts "plasma ball 15"; a red "7.11850E09" pops out.

The dragon runs away casting cure on itself. Cure has the same effects as the second half of life-cure (with the sparkle spiraling up), only without the scene darkening, the angel, or time stopping. A green "7.05713E09" pops out of it the moment the effects start. The dragon casts lightning on Knuckles and a green "25,781,087" pops out.

The dragon casts ice4 on Knuckles and a green "49,550,862" pops out. Knuckles casts ultimara6 during ice4's effects. When time resumes, ice4's popup and its effects finish. A red "9.04116E80212" pops out of where the dragon used to be.

Announcer

What a fight that was! Why all the "immune" popups? What is that for?

Knuckles

I'm immune to all negative and neutral status effects. And before you ask, I absorb all ten elements which is why the dragon cured me.

Announcer
Even with our 20 best masters working together, they couldn't defeat the dragon; yet, you come along, small, single, and you take it out like there's nothing to it. How do you do it?

Knuckles
There's more to the dragon than meets the eye. I cast the "full scan" spell on it, bringing up the stats window you saw which shows more than just stats. It shows the strengths, weaknesses, origin, age, background, abilities, and many, many more things. I almost always only look at the first screen, the overview as I call it. With the dragon extremely resistant with seven dot four billion hit points, your masters aren't going to do much to it. Its cure spell will quickly recover it, as you saw. With the ultimara series, I can take out anything with ease. Just look at the damage ultimara6 caused....

The monitor replays the battle from the moment the stats window disappears. The replay stops when the "plasma ball 15 spell" was cast only without the spell effects playing.

Knuckles
Wrong one, that's plasma ball 15. Time stops for its effects so you couldn't see them. It's three upgrades above fire.

The replay continues until the ultimara6 spell was cast.

Knuckles
That's the correct one.

Announcer
What does that mean anyway? I've never seen damage values like that.

Knuckles
The value after the "E" means "times ten to this power". Basically, it's a number over 80,000 digits.

Steve
Is that the ultimara6 spell he was referring to?

Announcer
How does that spell do so much damage?

Knuckles
It uses very extreme energy levels obliterating the atomic make-up of anything, converting it to pure energy. Only the imprecision of spells and quantum fluctuations cause some stray particles to survive. The smaller the object, the better the chance of an infinity symbol appearing instead, but it has to be the size of a grain of silt for a reasonable chance. All that matter is converted to pure energy and gets sent into a parallel universe.

Chris
What are the spell effects like?

Knuckles
With third grade spells and higher, you can't see them since time stops. I've been hit by the spell many times. My max defense makes me immune to everything, including it, so I can describe them.

Announcer
Since the computer here seems to have stopped making sound, do you know what happened?

Knuckles
It thought I was Seth King so I cast the mute spell on it. With my high magic attack and "long effect duration" ability, the effect lasts 67 minutes. A quick "unmute" or "heal" spell will cancel it earlier.

Announcer
I don't know why it thought you were Seth King, outside your high level, but would you fix it?

Knuckles casts "unmute" on the computer outside. The spell effects and related popup cannot be seen as walls block it.

Knuckles
The fix is done. Now I want to return to the outside to take on Seth King. You saw what I could do with that super dragon and how easily I defeated it, you'll have a good idea on just what I could do with Seth King when I do figure out how to get to him and I think I know how thanks to my visit here.

Josh
It was nice seeing you. Thank you for saving me though. You're my favorite because of your power.

Knuckles
Thanks for reminding me....

Knuckles casts create. The effects are not seen.

Knuckles
I cast the create spell to make more life and cure potions, 10,000 of each to be exact. This should last more than long enough until your factory runs again. I spread them out evenly among each of the fighting arenas. My magic potency and accuracy make defective items otherwise improbable. Unless I'm using a spell I haven't used in more than a century, I have no chance of failure or missing.

Chris
It would be so awesome to be at your level! Those water ones would look like a piece of cake! Bye!

Knuckles casts teleport and appears in the audience stands next to the rest of the group.

184

Steve
I have totally underestimated your power! But, if you must go, take care. That Seth King is a real pain to deal with but with what I saw, you should make quick work of him. You should remember that he has been sentenced to death. Do whatever it takes to get rid of him.

Knuckles
Ultimara6 would make quick work of him. Bring my friend Speed in, who is much more powerful than I am, and he stands no chance since Speed, essentially, can't get hit due to four-figure evasion.

Steve
Everyone here, myself and the mayor included, unanimously voted for the death penalty along with most of the whole city. One in sixteen hundred wanted a life sentence; the rest were for the death penalty, the most extreme voting I've ever seen and I've been to many cases. I and the mayor would appreciate your efforts in helping our city. Bye.

Act 7: Solving the mystery
Scene 19: The rescuer's great race

May 29, 1999 at 9:25 PM UTC – 1 hour, 34 minutes remaining

After one second, the city fades away in three seconds and the team appears at the same location they entered the city from. Time flows again. Knuckles casts teleport and the team appears in Knuckles' unchanged house. The three humans return to playing Uno, but reshuffle all of the cards.

Knuckles narrator
My visit to Amazonia, though unexpected, answered numerous questions I had. One still lingered. If the evil force, now known as Seth King, was 1800 years into the future and time was to expire in less than two hours, how was I supposed to get to him? For now, I focused on saving the last few elemental masters. A race to save them started, but had a few problems, until I had unexpected help.

Master Laqualent
There are still five other elemental masters yet.

Knuckles
Where are they?

Master Laqualent
You'll find the Master Lavalent at the top of the Pyramid of Giza in Egypt.

Seth King
And I'll get him first. Take this!

Master Laqualent
I knew that that thing would return.

Knuckles casts teleport but nothing happens.

186

Knuckles
Great, another teleport barrier.

Knuckles casts "cancel teleport blocker 70". He then casts "teleport barrier blocker 47" on everyone, even himself. A gray "47 teleport barrier blocker" pops out of each, including Knuckles.

Knuckles casts teleport and the team appears at the base of the Pyramid of Giza. Rumbling is present and the ground cracks apart two seconds later. It caves in ten seconds after this revealing the same black, hazy ground from before.

Knuckles takes the platform out of his chest upon arriving. The team gets on. Knuckles casts "levitate74", "barrier89", and "teleport blocker barrier 47". "Barrier89" is used on the three humans in addition. The usual gray popups appear. The humans get a gray "0 defense up" and "0 magic shield" instead.

The platform rises, stopping at 5000 feet. When the ground caves in, Knuckles casts "fire shield 88" on the three humans and the platform with the expected gray popup appearing for all.

Seth King
(two-second pause) How did you get here? Come out my friend!

Knuckles
Think before acting. You act well before you think.

Seth King
Advice huh? Come here Master Lavalent.

Master Lavalent
Get out of here! You do not belong here!

Knuckles
I'm here to save you.

Seth King
Don't believe that pink blob.

Master Lavalent
Knuckles? Is that you?

                    Seth King
(with Knuckles) No.

                    Knuckles
(with Seth King) Yes, I'm here.

    Knuckles casts "possession blocker 82" then "barrier89" on the
still-hidden Master Lavalent.

                    Seth King
    Not again! Why do you want to save these large,
    powerful monsters as it is anyway? They are evil
    and on my side.

                    Knuckles
    Do you know what light green dots or aura mean?

    The Master Lavalent rises out of the mist.

                    Seth King
    You have yet to learn.

    A green "blocking possession", "defense up", and "magic
shield" pop out of the Master Lavalent. Knuckles recasts the
same spells. A second later, the same green popups appear and
Knuckles recasts the effects again immediately.

                    Knuckles
    Give it up already, Seth King. You're too slow!

                    Seth King
    I'm faster than you think I am.

    A green "blocking possession" pops out and Knuckles
immediately recasts the spell. When the Master Lavalent rises
above the top of the platform, it disappears.

                    Master Lavalent
    Whew! Thank you Knuckles! So Seth King is that
    thing's name?

188

Knuckles
Sorry about defeating you earlier. I didn't know that Seth King could possess you and I forgot to check my radar and your aura.

Master Lavalent
That's okay. Seth King is very irritating. I've warned all the other masters about this.

Seth King
I'll get the masters before you so bye!

Master Lavalent
Quick, go to Zimbabwe in a small village. You'll encounter the Master Lachemalent there. (hollering) Lavalent land to normal!

The ground returns to normal. Knuckles casts teleport and the team appears 3000 feet above and 500 feet outside a small village in a grassland area in Zimbabwe. The village, hard to see, has straw houses and a small bonfire in the town's center. It is night. The ground, upon arriving, cracks apart.

Knuckles
How come I can't sense anything beyond ten feet from me?

Knuckles casts "cancel sensing barrier 80", which has no effects or cast time.

Knuckles
No effect?

Master Larockalent
I can't figure out that sense barrier at all.

The ground caves in revealing an endless pool of green slime with a 15-foot visibility. It looks and behaves like Jello.

Master Lavalent
I know where the others are.

Knuckles

But, how do I save them all if I can't sense where
Seth King is going?

Knuckles casts "full normalize 46". A ball of white light forms
around Knuckles and gets smaller at an accelerating rate. At the
smallest possible, a burst of several large white sparkles fly out,
fading away in a second. A green "teleport barrier blocker" pops
out. Knuckles recasts "teleport barrier blocker 47" on himself.

Knuckles

It's not me that has the sense barrier status effect.

The Master Lachemalent rises out of the slime causing it to
spray all over, but it smoothly blends back to a smooth surface.
The monster resembles the small version but 30 feet in diameter.
Knuckles casts "possession blocker 82" on the monster.

Master Lavalent

Even I can't tell. It moves with you if that's a hint.

Knuckles

Say, you're right!

Knuckles casts "cancel sensing barrier 53"; nothing happens.

Knuckles

Nothing, no effect. I targeted an area one mile all
around which should've definitely got it. It might be
something else though.

Master Lavalent

That is weird. Using full scan on you doesn't show
you having any negative status effects, but a few
very intense beneficial ones.

The Master Lachemalent disappears when above the platform.

Knuckles

Gotcha! You're safe now.

Master Lachemalent
(shocked) Oh, thank you Knuckles! You scared me for a bit there!

Knuckles
Sorry, I didn't mean to. (hollering) Lachemalent land to normal!

The ground instantly returns to normal.

Master Lavalent
Great! Six down, three to go and no Seth King! The Master Lampalent is on the eastern side of Lagos, Nigeria.

Knuckles casts teleport and everything appears 3000 feet above a rural area near the ocean outside Lagos, Nigeria. The ground, upon arriving, cracks apart. Eight seconds later, it caves in revealing an endless area of dense lightning strikes and sparks that cannot be made out individually. They are generally blue-white (FFD0D0FF) with a few yellow-white (FFFFD0D0) or blue (FFA0A0FF). The visibility through them is only two feet. They are so bright, 40,000 lumens, that, when in the camera view, everything else darkens (from the camera adjusting).

Knuckles
Do not look over the edge or you'll be blinded.

Master Lavalent
I still don't understand it.... Wait! Cast full normalize on everything around you then re-add the good status effects again.

Knuckles
Good idea!

Knuckles casts "full normalize 46". The camera gets 400 feet back from the platform underneath it looking up and the effects occur, now 200 feet in diameter. The camera returns to normal when the effects are over and green popups appear. On the three humans, a green "blocking possession", "defense up", "fire shield", "magic shield", "teleport barrier blocker", and "wind barrier" appear. On Knuckles, a green "teleport barrier blocker" appears. The platform has a green "defense up", "levitate", "magic shield", and "teleport barrier blocker".

Knuckles casts "levitate16" on the platform preventing any noticeable fall. The other status effects are added after in the following order (the spell cast): "teleport barrier blocker 46", "barrier89", "wind barrier 81", and "possession blocker 82".

Knuckles

That was everything and I still can't sense the Master Lampalent anywhere!

Master Lavalent

I can't either, and I can't speak to him either.

Master Larockalent

Same here.

Master Laqualent

No different. Did (one-second pause) Seth get him?

Master Lavalent

I hope not! Gravity and light still remain though.

Knuckles

(hollering) Master Lampalent, I'm here for you!

Master Larockalent

I'm not sure if other masters can hear you when in their element where the ground used to be.

Knuckles

Short of diving down there and looking around, I don't know what's taking him so long. It's always been no more than 20 seconds, usually ten, but this is going on much longer.

Five seconds pass without anything. Knuckles walks around the platform's edge in 15 seconds looking down.

Knuckles

(3/4 of the way around) I'm not seeing him.

Master Lavalent

I don't either.

Master Lachalent

Zip.

Master Lairalent

Zilch.

Master Laqualent

Nada.

Master Larockalent

Nothing at all.

Master Lavalent

It appears as if Seth King got here first. Let's go to the Master Lalightalent. He's on that new continent on a mountain peak near his weird house. It's on the eastern side near the U-shaped alcove. Be warned that it is dangerous there.

Knuckles

I have a map of the area, due to sensing it when I could. (hollering) Lampalent land to normal!

The ground returns to normal. A two-second pause occurs. Knuckles casts teleport and everything appears on a peak 9600 feet above the rest of the land.

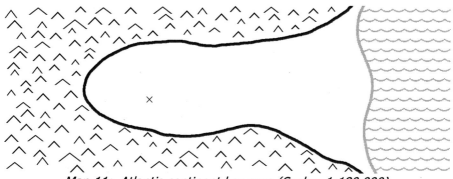

Map 11: Atlantis continent key area (Scale: 1:180,000)

All of Atlantis is bare rock. There are no life forms outside the occasional dead, decaying deep sea creature. The team is in an area where 10,000-foot mountains are. The mountains form a "U" shape. In a large, flat, open valley inside the "U", a 25x10-foot wooden shack is found (the X). A 400-foot-deep valley surrounds the "U". The mountains and valley have very steep, near-vertical cliffs. The mountains are generally higher further from the valley. Barely visible, scattered few and far between, are smaller versions of the elemental masters. Only lalightalents and lagravalents are visible, of which new ones burst out every three seconds, appearing in a five-mile radius around the shack.

Master Lavalent
Wrong peak! Go north, northwest of the shack.

Knuckles casts teleport again and appears another four miles north on the other side of the "U", now on a peak 10,800 feet above, the highest in the area.

The ground cracks apart three seconds after arriving. Before this, Knuckles casts "hypernova9" on the monsters. The popups cannot be seen due to too much distance.

Master Lavalent
The Master Lalightalent should be here, I hope.

The ground caves in in ten seconds after cracking apart. An endless serene scene of cumulus humilis clouds replaces the ground. The clouds have openings where various other types of clouds are below. It's as if the team is above an overcast sky. The clouds drift along at 30 mph all in the same direction.

Knuckles goes to the edge of the platform and looks down.

Knuckles
Nice scene. It's, in a sense, heavenly.

The Master Lalightalent appears and Knuckles casts "possession blocker 82" on him.

Knuckles
Good, he's safe. Hopefully I can get to the Master Lagravalent in time!

The Master Lalightalent disappears when above the platform.

Master Lalightalent
What happened?

Knuckles
I saved you from Seth King. (hollering) Lalightalent land to normal!

The ground returns to normal.

Master Lavalent
The Master Lagravalent is in the valley south of here, southwest of the house.

Knuckles casts teleport and everything appears in a valley 400 feet below the rest of the land but 3000 feet above it. The ground has already started cracking apart.

Seth King
(in a child's bullying form; singing) I got the lampalent, na, na, na, na, na!

Knuckles
How dare you! You aren't getting the last one!

The ground caves in revealing a dark gray (FF505050), textureless ground. The gravity also increases at a constant rate, making the three humans struggle to stay upright.

Ivan
(yelling) Help! The gravity! (almost out of breath) Too strong!

Knuckles casts "gravity shield 78" on the three humans. The spell is the same as "fire shield", only with a gray (20808080), nonmoving wall instead. A gray "78 gravity barrier" pops out of each. Knuckles and the platform are not affected, even at 50 G, the maximum it reaches, within 15 seconds.

Ivan
Thank you. I feel light-headed now.

Knuckles
You can't glide with this status effect active so watch it so you don't fall.

The Master Lagravalent appears from below. Upon it appearing, Knuckles casts "possession blocker 82".

Seth King
The Master Lagravalent is mine! It's all mine!

A green "blocking possession" pops out, but Knuckles recasts the spell to get it back.

Seth King
So you want to play hard-to-get huh? Try this!

Seth King casts "death" on Knuckles and the three others. The effects play, one copy for each. The ax bounces off Knuckles but slices through the humans. A red "immune" pops out of Knuckles, and a gray "1 fatal" pops out of the humans. Before the humans fall, Knuckles casts life-cure to revive them, with the same effects as before, though the green numbers at the end are "308" for Ivan, "274" for Tu, and "321" for Tyler.

Knuckles
Good try, but you're wasting time.

The Master Lagravalent disappears when above the platform.

Knuckles
Got him, so I'm good to go there.

No you're not.

Seth King casts ultimara3 on everything; only Knuckles remains. A red "0", pops out of Knuckles, "1.31265E595" for Ivan, "1.35927E595" for Tu, "3.7564E652" for Tyler, and "2.12046E599" for the platform. Knuckles, when time resumes, casts "recall". Everything reappears as if nothing happened.

Knuckles

Give it up already!

Seth King

You'll love my house. Really! You will! It's filled with all kinds of decorations that make it look pricy. Oh, and my friends there will be welcoming you, if you don't mind. See if you find my....

Knuckles

Oh hush! I already know what the house looks like, inside and out. I'll get Speed on you too and you're not going like him.

Seth King

You hush yourself too! I see you haven't figured out my sense barrier! It's Amazonia's greatest treasure and I think I found its weakness now.

Knuckles

I think I found your weakness: stupidity. (three-second pause) He left I guess. (hollering) Lagravalent land to normal!

The ground returns to normal.

Master Lavalent

Well, we got three of the four, still good. Once we get to his realm, we'll need to grab both the Lampalent and Ladarkalent while there, if they are at that house of his.

Tyler

What is meant by "Amazonia's greatest treasure"?

Knuckles

Good question! He thinks he found a weakness and given this, I suspect that this is the barrier around Amazonia that prevents him from entering. (shocked) Yikes! Did he find a way to get in!? I sure hope not! (normal) Then again, if I couldn't sense the barrier when we were about to go there, then I suspect that that's the cause of the barrier. But what spell was it that was used to take down such a sensing barrier?

Ivan

Remember, at the library, you stated of having to read the computer stuff to figure out how to add the details about the elemental masters? Would it be in any of that?

Knuckles

Oh, I should still have those details too! (three-second pause) I found the weakness for the sensing, but none that I can see for the barrier.

Knuckles casts "cancel sense-proof barrier 18", a spell with no effects. A green "18 sense-proof barrier" pops out of a point a foot above Knuckles. Another cast gives the same popup but the third causes a green "sense-proof barrier".

Knuckles

That's a spell I haven't used for almost 300 years by now, at such an extremely low level. It leveled up twice from this as it's so low, just seventeen-fourteen now! I can sense things again too!

Ivan

I want to use those coupons I got at the party for pizza. I'm hungry!

Knuckles looks at the shack below.

198

Knuckles
(three-second pause) That house is our final destination, and it's certainly not a pretty one to me. It's got all kinds of traps and even high-level evil spirits, both of which not a problem for me.

Scene 20: A pizza break

May 29, 1999 at 9:42 PM UTC − 1 hour, 17 minutes remaining

Knuckles casts teleport. Everything but the platform appears inside the building. The team waits to be seated. The place has moderately-low activity and increases; it's 4:42 PM local time.

Knuckles narrator
With eight available elemental masters saved, I decided that we should use those free pizza coupons. I was disappointed that I couldn't get one of them. After the meal, I intended on getting Speed and heading over to that mysterious little shack I saw when getting the last two masters.

A waitress comes to the team.

Waitress
Hi Knuckles. Are you here to eat?

Knuckles
I don't eat, but these three are.

Waitress
Would you like a table or a booth?

Ivan
I prefer a booth, but I generally don't care.

The waitress leads the team to the nearest booth. Ivan and Tyler are together and Knuckles and Tu are on the other side. Knuckles stands instead, so he can see the table top.

Waitress
Would you like anything to drink?

Ivan
Mountain Dew or Mello Yello, whichever you have.

Tu
I want what you get when two atoms of hydrogen covalently bond with one of oxygen. That is, water.

Tyler
Sprite or 7up, whichever you have.

Knuckles
I never need to drink anything, nor eat anything.

Waitress
Do you know what you want to order?

Knuckles
Ivan and Tu won a free, one-topping medium pizza.

Knuckles takes a coupon out of his chest and hands it over.

Knuckles
Erik Ramstad Middle School gave two of these to them at the graduation party.

Waitress
Okay. What do you want to order?

Ivan
I want a plain cheese pizza, thin crust. I'm a vegetarian – I hate meat.

Tyler
I want a thin-crust pepperoni pizza. Could I have an extra topping of pepperoni though?

Waitress
You'll have to pay for the extra toppings beyond what the coupons allow.

Tu
I guess I'll go with pepperoni as well. Then again, split it between half cheese and half pepperoni. Although I would prefer thick crust, I wouldn't mind going with a thin crust.

Knuckles
Basically then, have one pizza a cheese-only and the other as pepperoni. Tu will get one-third of each while the others get two-thirds of their type. That way, it's fairly split and easier to make. I'll pay for the second pizza, drinks, and the extra topping.

Tu
I can agree with that. You're smart!

Waitress
So, that's two thin-crust medium pizzas. One is cheese and the other is pepperoni with an extra topping of pepperoni. For drinks, I have Mountain Dew, Sprite, and a water.

Knuckles
Correct.

Tu
Oh, no frozen water, ice, with my water, please.

The waitress leaves to go back to the kitchen.

Suddenly, out of nowhere, Ivan spots a large pile of random cars stacked in the ditch where seven cars are stacked, forming a partial pyramid with four on the bottom and decreasing by one each step. Crossing the frontage road and two lanes of the four-laned highway is a red 1992 Ford truck hovering in mid-air ten feet above the ground going ten mph as if being hauled by an invisible crane at a junk yard. When the truck lands, a 1989

Buick is lifted out of the Pizza Hut's parking lot and is moved over to the pile as well. No one is inside any of these cars.

Ivan
(sees the cars; confused) Now how can cars hover in the air without a crane? That's strange.

Knuckles looks out the window and sees the cars moving.

Knuckles
Huh? Is that you Seth King? (one-second pause) No response, but I can sense his black dot.

Ivan
Why is Seth King doing that?

Knuckles
I don't know, but it's probably to grab my attention. No one is inside any of the cars but the fix is easy.

Knuckles casts teleport. The cars reappear in their original locations, including the one in mid air. Five cars appear in the Pizza Hut parking lot and three appear by adjacent buildings.

A cure spell follows. Green numbers pop out and range from 1700 to 3900, increasing with mass (double means double). The cure spell's effects play at the same time – one sparkle each.

Seth King
You better hurry! Seventy minutes remain! I've set numerous traps at my house. Have fun with them!

After a five-second pause, two robbers wearing ski masks and gloves enter the store armed with metallic baseball bats. They demand cash from the cash register using a type-written note. At this moment, Knuckles casts "glue" on them and become statues, unable to move. A gray "1 immobilized" pops out.

Knuckles
Don't worry about them, I've got it under control.

A half second later, a green "immobilized" and "charmed" pop out. Knuckles casts teleport and they disappear before moving.

Knuckles
I've teleported them to jail so he's not a threat anymore.

Waitress
Thanks for protecting us and the store.

A red "missed!" pops out of Knuckles. A red "immune" pops out of him a quarter second later. After another quarter second, one of the waiters, attending a couple, suddenly falls, as if having cardiac arrest. A gray "3 cardiac arrest" pops out of the waiter.

Knuckles
Stop it Seth King!

Knuckles casts "heal11" on the fallen waiter. A brief-case-like first-aid kit 18 inches long by 12 inches tall and 3 inches deep fades on over the waiter in a half second. In red, and centered, "first aid kit" is written above a "plus" sign. After a half second, the kit opens in a half second revealing various things found in first-aid kits like band-aids and various medications. The kit remains open for one second and fades away in a half second. When the spell's effects start, a green "cardiac arrest" and "flu" pop out of the waiter and he gets up as if nothing happened. Knuckles casts "cure" on the waiter. A green "257" pops out.

Knuckles
You aren't going to fool me Seth King!

Seth King
(mad) That does it! I'll add a trap you'll just love to be in, three actually! Good bye forever! Ha, ha!

Knuckles
Well, he left.

Waiter
What was that all about?

Knuckles
He's just some highly advanced criminal from the distant future wrecking the present named Seth King that I'm about to get. He's causing a lot of mayhem but always underestimates me.

Waiter
He sounds scary, but good thing you were around.

Fifty minutes pass. The pizzas, except for a slice of cheese pizza, are eaten. A pile of napkins with soaked up grease on them (from fat) by Ivan an inch tall is on a plate. The waitress is walking to the group. The place is now busy with customers.

Ivan
I'm full!

Tyler
That was a good meal, before the big battle with that moron.

Waitress
Would you like a to-go box?

Knuckles
Nope. I'll just delete it with the delete spell. It's a better form of recycling – it becomes atmosphere.

Knuckles casts "delete". The extra items disappear.

Knuckles
I'm now going off to eradicate that stubborn Seth King once and for all.

Knuckles casts teleport and the team appears inside his house, now dark. Knuckles casts "lighten" and the house lights up in the center of the ceiling like before. A four-second pause occurs and Speed appears in front of Knuckles.
Speed revolves around speed, hence his name. He resembles Knuckles, only with green (FF30B050) fur an inch thick. He is just 23 inches tall, has normal-sized hands (for his size), has the

haze around the pupil, uses the selective speech ability, and can put things in his chest like Knuckles. When Speed moves, he instantly appears at his intended location, unless noted.

Speed

What is it Knuckles?

Knuckles

I'm about to enter battle with Seth King who seems to be a very powerful foe. I'll need your assistance.

Speed

Okay then, let's get a move on.

Scene 21: The death house

May 29, 1999 at 10:47 PM UTC – 12 minutes remaining

Knuckles casts teleport and the team appears 15 feet outside the wooden shack's east side seen earlier. They look at the 25-foot wide, 8.5-foot-tall, 10-foot deep shack standing still for 15 seconds then walk to it, including Speed, stopping upon entering.

Map 12: The death house's ground floor (Scale: 1:75)

The shack's two-foot-wide, door-free entrance is 6.5 feet tall. Inside, the three-foot-wide, easily-crumbling floor splitting in two is made of badly-prepared concrete. The ceiling is 7.5 feet high.

Knuckles narrator
With everyone set to go, it was time to get to Seth King. I still had the problem of figuring out how to get him, but the strange house on Atlantis was the only clue I had. Thankfully, Speed's ability to distort and travel through time and space solved the problem. The last few minutes ticked by faster than I realized and this trap-filled death house wasn't much of a problem (one-second pause) at first.

Speed
(upon entering the house) Oh I see what you're doing. There's a certain area in this house that will allow you to successfully get into Seth King's realm. I went through the house 15 times to find the traps and the easiest route. The pathway to the right is just a dead end that leads to a pool of quicksand. The pathway to the left leads to a basement filled with traps but has the key area. So, go left.

The team takes the left path where they encounter a set of unstable-looking concrete stairs to the north.

Ivan
Knuckles, I have a question. When I watched you in the fighting arena, I saw every one of the human fighters casting spells. How can I do it?

Speed
(upon Ivan finishing) Go down these stairs into the basement, turn right, and get on the white platform.

The team goes down the stairs, which crumble as they descend. With two steps left, all stairs break apart in a chain reaction and fall. The team turns right and heads to a white platform six feet long by four feet wide six inches above the sand in the opposite corner across 12 1/4 feet of soft, fine, flat sand.

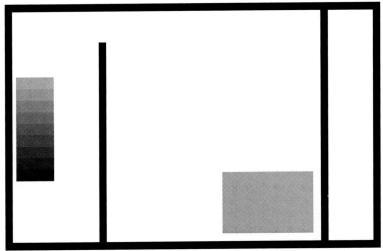

Map 13: The death house's basement (Scale: 1:75)

<u>Knuckles</u>
(while going down the stairs) Naturally, you'll need to gain some very powerful abilities, most notably the "energy management" one in addition to the spells themselves. This'll take humans at least a century of constant wars. Let's get through this house first then I'll give you the basic set of spells.

Five seconds after the team steps on the platform, the sand becomes a grayish yellow (FFD0C060), viscous liquid with a white (FFFFFFFF) glittery look. It bubbles intensely and has three-inch waves. The visibility through it is six inches.

<u>Seth King</u>
Welcome to my home, uninvited guests. Oh, I see you have a new one. Let the games begin!

Seth King casts "blind" then "ice4" on Speed. A red "missed!" pops out instead of spell effects both times.

<u>Seth King</u>
Hmm. A sneaky one apparently. Come out my servants and show these morons what you've got.

Suddenly, an egg-shaped monster with five arms, three legs, and a rounded "hill" for a head made out of the liquid rises out in five seconds ten feet southwest of the team. It is eight feet tall. After a second, it takes a step toward the team, going one mph.

A half second later, it becomes a fireball resembling a meteor punching a hole in the southwest corner at four miles per second. At this moment, a red "2.98257E19" pops out of it. This is Speed's "speed busher" attack. The fireballs' speeds vary but they have the same kinetic energy with slight fluctuation.

<u>Speed</u>
Simple monsters! Got something more at my level, 11,058? I could use a level up.

<u>Seth King</u>
So you want real demons then? Alright, fine. Come out wherever you are!

A one-second pause occurs. A seven-foot area of the north wall has facial and arm indentations extending inward three feet as if someone was lying down on them as if very soft.

The demon casts "dark beam 27" on the entire team, a spell, to it, with no cast time. Time stops and the scene, except the team, fades halfway to black in a half second. None of the spell effects play on Speed, except the fade and time stop. A flame resembling that from flare erupts over the team in the same way but all black, lasts longer, and without an explosion. A circular, black ray of light comes from below the center of each a second later, widening to 60 inches wide for the humans and 21 inches wide for Knuckles. It grows and shrinks, resizing linearly by area, in a second each. The ray of light is infinitely high. When gone, the black flames fade away in a second. One second later, the scene fades to normal in a half second. Time resumes. A green "2.46729E10" pops out of Knuckles, a red "2.48728E10" for Ivan, a red "2.48783E10" for Tu, a red "2.54920E10" for Tyler, and a red "missed!" for Speed. Speed is avoided due to the miss. Knuckles casts life-cure; a green "309" pops out of Ivan, a green "275" on Tu, and a green "323" on Tyler at the end.

Knuckles casts "moon blast 86" on the demon with the green numbers still present. Time stops and the scene completely fades to black, except the walls. Extremely bright rays of white light a half inch in diameter and five to eight feet long, increasing with speed, bombard the target from random directions 15 times a second from 250 to 400 mph after a one-second pause. The camera adjusts for the very bright light making the walls look black. A large ray of white light, similar to the second half of "dark beam", appears. It grows to 70 feet in diameter instead then shrinks taking two seconds for each. The bombardment continues until the large beam is gone where they abruptly stop. The wall is no longer blackened. After one second, the scene returns to normal and time resumes. A red "5.37003E16" pops out of where the wall indentations were and they return to the way they were originally in a quarter second.

Tyler

What is this all about anyway?

Seth King

You must like traps if you wanted to come here.
You have no idea what you got yourselves into.

Knuckles

I've known ever since we first came to Atlantis.

Seth King

If you're so smart, figure this one out!

The eastern wall closes in at a foot per second. A very large, jagged hole instantly appears a half second later, big enough to allow the team through safely without touching it. It becomes a fireball and digs a cylindrical-shaped hole in the dirt wall 11 feet behind. A red "2.92625E19" pops out of the hole's center. The walls continue moving until they completely close then return to the original position after a two-second pause.

Knuckles

The crushing wall trap won't affect me or Speed.

Plus, I can easily get out of the way. You're such a simple enemy that you're not worth much effort.

Seth King
I think you'll love my beautiful castle I made. You'll meet me there, if you can make it out alive!

A one-second pause occurs and the scene flashes white for a half second. The liquid has no more bubbles, the waves are four inches high, and it has a one-foot visibility through it.

Knuckles
What was with the bright flash? I should refresh some status effects.

Knuckles casts "barrier89" on the humans and Speed. A gray "0 defense up" and "0 magic shield" pops out of the humans and a gray "89 defense up" and "89 magic shield" pop out of Speed.

Ivan
What did you target Speed for?

Speed
I'm not immune to damage like Knuckles is. My extreme, generalized 2000% evasion makes me practically impossible to hit which has almost the same effect. If I lose my concentration at the right moment, I can take hits. I'm focused mostly toward statistical development than abilities and spells. My speed busher attack is my primary attack and it's more powerful than Knuckles' spells, except the ultimara series. It's useless with spiritual enemies as only spells work on those but I can also cast spells too, far, far faster than Knuckles can, approaching Planck time for the fastest if I warp space-time in the right way, something Knuckles can't do which really limits his speed. I should cast hasten on myself, just to be safe. This increases my physical evasion further.

Speed casts "hasten107" on himself. A gray "107 haste" pops out. Speed, like Knuckles, always skips the middle part of spell-casting. Unlike that in the fighting arena, Speed's voice is not affected by the time effects – he changes it to cancel the effect.

Ivan

So, now what? What's this castle he's mentioning?

Speed

I know where its at and the whole world outside is drastically different, and scary. Basically, let's just get out of this death house of his.

Speed appears past the exit. The rest of the team jump and glide to Speed over the liquid. Just before reaching the entrance, a concrete slab two inches thick crashes down blocking the exit. Ivan, Tu, Tyler, and Knuckles slam into it, fall, and quickly get into an upright position upon landing. The humans land in the liquid causing a big ripple but no real splash. After a half second of standing on it, the humans sink four inches per second until they hit bottom, when the waves' crests reach Tu's upper neck. The liquid is a lot less dense than water but its very high viscosity causes the slow sinking. Knuckles stands on it, going up and down with the waves, as if solid. A red "0" pops out of each.

Ivan

(one-second pause; scared) Help! I'm sinking!

Knuckles

(with Ivan) That's a dirty trick!

The concrete slab becomes a fireball headed toward the white platform. A red "2.83632E19" pops out but another identical slab instantly slams down to replace it. Speed appears by Knuckles.

Ivan + Tu + Tyler

(all three at the same time; scared) Help!

Speed
Don't worry. This stuff doesn't hurt you and you'll
bottom out safely. Pulling you out is not possible as
we'll rip you apart. I'll need to bust these doors.

Tu
(worried) You'd better be sure on that.

The slab that just replaced the previous becomes a fireball
headed east and slightly downward. A blue "6.20077E19" pops
out and another one comes. After a half-second pause, it, too,
becomes a fireball heading south going through the ceiling a foot
before hitting the wall. The hard-to-see outside sky is black. A
red "2.7427E19" pops out and another slab appears.

A half second after the humans hit bottom, Ivan walks in the
liquid at five inches per second. The others follow a second later,
but at four inches per second. They walk away from the entrance
watching Speed and Knuckles. Ivan tries swimming, but can't get
in the right orientation. He tries treading it like water for four
seconds, but doesn't rise as he can't do it fast enough.

Knuckles
(as the humans move) So it appears he finally used
his peanut brain. How many of these are there?

Speed
Since my reaction time is instantaneous, you bust
these while I get under one to see what's going on.

Knuckles
Right. Ready?

Knuckles punches the slab a second later. It bursts into many
small fragments and dust scatters; a red "877,433,704" pops out.
As damage increases, there's more dust and the fragments get
smaller and more numerous. Speed appears under it as another
slab comes down on top of him. Speed holds it up.

Knuckles
Anything?

212

Speed

I saw another one, the one I'm holding. Try again.

Knuckles punches the slab Speed holds up. A red "899,469,052" pops out and another one comes.

Knuckles

Anything yet?

Speed

Same thing. Keep busting more repeatedly.

Knuckles busts the slabs once every half second. Another one falls to replace it when broken. In order of occurrence, the popups are as follows: blue "3.41451E09", red "845,580,894", red "905,199,871", red "834,538,222", white "2.59891E09", red "841,394,535", red "840,478,283", then a red "895,332,129".

Speed

I'm still not getting anything. There's always another one directly above it.

Knuckles

I got an idea then.

Knuckles casts hypernova on the slabs, the one Speed holds up and one hidden in the wall directly above. The slabs shatter when time resumes and some fragments fall in the liquid sinking a half second after landing in it. Ivan grabs a large piece before it sinks and throws it upwards to his left. A red "161,416,890" pops out of the lower one and the other number cannot be seen. A slightly longer delay occurs before another slab appears.

Knuckles

I blasted both the lower one and where the upper one is supposedly at. Anything?

Speed

I saw something completely different 14 feet above.

Knuckles

Okay then.

Knuckles casts hypernova, targeting the slabs and a webcam-like device directly above. A blue "350,579,225" pops out of the lower slab; the others cannot be seen. Another slab slams down.

Knuckles

Still nothing?

Speed

You got rid of that thing up there.

Knuckles punches the slab. A blue "2.08099E09" pops out, but no more appear.

Speed

That was it. Let's go!

Act 8: The finale
Scene 22: Finding the enemy

Unknown time

    The humans walk through the liquid to the entrance. Tu gets out by pushing down with her hands on the solid floor where the entrance is. She pulls herself out at a foot per second. The glittery material sticks all over her skin and clothes. Tyler gets out then Ivan. Ivan's hands slip when two feet out and sinks four inches before he gets his hands back and makes it out.

    When out, the team goes to where the stairs are, which are in ruins. Speed disappears. The team steps over the fragments from the busted slabs. They jump up to get up the stairs then follow the path used to enter the house in reverse.

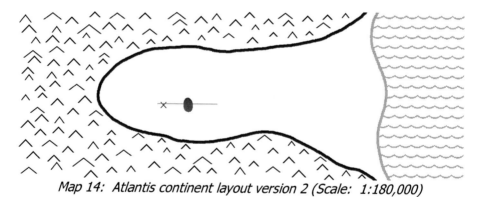

Map 14: Atlantis continent layout version 2 (Scale: 1:180,000)

    There are 500-foot hills instead of mountains. A long row of withered trees are 225 feet north. The valley is nearly absent, and the land is black with a few areas of dark brown.

    Outside, the world is scary and evil-looking. Fires; pointy, black (FF000000), bent metallic fences three to five feet tall; lava; and a few evil spirits are scattered around. The sky is black, but the stars and Moon are not visible. The clouds, 1/2 scattered cumulus humilis and 3/8 scattered altostratus, glow an eerie red-orange (FFD06000) at 50 lumens as if made of embers. The brightness of the area is 30 lux, but increases to 150 by the lava and fires. A very severe lightning storm with six big strikes per second is visible just over the black ocean. The wind is calm.

Knuckles narrator

(as the humans get out) That was a strange shack, but that was only for starters. I now knew I was in Seth King's realm, but it looked very scary and evil, the stuff of the worst nightmares. I knew I needed to keep my guard up. That creator pod and the very viscous liquid were the most intelligent things that Seth King did so far. Speed is of great help to me. Now my mission was getting to Seth himself, but more challenges awaited me and the others.

Tyler

(upon exiting) Where do we go now? What happened? Where are we?

Tu

Yeah, why is everything so dark and evil-feeling?

Knuckles

I think I can see why everything is eerie and evil-looking. Remember how I went around saving the elemental masters and that the tenth, the master of dark, is not around? Dark is the element of evil. Light is the opposite. With the electric element lost, the storm is present. Since eight of the elemental masters are safe, these elements are kept in check. Since those for dark and electric are gone, evil and electricity have gotten out of hand. As to what time it is, I don't know. The world is about the same in terms of land and ocean, though the continents have moved about 250 feet or so. Given this, it's seventeen hundred to nineteen hundred years in the future, and knowing Seth King being eighteen hundred years, it checks out very well. We're still on Atlantis, the eastern coast to be precise.

Speed
Seth King's castle is on Mount Olympus in Greece.
The land has a few differences, but the layout is
generally the same. There are no cities, and, unless
you consider the billions of evil spirits as living, Seth
King is the only living thing that I can see.

The line of withered trees, from the west, start being pulled
under in a quarter second, as if brought down by a gopher, and
completely disappear into a hole. A second later, the next one in
the row goes under. The rate accelerates at 10 mph per second.

Ivan
(after the third tree goes down) Why are the trees
getting plowed under so fast?

Knuckles
(yelling) Run for it!

Knuckles takes the platform out and casts "wind barrier 81",
"levitate74", and "barrier89" on it, with the same popups, as the
team gets on it; Speed appears on it and Knuckles jumps on.
The platform moves east, 30° upwards, and stops at 20 mph
upwards. It keeps going horizontally. When at 200 mph, 8.066
seconds later, the platform stops going up, now 280.6 feet high,
but goes east at maximum speed 2100 feet from the shack.
A dark forest of withered trees is 1200 feet ahead. The line of
trees continues beyond it for 3/4 of a mile. When the team gets
across the 1500 feet of forest, the trees being pulled under get
within 200 feet of the team. Past the forest, the trees suddenly
speed up, approaching and passing them at 400 mph.
When the last tree goes down, the entire island becomes a
pool of glowing red-orange lava within five seconds. A series of
geysers of lava burst below the team. When near the ocean, a
lava geyser hits the left side of Ivan's seat, melting it a little. A
red "7" pops out. Another goes over the top of the platform
missing everything. A red "missed" pops above the center of the
platform. The team, two seconds later, is over the open ocean,
glittering in the dim, red-orange light, but looks and acts normal.

218

Knuckles

That was close! I wonder why that happened. Oh, a powerful evil spirit. Oddly enough, the house survived! Now, where's that castle at?

Knuckles casts "teleport" but nothing happens.

Knuckles

Great, another teleport blocker.

Knuckles casts "cancel teleport blocker 70"; nothing happens.

Knuckles

No effect? That's strange.

Speed

It's not a spell or status effect causing it; it's just plain evil that's causing it. You won't be able to remove this one. Then again... nope, cannot be removed. I'll lead you to where Seth King's castle is. You know how I can warp space-time.

Master Lalightalent

I just realized that I forgot to give you the "hyperleviburst" ability when you rescued me. But, I'm scared. I only have four though, not five.

Speed

If it involves high speed, you can leave me out, unless it goes faster than the speed of light, of which I highly doubt.

Master Lalightalent

Man, that's the fastest possible! Well, I guess I can leave Speed out. Hyperleviburst allows you to go sixteen hundred m-p-h and accelerate at 500 m-p-h per second, well beyond superleviburst. So, I guess, in that case, I can leave Speed out.

Master Lachalent
You should transfer the abilities to Knuckles then
have him transfer as needed. He's got better safe-
guards against evil than we do, considering his level
is higher than ours and he's immune to everything.

The ability transfer effect occurs on Knuckles, with a density
of 20 sparkles per square foot. After a one-second pause when
the ability transfer effect ends, Knuckles takes out three green
marbles from his chest. He transfers first to Tu, Ivan, then Tyler,
with a density of five sparkles per square foot.

Ivan
How is this ability used?

Knuckles
Ah, I see how. You need to get into a somewhat
egg-shaped position. Basically, get down on your
knees, then sit on the back of feet. Curl your body
over so you're almost inward and have your arms
tucked inside. From there, just think about the
direction you want to go and off you go. You only
go up at ten mph, but in all other directions, you
peak at sixteen hundred m-p-h. The acceleration is
300 m-p-h per second so, according to the in-depth
description of usage, it checks.

Speed
Boy is that slow! But for you, it's worthy. The
hasten spell also helps.

Several hours pass. The team is still on the platform, now
over Mount Olympus. Seth King's 70-foot-high, medieval-style,
dark red-orange (FFA03000), brick castle 800 feet wide by 1200
feet back is seen from 6000 feet away. It has four watch towers
(where guards would stand) 130 feet high. The castle has a 12-
foot-high door that looks like the bottom of a drawbridge with a
large "do not enter" sign on it. Lava ten feet wide surrounds it
(like moat). The castle has no windows or openings.

Two seconds later, rays of blue-white (E0A0A0FF) light are fired at the team, five per second for two seconds. One gets five inches above Tyler's head; the others miss but are fairly close.

Incoming attack!

The light beams suddenly stop. When the platform gets 1480 feet from the castle, it slows down to a stop with its edge 8 feet away from the entrance to the castle. When the platform stops, the team gets off and it disappears a second later.

I fixed it. An evil spirit did it. Cheap enemies!

That is one huge castle!

I agree. Why so big though?

It almost reminds me of the medieval times as it looks very close to one of those kinds of castles.

It reminds me of history class. I don't like history class, but now that I've seen a medieval castle, I think I've gained a renewed interest.

(when the platform stops) Welcome to my castle, uninvited guests. Leave this place immediately!

That's just a recording, ignore it. The doors are locked, but who needs a key when the speed busher does the same, only better?

The doors become fireballs aimed toward the floor. A blue "6.16117E19" pops out of the center of where they used to be.

A black carpet ten feet wide by seven feet back is inside in the area facing the entrance. Bordering the whole carpet is a flame two feet high with a black, metallic fence in it. A red-glowing hole is in the center of the black area (from the fireball).

An old-looking staircase is to the west; the top is unseen.

A nightstand two feet on each side is 12 feet ahead centered against a wall three feet wide. A vase with a yellow, scary-looking flower inside is on top. The flower is a foot tall and resembles a sunflower, but with spikes in the central area.

To the left and right of the entrance hallway are two paths six feet wide. They are parallel to each other but are both different. The left path has a large pool of glowing yellow (FFFFD040) lava. The right path is simple flooring with a few odd spots. The entrance hallway is 15 feet long from west to east by 12 feet wide. The ceiling is 15 feet high, including that in the pathways.

Speed

I've gone through this castle about 15 times so I know where all the traps are and also where Seth King is. Although his door is locked, the speed busher works wonders for physical barricades, but I grabbed the key anyway. The left path takes you through spikes and lava. The right path takes you through that liquid you were in while in the shack but very deep. From what I'm getting on studying traps, if you go one way to get in, you must use the other to get back. From what I'm seeing, there's no way to fix it due to this strange, pure evil world that we got ourselves into. We might need the left path to flee, since it's straight, so we'll take the right path. I'll lead the way since I memorize it.

Knuckles

Go right on ahead.

Ivan

Wait! What about the spells you said you were going to give us three?

Knuckles
Oh, yeah.

Knuckles takes 16 marbles out of his chest. He gives them to Ivan, Tyler, then Tu, with 80 sparkles per square foot this time.

Knuckles

(while transferring abilities) I'm giving you ten basic attacking spells: "fire", "ice", "lightning", "earth", "acid rain", "gust", "water", "light", "gravitate", and "blaster". I left out "dark" as that's attacking using the power of evil and it has almost no effect. "Blaster" is non-elemental. In addition, I'm also giving you three support spells, "light cure", "heal", and "spell power draw". I gave you "energy management" so you can cast spells and also "status management" so you attempt to gain more spells and abilities on your own. Lastly, "view damage" will allow you to see what damage you and others do, directly and indirectly. I'll explain the ability-learning later. For spells, I need a target.

Knuckles casts "create". A target like those used in archery appears a foot in front of the night stand.

Knuckles

It can take a bit to get used to it as you're going to get a few failures on your first attempts. To cast a spell, all you need to do is focus your energy in an area in front of you, then release it onto your target. The part of releasing it often causes failures in beginners. High-level spells require a high magic potency to reduce the failure rate. You should be able to get about three or four casts, whether successful or not, before you run out of spell power. As you use the abilities, they'll level up and the more powerful spells become available. Unlike me where spells take nanoseconds to cast, you'll take probably a half second or so to do so. This is expected due to a significantly lower action rate and magic potency. Go ahead and try it on that target I used the create spell to make.

Ivan casts lightning; nothing happens and no popup appears.

Knuckles
You're not gathering the energy. Ah, a quick fix!

Knuckles casts "memory alter" on the three humans, a spell with no effects.

Knuckles
Try it now as you should know how to cast now.

Ivan casts lightning on the target taking 450 milliseconds to cast it. A lightning bolt strikes the target; a red "47" pops out.

Ivan
(excited) I did it! Thanks! I saw the 47 too!

Knuckles
Hmm. Weaker than I thought. Ah, the target is quite resistant to electric-elemental attacks.

Tu casts fire on the target but a red "missed!" pops out of it without any effects. She has a 480-millisecond cast time.

Knuckles
You missed the target. Try again.

Tu tries again and is successful. A red "61" pops out of it and the target slowly begins to burn.
Tyler casts water on the target in 450 milliseconds. The fire is put out and a red "16" pops out of it.

Knuckles
If you run low on spell power, you can cast spell power draw to draw it out of your enemies and

replenish it. Either that, or wait a few hours where it'll slowly recover. Anyway, let's go now.

The team walks to the right pathway. When lined up, they glide level. When five feet above the ground, they slow down to land. Speed appears 300 feet down the pathway. The team stops when they get to where Speed is.

Seth King

(when the team glides) Welcome to my castle. I'm surprised you made it. Did you like the sand pit?

Knuckles

Your little brain was working that time, surprisingly.

Speed

But it wasn't good enough as you forgot to take me into account. Be warned though, I know exactly where you and your traps are.

Seth King

You have to find the 15 keys in order to enter, and my door is indestructible. Ha, ha!

Speed

The speed busher can fix indestructible doors easily. Anyway, there's a trap door here. If you step on it, it'll open up and you'll fall into a deep lava pit.

Speed appears on the spot and, a half second later, returns. When Speed returns, the trap door opens and a pool of red lava is visible below. The trap door is six feet wide and five feet back.

Speed

That's what I mean. I'll go to the next trap.

Speed appears 180 feet further down the course. The team glides over the lava pit. The team comes across a brick wall that extends from floor to ceiling and fills the entire area.

We will need to get past this wall, but a cage will crash down upon finding the secret brick that functions as a button to get rid of it. We don't need this as my speed busher will take care of both.

The wall becomes a fireball headed straight across. A red "2.85123E19" pops out.

A square cage with black metal bars an inch in diameter five feet wide by nine feet tall drops on the team. It, upon landing, becomes a fireball headed straight across. A white "1.35828E20" pops out of the cage's center point.

A pit four inches below the ground with the viscous liquid in it is ahead. The liquid is blue (FF0000D0), has two-inch waves, a two-foot visibility, and is nine feet deep.

Walls drop an inch below the liquid's surface and cross over it. They are ten inches from the walls of the pathway on one side.

Ivan
Oh great, more of that liquid stuff, only blue.

Speed appears in both his current location and centered against the wall at the same time for 800 milliseconds.

Speed
Hmm. That's odd, my speed busher won't bust the walls. There's some kind of magic barrier doing it.

Knuckles
Are they solid?

Speed
They are solid, but they won't budge with my speed busher and I tried ten billion times. Even high-end supercriticals aren't enough.

Knuckles casts "cancel magic barrier 86"; nothing happens.

Knuckles
Huh? No popup? That means nothing happened.

226

Speed

It's still there as the speed busher still won't bust it.

Ivan

Maybe we could just hop in, sink to the bottom,
then walk through it, like we did at that shack.

Speed

That isn't going to work – it's nine feet deep.

Ivan

Oh, what about Knuckles' delete spell to delete it?

Knuckles

Good idea.

Knuckles casts delete, but nothing happens.

Knuckles

Nothing happened, not even a popup. Ultimara!
Speed, cast your ultimara8 spell.

Speed casts ultimara8. The blue dome at the end, compared
to ultimara6, is extremely hard to see (20000080). No popup
appears and the liquid remains.

Speed

There's some magic field around here preventing it.
It's apparently going to stay from what I can tell.
Oh, it's the evil of this world that is causing it.

Ivan

Uh, so, how do we cross it then? What about this
hyperleviburst ability?

Knuckles

You're too wide to fit through that narrow gap.

Ivan

What about gliding toward it then making an abrupt
turn sideways?

Tu

I don't know how you do it, but you seem to be smarter than me in regards to problem-solving.

Speed

Won't work. Another wall is just three feet beyond this, too tight.

Knuckles

Ivan does have the right idea. It can be done even with just one foot, but you'd have to go so slow that you'll just land in it.

Tyler

Ya know, I saw that you walked on that liquid while at the house. Is it possible that you could carry us across? Can you lift 75 kilograms?

Knuckles

Say! Not a bad idea! I can easily lift up to 9000 times that much weight, more if I equip some strength pluses. Standing on me is going to be a problem though as I'm very small.

Ivan

Hmm. I guess we should do a practice run near the edge so that, if we do fall over, we can get out. How about creating a walkway over it?

Knuckles casts create, but nothing happens.

Knuckles

Strangely enough, that doesn't work here. Why it worked at the entrance, that I don't know.

Speed

I went on the other side of the world 200 miles above and even I can't so it's got to be the evil of this world that is causing it.

Ivan
So, I guess it's the balance idea? Can you stand on the liquid with us on top of you?

Knuckles
Good question. I don't know in that case. We'll have to try it instead.

Ivan
I'll try first.

Tyler
Being brave? I'll let you.

Tu
I'm a bit scared myself. Go ahead.

Knuckles steps on the liquid, standing on it, and goes up and down with the waves. Ivan slowly puts more weight on Knuckles a second later. When his full weight is on Knuckles, Knuckles sinks in it at an inch per second and Ivan loses his balance. He steps backwards to correct it, but pounds his feet on the liquid's surface jumping up into the ceiling as if the liquid was solid. A red "0" pops out. A ripple like a splash eight inches high spreads out quickly. He lands back in it at the edge and a half second later, he sinks six inches per second. When waist deep, he puts his hand on the edge behind and uses it to twist and turn around. He pulls himself out using the ledge. Blue glitter covers him.

Knuckles
It's a lot less dense than I thought it was so my walk-on-water ability is not effective enough.

Ivan
And I have the solution. When I lost my balance, I hit the surface hard and jumped up into the ceiling. I've also noticed a delay before you start sinking. It seems like if you pound on it hard and repeatedly, you won't sink and could thus walk across it.

Ivan steps over the edge and begins pounding the surface of the liquid, causing ripples to spread out each time, but without sinking. He starts fast, turning around, but gradually slows down until two pounds per second where he sinks enough to prevent lifting his foot. When waist deep, he pulls himself out.

Ivan

(while pounding) See, just like this. Walk up to that gap, turn to the side, jump sideways, then turn as needed and repeat until you've crossed it. Don't go too slow or slip, or you'll sink in it.

Knuckles

Great find!

Speed

There are four of these walls with narrow gaps. They go left, right, left, center in that order.

Ivan crosses the pool successfully constantly stomping four or five times a second. Knuckles runs across and Speed appears at the end. Knuckles' steps don't cause the ripple effect. Tu goes with. Tyler is last, but on the last gap, his sideways jump is awkward and tilted causing him to lose footing and land on his knees. He faces the team, quickly getting up, and sinks.

Tyler

(scared) Oh no! I lost my footing! Help!

Ivan quickly goes to the edge but can't reach for Tyler.

Ivan

(while reaching out) I can't reach you! (quickly) When you reach bottom, walk straight, raise your hands, and I'll grab you, pulling you up.

Tyler

Got it!

Tyler gets a big breath of air then goes under.

Ivan
Hold onto my left arm. I'm jumping in to grab him.

Tu grabs Ivan's left arm. Ivan jumps in, pounds it, turns around to face the edge, then stops pounding. A half second after stopping, Ivan sinks, but Tu prevents him from sinking more than four feet deep. Eight seconds later, Tyler's hands are barely visible. Ivan reaches in with his right hand, grabs Tyler's hands, and pulls him up. Ivan sinks while doing so and Tu moves closer to the edge. Knuckles and Speed hold onto Tu's foot. At a foot per second, Tyler rises out of the liquid. When above the surface, Tyler gasps for air. When four feet in, Ivan lets go of Tyler and Tyler grabs the edge. Tu lets go of Ivan and Knuckles and Speed let go of Tu. Both pull themselves out.

Tyler
That was scary! Thank you so much!

Suddenly, a meteor-like object four inches in diameter 20 feet ahead strikes Tyler at 30 mph knocking him back into the liquid. He sinks to waist deep then pulls himself out again.

Evil spirit
This is Seth King's territory. Do not enter!
Knuckles
Bye!

Knuckles casts "light". A single beam of light from the "moon blast" series strikes a point 20 feet ahead. A red "18,831,229" pops out of the point the meteor-like object originated from.

Knuckles
Cheap enemy. Let's get going.

Speed
There's one more thing up ahead, but it's easy.

Speed appears 200 feet ahead. Here, there's a pool of soft, water-rich, gooey mud 20 feet across. The team walks to it.

<u>Speed</u>
(when the team arrives) A pool of soft mud four
feet deep. Just glide over or walk through it. This
is the last part.

Tu and Tyler get a running jump then glide across without
problems. Knuckles runs over it as if solid and Speed appears at
the other side. Ivan follows by getting a running jump and glides
across higher. He hits an invisible wall 12 feet from the end and
falls in. Ivan walks through the mud at one mph to the end.

<u>Ivan</u>
(upon landing in the mud) This feels weird and
gooey! I hit something, but I don't know what I hit.

Ivan gets out of the mud, covered by it.

<u>Tu</u>
I think we should practice that hyperleviburst thing.
I've never seen it in use yet.

Everyone but Speed gets into the leviburst position and rise at
ten mph until two feet below the ceiling. They make a few small,
slow maneuvers for about five seconds then fall to the ground by
getting out of the leviburst position.

<u>Speed</u>
I forgot about that. Wait a minute! It's the evil of
this world that caused me to forget! Beyond these
doors is where Seth King is. Start preparing.

Scene 23: The final secrets

Unknown time

Everyone but Speed use leviburst. Ivan throws mud around
by getting big bursts of speed. He slams into a wall over the

mud; a red "0" pops out and he returns. Tu and Tyler, near the end, crash into each other mid-flight; a red "0" pops out of each.

Knuckles narrator
(while the team practices) Having reached Seth King's domain and dodged his thoughtful traps, the battle was about to begin. I was eager to use ultimara6 on him to eradicate him for good!

Speed
Ready?

Everyone but Speed head to where the door is then fall. Most of the mud is off of Ivan.

Speed
Although this door is locked, the speed busher is an easy fix, hopefully.

The door becomes a fireball that strikes Seth King inside. A red "2.74936E19" pops out of the door and a red "3.2068E12" pops out of Seth King.

Seth King, sitting in his black and red throne, looks exactly like that shown on the monitor in Amazonia during the library visit.

Seth King
Ouch! So we finally meet! Did you like my castle?

Knuckles
Bye!

Knuckles casts ultimara6 on Seth King; he doesn't disappear at the end like with Knuckles. A red "immune" pops out.

Speed
How's that possible!? Immune?

Seth King
Let's go into the arena.

A red "2.94895E19" pops out of Seth King, but unlike previous uses of the speed busher, Seth King does not become a fireball.

The scene of the castle fades to black in two seconds after a quarter second pause; time doesn't stop. A scene of Earth in space fades into view in two seconds. The Earth is 10,000 miles below and is all black except for a few fires and patches of lava which glow orange. The land is slightly brighter than the water. Earth is 15° down and straight across. Earth's Moon, unchanged, is visible rising a degree above Earth's top side in the black atmosphere. The Sun, unchanged, is 120° to the right. Stars from the Milky Way Galaxy are easily seen.

At 1000 miles distance, Amazonia, with the sky scrapers barely visible and a grayish (60A0A0B0) dome around it, is 70° to the left and 5° above. It tilts 10° toward the team. The buildings are easily seen, but are much too small to make out individually.

After a half second into the black-to-space fade, the humans gasp for air. Knuckles casts "oxygen shield 67" on them and they begin to breathe again. A gray "67 oxygen shield" pops out.

Ivan
Fighting him in space? Why there?

Ivan casts "spell power draw", in 400 milliseconds, on Seth King. A black and gold "0" pop out. Seth King casts "full scan" on Knuckles and he views Knuckles' stats.

Seth King
No wonder you're tough! Level 9000!? No way!

Knuckles casts full scan on Seth King and his stats show.

Two seconds later, Seth King casts "full scan" on Speed eight times, once each half second. A red "missed!" pops out on the first seven but Speed's stats show up on the eighth.

Speed
You are not going to hit me with anything bad. My stats aren't going to help you. Don't bother trying to hit me; note my evasion, level, and speed.

234

Knuckles	
Level: 9218	Origin: Virgo Supercluster, Local Group, Milky Way, Criscoma Korona, Ramusi, Uametik
HP: 1.00084E19/ 1.00084E19	
SP: 8.82347E27/ 1.2996E28	Strengths: Defense, magic efficiency, magic, spell power, magic accuracy, absorbs all elements, immune to all status effects, equip slots, abilities, intelligence
Aura:	Weaknesses: Physical, magic attack, no emotions
Age: 9.93902E09	

5.4 ☆		24.8 ☆		13 ☆		15.6 ☆		12.1 ☆	
15.3 ☆		10.4 ☆		9.9 ☆		4.8 ☆		9.5 ☆	
12.1 ☆		12.2 ☆		11.6 ☆		10.7 ☆		12.4 ☆	
7.6 ☆		8.5 ☆		11.3 ☆		13.3 ☆		10.8 ☆	
7.2 ☆		10.3 ☆		9.7 ☆		14.6 ☆		8.8 ☆	
18.4 ☆		17.9 ☆		21.7 ☆		13.5 ☆		6 ☆	

Physical attack	870,106,894	Magic attack	19,726,182	Strength	683,498
Melee accuracy	294	Magic efficiency	4.02724E35	Speed	378
Ranged accuracy	291	Magic accuracy	467	Hit points	1.00084E19
Physical defense	∞	Magic defense	∞	Spell power	1.2996E28
Physical evasion	212	Magic evasion	248	Level	9218
Actions/second	13,544,252	Magic potency	1.5904E21	Experience	2.94627E22

Figure 10: Knuckles' stats (Scale: 1:3.75)

Seth King	
Level: 6174	Origin: Virgo Supercluster, Local Group, Milky Way, Sol Earth, Brazil, Amazonia
HP: ERR/ ERR	
SP: 3.29161E16/ 4.26005E17	Strengths: Hit points, spell power, level, magic accuracy, accuracy, magic efficiency, magic potency, immune to all status effects, elemental immunity, absorbs dark, intelligence
Aura:	Weaknesses: Light, physical evasion, physical attack, speed
Age: 1.23478E09	

12.2 ☆		16 ☆		11.5 ☆		12 ☆		10.2 ☆	
7.8 ☆		9.6 ☆		9.2 ☆		8.8 ☆		7.6 ☆	
14.5 ☆		10.4 ☆		10.3 ☆		10.9 ☆		12.8 ☆	
13 ☆		8.1 ☆		10.1 ☆		13.2 ☆		13.5 ☆	
10.6 ☆		10.5 ☆		7.4 ☆		14.4 ☆		11.3 ☆	
16.2 ☆		15.8 ☆		ERR ☆		9.5 ☆		19.4 ☆	

Physical attack	98,480,158	Magic attack	117,869,044	Strength	15,024
Melee accuracy	280	Magic efficiency	3.21824E12	Speed	148
Ranged accuracy	275	Magic accuracy	336	Hit points	ERR
Physical defense	70,476,080	Magic defense	64,026,702	Spell power	4.26005E17
Physical evasion	118	Magic evasion	140	Level	6174
Actions/second	12,696	Magic potency	7.24105E11	Experience	2.41349E16

Figure 11: Seth King's stats (Scale: 1:3.75)

Speed	
Level:	11,058
HP:	2.63043E25/ 2.63043E25
SP:	1.81575E21/ 1.81843E21
Aura:	
Age:	1.55449E17

Origin: Virgo Supercluster, Local Group, Milky Way, Criscoma Korona, Ramusi, Bazipenna

Strengths: Speed, reaction time, evasion, action rate, physical attack, melee accuracy, level, strength, magic efficiency, intelligence, hit points, immune to all status effects, absorbs all elements

Weaknesses: Magic attack, magic, ranged accuracy, no emotions

7.4	30.6	16	20.1	12.6
18.6	9.7	9.2	30.1	7.8
14.5	13.1	14.1	12.4	15.2
10.4	10.8	16.4	16	11.1
8.7	12.4	8.6	16.8	10.3
20.6	20.8	29.4	32.6	6.5

Physical attack	3.58837E18	Magic attack	1,097,174	Strength	648,316,345
Melee accuracy	865	Magic efficiency	3.32522E27	Speed	299,792,458
Ranged accuracy	430	Magic accuracy	568	Hit points	2.63043E25
Physical defense	1.05294E12	Magic defense	9.01934E11	Spell power	1.81843E21
Physical evasion	2317	Magic evasion	1443	Level	11,058
Actions/second	1.2454E10	Magic potency	6.81911E20	Experience	1.41465E26

Figure 12: Speed's stats (Scale: 1:3.75)

Seth King takes a bow and arrow out of his chest as Knuckles does. He aims for Speed and shoots. Speed moves off the side a few inches and catches the arrow. A quarter second later, the arrow disappears. A blue "2.30416E21" pops out of Seth King.

Speed
Thanks for the extra weapon, an easy catch.

Knuckles' and Seth King's full scan results window disappears.

Knuckles
Now, tell me, why did you cause destruction and mayhem in Amazonia?

Seth King
I wanted to control Amazonia. I ran for mayor in the thirty-seven eighty-eight election, but was turned down by a pretty lady who did.

Knuckles
(one-second pause) I recall seeing details about the mayor when I was there, by sensing. Being

mayor doesn't mean you can control the whole city or have anything you want. Bad mayors do get fired from their job ya know.

Seth King

Well, yeah, but I only wanted to be mayor.

Knuckles

And do you have the ability to make wise decisions related to legal concerns and city design?

Seth King

Yes.

Knuckles

Wrong. You are skilled at problem-solving from what I saw in the library there and in my "full scan" data window, but they aren't geared toward that of being mayor. (one-second pause) It seems like you're also limited in many other regards so mayor is not a job for you. You'd be good at construction.

Speed

I'm, in a way, mayor of my planet. I don't just watch over everyone or travel around the world, I also must defend it from alien invaders. When the Great War struck, I had to focus on fighting them off and it took well over 200 years to do so, until all of them were defeated or fled. I've since closely watched over everyone on my planet, and also investigated stars within 100 light-years of home. So, it's not easy. I didn't experience Amazonia.

Seth King

But, I could if I was just elected.

Knuckles

With lots of time and practice, yes, but as you were at the time, you were far from it. Instead of coming up with your plan to capture the elemental masters to destroy Amazonia, there are much better ways to resolve your issue.

Seth King
Well, I needed the elemental masters for power so I could get back into Amazonia.

Knuckles
If you didn't commit all of those crimes in the first place, you wouldn't have been evicted. See, that's your weakness and why you weren't elected and later sentenced to death.

Seth King
Death!? Why such an extreme punishment? I'm indestructible anyway!

Knuckles
You have committed so many crimes in Amazonia, very serious ones, that, of Amazonia's residents, all but one in sixteen hundred agree to sentencing you to death. I got this from visiting their library so I know. Steve read right off the document about you on their information supernetwork. I got more details about you by sensing how their computers worked and read much more than Steve read out.

Seth King
They let you do that!?

Knuckles
Enough now. Give the Master Ladarkalent and Master Lampalent to me.

Seth King
They are my power source; I can't go without them.

Knuckles
They are not yours. The eight I have aren't mine. They belong to the Earth. Strike one. Give me the other two elemental masters so I can return them to where they really belong.

Seth King
They aren't yours; you don't need them.

Knuckles

They aren't yours or mine, but I'm going to be returning them to where they belong, not keep them. I have my own power, even more than they do, so I don't need them, directly. Strike two!

Seth King

Directly? Ha ha!

Knuckles

Unlike you, using them for your power, I'm offering them protection from you in exchange for returning them to where they belong, and it's not inside my chest, far from it. I earned my high level through centuries of war. Speed is the same.

Speed

No kidding! Forty thousand total years in war out of my over four dot nine billion is enough to allow me to be over level 11,000. I don't see anything passing the 10,000 mark at all.

Knuckles

So, are you going to hand them over so I can return the elemental masters to where they belong?

Seth King casts slow4 on Ivan. A gray "4 slow" pops out. Knuckles casts "hasten4" on Ivan and a green "slow" pops out.

Knuckles

Strike three, yer out!

Knuckles casts "meteor storm 91" on Seth King. Time stops and the space scene completely fades to black in one second leaving only Seth King. Another space scene fades in in one second, with a few colorful nebulas in the background instead. A second later, a meteor storm comes into view where large rocks five miles across head toward Seth King at 20 miles per second. The rocks slam into Seth King frequently for five seconds. The meteor storm scene fades completely away in one second with the strikes continuing and Seth King's space scene fades back in one second. A red "3.12184E17" pops out as time resumes.

Knuckles

Man, how many hit points do you have!?

Seth King's stats appear in front of Knuckles. Speed casts "meteor storm 105" on Seth King. A white "2.33028E18" pops out. A red "2.99156E19" pops out a second later.

Knuckles

Hey Speed. What is this E-R-R in the stats?

Speed

I never saw that before.

Knuckles

Huh? You haven't? Both H-P and elemental defense against light have this.

Speed

I seriously don't know. I never saw it before.

Knuckles

The stats show that light is his primary weakness.

Tu casts "light" on Seth King in 450 milliseconds. A red "5.21077E2.18069E09" pops out.

Seth King

Ouch! Don't do that!

The team

(everyone but Seth King; when the number appears; very shocked) What the!?

Knuckles

What does that mean? Excellent idea Tu!

Speed

Oh, I get it. The exponent reached a billion and it, too, was transformed into exponential form. Why so big though?

240

Knuckles

Remember how everything, after the shack, was dark and evil? Light is the opposite of dark. I would suspect that this is the cause and because Seth King and the world are purely of dark, light-elemental spells put a "hole" in this of sorts.

Knuckles casts "spell power draw 85" on Seth King. A black and gold "1.79314E14" pop out of Seth King. Knuckles casts "spell power massdraw 83" on Seth King. A sparkling, magenta-colored (A0FF00E0) beam of light two feet in diameter connects Seth King to Knuckles, appearing instantly and remains for three seconds and instantly disappears after this. The scene vibrates vertically five times a second while the beam is present. A black and gold "2.14252E16" pops out as usual. Knuckles casts it again. A black and gold "1.13116E16" pops out.

Knuckles

I don't like wasting spell power and could use it. Everyone, fire away with light-elemental spells!

Seth King

No!

Knuckles uses "moon blast 82", Speed uses "moon blast 104", and the humans use "light". The order of casting and the popups are as follows: Knuckles red "8.42204E2.18069E09", Speed blue "6.31447E2.18069E09", Ivan red "5.96585E2.18069E09", Tyler red "5.00289E2.18069E09", Tu red "5.0879E2.18069E09", Speed red "2.75108E2.18069E09", Knuckles red "8.39638E2.18069E09", and Speed red "3.20482E2.18069E09". There is a half-second delay after the first two casts, the humans go together, then the rest follow side by side without a break in the time.

Seth King begins to emit bright white light of 2000 lumens and grows brighter slowly at first, but accelerates.

Tu

What's going on?

Knuckles
I think he's defeated.

Speed
Yes, he's defeated. Get ready to run though.

The space scene fades away in two seconds and Seth King's castle fades in in two seconds. When the castle scene returns, from the same area where the team encountered him, the Master Ladarkalent and Master Lampalent come out of Seth King at 20 mph and gravitate toward him. They disappear a second later.

Knuckles
Run for it! Use hyperleviburst!

Speed
Take the path to your right. Avoid the lava.

Speed disappears. The team uses hyperleviburst after jumping to dart through the other path. A pool of yellow lava is below with thin, sharp spikes three feet high on the edges and ceiling during the entire route. The team, at the end of the pathway, sees Speed at the entrance and stop above him.

Speed
Go straight and keep going.

Speed disappears and the team goes to the full 1600 mph in 5 1/3 seconds and remains there heading away from the castle. A second after the team leaves, the castle gravitates toward Seth King breaking apart. The surroundings are all black since Seth King emits an extremely bright light. Four seconds later, Seth King explodes sending a huge blue (B00000E0) shockwave in all directions going 2400 mph slowing down and fading away over time. After several seconds, the shockwave gets within 15 feet of the team. Five seconds later, it is no longer visible; atmospheric distortions still are which go away after 30 seconds. The team, almost together (the humans 280 milliseconds later), decelerate to a full stop in 5 1/3 seconds. The shockwave is a 50 mph gust.

Upon coming to a complete stop, the darkness and evil slowly disappear as another shockwave-like case occurs. The evil world is replaced by a natural, bright, colorful world without anything manmade like planes and cities. Life, except the team, is also absent. The visibility is 100+ miles and the air is pollution-free.

The scene goes to where Speed is, 1000 miles above where the castle was. He watches the world lighten up in concentric circles spreading at an accelerating rate; the entire world returns to normal in 30 seconds. The land below is nearly the same as it is today, only with many more forests, glaciers, and lakes. There are no manmade developments. Sea level is a foot lower thus coastlines are slightly different.

Speed

(as the darkness goes away) What a pretty sight!

Scene 24: Finishing the mission

Unknown time

Knuckles narrator

(after Speed) With Seth King history, I needed to return the elemental masters to where they belong. That Seth King battle was weird and unique. I saw damage values I never saw before, E-R-R showing up in full scan stats, and what happened when he was defeated. Fortunately, however, I copied his brain's memory contents as we spoke together. Speed has a backup, but had to leave.

The scene switches to where the team is, now on the ground near the sea in southern Greece.

Tu

So, what now? The Earth seems to be back to normal.

Ivan
Where's Speed at?

Speed appears where the team is.

Speed
The entire world has returned to normal. It's no longer evil. It's only dark due to night.

Knuckles
I can sense that.

Master Lavalent
We need to be placed back in our worlds, like you stated, and in our own time.

Knuckles
So, we need to go to May 29, 1999 at 22:59 U-T-C?

Master Lavalent
Correct.

Knuckles
Let's go! It's time for the time warp spell!

Knuckles casts "time warp". A lens effect occurs; everyone, including Speed, appears distorted in a whirlpool shape which intensifies over time. Their colors are in tact but some areas are magnified while others are unmagnified, some are brighter and some are darker. The background scenery is not affected by this. This lasts five seconds; the team fades away in the last two. After a half-second pause, the scene changes to an area in a forest next to a small, gentle, clear stream. The team fades into the view, now with the effects reversed. Tu stands in the stream two inches deep upon returning; she jumps back to get out.

Knuckles
How do I get into your elemental worlds?

Master Lavalent
What, you haven't been told?

Knuckles
Unfortunately, I wasn't told. I can't sense it either.

Master Lavalent
You meet the level 3000 requirement so all you need to do is say the name of the master, then "land to", then the element of that master and you're there. You can bring friends with.

Knuckles
So, it'd be "lavalent, land to fire"?

Master Lavalent
Yes, but you need to holler, just as you did to leave our elemental worlds.

Knuckles
Alright, but I need safety so out comes my platform.

The platform appears on the ground. Knuckles casts "levitate" and "wind barrier" on the platform for a gray "0 levitating" and "0 wind barrier" and casts "fire shield", "ice shield", and "gravity shield" on all but himself for a gray "1 fire shield", "1 ice shield", and "1 gravity shield". He casts teleport and everything appears 3000 feet above the ground. The ocean shore can be seen 180 feet straight ahead. This offset is due to continental drift going backwards 1800 years.

Knuckles
I'm all set now. (hollering) Lavalent land to fire!

After hollering, from here on, the ground cracks apart and caves in, without rumbles, in one second revealing the elemental world of the master unchanged from the previous encounters.

Knuckles
Alright, you can go now.

From here on, the elemental master referenced in the hollering appears 150 feet in front of Knuckles.

Master Lavalent
Just so you know, I was the one that caused the airplane on your first encounter to arrive so early. You should be able to do the same to access the other elemental worlds to release the other masters. Thank you for saving us though.

Knuckles
No problem.

Master Lavalent
Oh, and you know how to leave the elemental worlds, right?

Knuckles
Yes, by hollering "lavalent, land to normal".

Master Lavalent
Good. Bye now!

Knuckles
Bye. (hollering) Lavalent land to normal!

The ground returns to normal.

Knuckles
(hollering) Lachalent land to ice!

The Master Lachalent appears.

Master Lachalent
Thanks. You are an amazing being!

Knuckles
You could say so. If only I was like Speed....
(hollering) Lachalent ground to normal!

The ground returns to normal.

Knuckles
(hollering) Lampalent land to electricity!

The Master Lampalent appears, but falls due to gravity. Knuckles casts life-cure on him. A green "3.86369E10" pops out at the end with the usual green "fatal" and "1" during the effects.

Master Lampalent
(scared) Stay away! (confused) Huh? How did I get back here?

Knuckles
I couldn't get to you as Seth King put up a sense barrier that I and the other masters couldn't break.

Master Lampalent
Oh there you are! Thank goodness you came... and revived me. I knew I could trust you!

Knuckles
No problem! Good thing I was around. (hollering) Lampalent land to normal!

The ground returns to normal.

Knuckles
(hollering) Larockalent land to earth!

The Master Larockalent appears.

Master Larockalent
Great work! I knew I could trust you!

Knuckles
The obvious, high-level, rare white dot says it all. (hollering) Larockalent land to normal!

The ground returns to normal.

Knuckles
(hollering) Lachemalent, land to chemical!

The Master Lachemalent appears.

                    Knuckles
Take good care now!

                Master Lachemalent
You too!

                    Knuckles
(hollering) Lachemalent land to normal!

The ground returns to normal.

                    Knuckles
(hollering) Lairalent land to wind!

The Master Lairalent appears.

                 Master Lairalent
That exploding castle was scary!

                    Knuckles
It was kind of scary. Speed was of great help.

                 Master Lairalent
Yeah, he was of great use.

                     Speed
I was just doing what I like doing, deleting evil.

                    Knuckles
(hollering) Lairalent land to normal!

The ground returns to normal.

                    Knuckles
(hollering) Laqualent land to water!

The Master Laqualent appears.

                 Master Laqualent
Despite being scared of you at first encounter due
to that stubborn Seth King, I would like you as a
body guard! You were very helpful in saving all the
elemental masters, even those Seth King took.

248

Knuckles

I just forgot to check my mind radar map and your aura. It's no big deal. Even at level 9000, I still forget on some occasions, usually what spell to use.

Master Laqualent

That's all right. I hated Seth King the entire time I was with you and I still will. Thanks though!

Knuckles

You're welcome. (hollering) Laqualent land to normal!

The ground returns to normal.

Knuckles

(hollering) Lalightalent land to light!

The Master Lalightalent appears.

Master Lalightalent

I've got a bit of cleanup to do because of that moron. Thanks for helping me though.

Knuckles

You're welcome. (hollering) Lalightalent land to normal!

The ground returns to normal.

Knuckles

(hollering) Lagravalent land to gravity!

The Master Lagravalent appears.

Master Lagravalent

You're a very skilled fighter! Good job on taking care of Seth King. What an idiot he was!

Knuckles

No biggie. (hollering) Lagravalent land to normal!

The ground returns to normal.

Now, what about the elemental master of dark?
Dark is evil. Should I revive him? The elemental
masters are friendly, aren't they? Well, at least,
they're an easy target, just in case. (hollering)
Ladarkalent land to dark!

The ground becomes the elemental world for dark. This
elemental world has not been seen before, but it very closely
mimics what the world looked like when the team left the death
house – a flat, endless span of fires, lava, bent black fences, red-
orange glowing clouds, and the related. The ground's surface,
3000 feet below, is where the tops of the clouds are. The blue
sky above is not affected, like the other elemental worlds.

Interesting elemental world. I recognize it very
well. Now that I've seen it, I can see how the loss
of the Master Ladarkalent caused problems. The
world continued to get more and more toward evil
rather than evil being absent. With the elemental
master for dark not around, the entire world
became exactly like this elemental world. I guess
it's worth reviving the elemental master.

The Master Ladarkalent appears but is tossed up at 30 mph.
It falls some due to gravity. It resembles the others, but a solid
black (FF000000) instead.

It's a greenish-white dot on radar, so that's good.

Knuckles casts "life-cure" on it. A green "3.86369E10" pops
out at the end.

(upon seeing Knuckles; confused) Who are you?

250

Knuckles
I'm Knuckles. I saved you from Seth King.

Master Ladarkalent
(confused) What happened? Where am I?

Knuckles
I put you back in your elemental world then cast life-cure on you. I don't know what happened or what you're referring to.

Master Ladarkalent
Well, as the story goes, I was doing my usual things then some strange being suddenly entered and cast "stop5" on me. I didn't know who it was. It was May 27, 1999 at 15:49 U-T-C. The next thing I knew, I was in some gloomy brick castle at some unknown location. I saw someone there and he forced me to make a potion to make him have an infinite number of hit points, impossible by the laws of physics. He'd cast light-elemental spells on me as I refused. They hurt so I gave him as much as I could. He drank it and the next thing I saw was you in my elemental world.

Knuckles
I think Seth King might have killed you and used you for his power. I'm surprised that he could've done so, which could explain his high level.

Master Ladarkalent
Seth King? That's who that thing was?

Knuckles
He's a human from the year thirty-seven-ninety-seven. He apparently read a discovery about ancient scrolls telling of elemental masters. While I have no idea how he figured out how to access your world, I was only able to, after everything, because the Master Lavalent, the master of fire, told me and with my extreme level, over 9000, I could.

Master Ladarkalent
What happened in the aftermath ever since I supposedly died and the time you revived me?

Knuckles
The first thing I noticed was someone unexplainably escaping from jail. There wasn't any spirit there either, as if it was, then I could get rid of it with light-elemental spells if evil and help it if good. A simple glue and teleport spell fixed it. The next thing was a lavalent bursting out of the ground in a school, a small one showing up as a dark red dot. All was peaceful for a while, then numerous strange events began to occur. A continent rose out of the ocean floating to the surface, and I began seeing the elemental masters myself for the first time, the first being for fire. As I saved the masters, the smaller versions of them disappeared. It all makes sense now. Seth King was behind it all too. It was only through an unexpected visit to his home city, which isn't evil, that I learned about him and his plans. Dodging his traps, I made my way to his castle having Speed help. I first wanted to find out why Seth King did this – he wanted to become mayor of Amazonia but was turned down. He refused to hand over the Master Lampalent and you so we fought him. I was shocked to find that, light-elemental spells did far more damage than even ultimara8 could, of which Speed has, way more. I saw E-R-R in my stats window for light elemental defense with a red star for weakness. Once he was defeated, I saw you and the Master Lampalent pop out in the very bright light. I grabbed them and we fled. With all masters in my hands and Seth King not around any more, I watched the whole world lose its evil. I cast "time warp" to return so I can return the elemental masters back into their elemental worlds and that's where I left off.

Master Ladarkalent

That seems hard to do all that. Thanks for saving and reviving me from that down-in-the-dumps Seth King. He should belong in the Sun's core!

Knuckles

He absorbs fire so that won't work.

Master Ladarkalent

Oh, I meant "the bin of nonexistence". Nice seeing you and I'll look forward to your assistance whenever I need it.

Knuckles

I should fully restore you and dump any negative and neutral status effects.

Knuckles casts "cure". A green "3.86369E10" pops out. Knuckles casts "normalize32". A ratchet and wrench fade in over the Master Ladarkalent in a quarter second. They rotate as if unscrewing a bolt making three 90° twists in two seconds. They fade away in a half second during the fourth. When the spell effects start, a green "fear", "distracted", then "dizzy" pop out. The Master Ladarkalent's behavior appears unchanged.

Knuckles

You're now pretty much as good as new.

Master Ladarkalent

Thanks for the assistance and restoring me. I have lots of clean-up to do, thanks to Seth King. Bye!

Knuckles

Bye! (hollering) Ladarkalent land to normal.

The ground returns to normal.

Speed

Well, I gotta go back to Korona and watch over it. Call me when you need me again!

Knuckles
Alright Speed.

Speed disappears.

Ivan
So, what do we do now? School's out.

Knuckles
I think we have a new home to go to.

Ivan
(confused) New home? Where?

Knuckles
You'll see, but I need to find it.

Scene 25: Returning home

May 29, 1999 at 11:15 PM UTC

A five-second pause occurs. Knuckles casts teleport. The team appears in a forest in Italy. It is night, the sky is clear, and the full moon shines brightly. Amazonia's dome's glitter is at its best glittering in the moonlight. The team walks around for ten seconds then the "doorway" opens up. The team enters and the fade at the same entrance location as before occurs.

A crowd of thousands cheering Knuckles line the area. The mayor, a pretty, short female with a pretty, fancy blue dress lined with lace, and smooth, brown hair eight inches long is directly in front with Steve to her right. A badge with a "1" and "Rachel" are on the mayor. Elizabeth, the announcer, resident of Janet, Josh, Chris, Sandy, and Hector, are behind.

Knuckles narrator
(a second into the pause) With all the elemental masters returned and the Master Lampalent and Ladarkalent safe as well, my mission was complete.

Having visited Amazonia earlier, I knew I wanted to return. The fighting arena seemed like a great place to gain levels. Everyone liked it there. Upon entering, however, I saw a huge, cheering crowd and even met the mayor Seth King mentioned.

Steve
(when the fade starts; surprised) Knuckles! You're back! Where's Seth King at?

Rachel
(happy with tears) I cannot thank you enough for eradicating Seth King and saving my city from him.

Knuckles
He's now only in history books.

Ivan
That death house he had was really scary. I helped Knuckles work with the clues and solve problems.

Tyler
It was quite an adventure! I liked it!

Knuckles
If you want, I can show you the entire story from chapter one. Well, at least from the start of the strange, unexplained events.

Josh
I'd like to see the story, too!

Elizabeth
Me too! I helped the city kick him out.

Rachel
You have a wonderful story. I'd like to see it myself and what he did after we kicked him out of my city.

Tu
Oh, you're the mayor?

Rachel

Indeed, yes. How can I see it? I watched you fighting him. How many levels did you gain?

Knuckles

Being over level 9000, even with 20 level-9000 experience pluses, it was hardly a scratch. As to watching everything, and since I have a spell for pretty much everything and a seemingly unlimited supply of spell power, I have a way. Let's all watch it in the library. I can use time lapse or leave out unnecessary content, but it's still nearly four hours.

Rachel

Would you show us all your adventures and what happened when we kicked Seth King out of my city?

Josh

Yeah, would you?

Elizabeth

Me too!

Knuckles

I'll do just that. We'll watch it together. Need more space? I got spells for that, particularly the spell-power-hungry create and edit spells. Your masters in the fighting arena don't have the kinds of spells I have, not even close. I'm 8000 levels above them. My teleport spell is faster than your teleporters so....

Knuckles casts teleport and the team, including Rachel, Steve, Elizabeth, the announcer, resident of Janet, Josh, Chris, Sandy, and Hector, appear in a dark room. The others are left out. Knuckles casts "lighten" at a spot behind a large monitor. A light like that used in Knuckles' house lights the 8-meter-wide by 16-meter-long room in the back. A table 3 meters in diameter is centered in the front. The door is closed. The hologram monitor is seven meters wide, five meters back, and goes all the way up to the ceiling 2.5 meters high.

Knuckles casts "mind thoughts to storage device". The scene from the beginning of the story, where Knuckles glides over the land 1500 feet above Lake Sakakawea at 800 mph, appears, but is still. Everyone gets seated around the table, forming a half-circle table. Knuckles is in the corner near the door standing.

Knuckles

Are you ready? I've added narration to my story at certain points.

Rachel

I'm ready.

Steve

I'm ready too. Let 'er run!

Suddenly, time stops. A one-second pause occurs. The scene backs away. The 3D monitor shows the scene at the moment time stopped, as if someone was watching this all along without realizing it. The room is unchanged. Ivan, Steve, Josh, Chris, and Sandy are eating buttered popcorn out of a large four-gallon bag that is circular in shape and red in color with orange dots. Tu is taking a sip out of a drink. Tyler and Hector just watch. Rachel and Elizabeth are eating a chocolate Hershey's bar, of which is one-third eaten. The resident of Janet and the announcer eat crackers. All food and drink are in movie-theater-style packages and containers.

Steve

That's it? Great story!

Josh

Yeah, really.

Chris

I'm very surprised about your history and talents.

Janet resident

Yeah, except when they almost hit me when gliding.

Rachel

That looked very scary at the end.

Sandy

That was scary! For you, it looks to be a good training ground for gaining levels.

Knuckles

When you absorb or are immune to all elements, dark especially, it doesn't bother you.

Steve

Your spells make good meals any day. What don't you have a spell for?

Knuckles

Creating objects too big for my spell power. This city is near or just beyond the upper limit when full.

Rachel

I have a special reward for you. You are rewarded an area 500 by 500 meters in the upper level. It is in the city's southern area centered at seven-point-two X, negative seventy-three-point-four Y. This area, normally, is not for residential use but I'm making an exception for our heroes. You have full control over this area outside the fact that you must still obey the law and do not disturb the neighboring buildings in any way. Of course, you can fix them if you spot problems. Seth King has caused a lot of problems in almost every location. Janet blowing up was one such problem. The tools to fix it were destroyed by Seth King. We've got a lot of rebuilding to do. Thanks for reporting that though.

Knuckles

Missing tools? Broken tools? The create, cure, edit, normalize, and recall spells are a good, quick fix for that. Anyway, I'd like to go into the master level for the fighting arena and see if I can gain some more levels, catch up to Speed's level. Level 7000 monsters are too weak for any reasonable growth. Level 8000 monsters are the low end.

Rachel
Rachel
I can see why. Bye though.

Steve + Elizabeth
(at the same time) Have fun!

Knuckles casts teleport. He appears alone by the fighting arena seen earlier. The camera points straight down eight feet above the ground and continuously accelerates upwards at five mph per second. Knuckles enters the building a second later.

Text appears on the screen in five groups. The first group states, "Knuckles continuously battles in the fighting arena, but the staff needed 13,492 years before they found something at his level. It would be another 2482 years later when Knuckles surpasses Speed's level."

The second group states, "Ivan gets involved with sports and becomes a professional at both matball and volleyball. His full control over learning abilities makes him tower over everyone else, easily beating the masters 200 levels below them."

The third group states, "Tu, with her dream of being a science teacher, uses the adventure simulators to do just that. She often throws big parties that everyone has fun with. Tu continued to explore the city's underside and used her scientific skills to help with city development and reconstruction."

The fourth group states, "Tyler began to study the rocks in Amazonia's underside to help the city's development and reconstruction. He occasionally went into the fighting arenas and worked his way up to the master level in 120 years."

The fifth and final group states, "Speed just kept guard on his planet. Another invasion occurs three years later, but this one was simple and the invaders make peace without any fighting."

A two-second pause occurs then the scene fades away in five seconds, now with the city's buildings indistinguishable from one another. The western side of the city is visible which turns into forest land. The "boot" of Italy is easily seen. The curve from the 180-mile radius is clearly visible. It gives a sense as how to big Amazonia really is. After the fade, the ending credits show.

Appendix
Appendix table of contents:

Appendix 1: All about the ten elements

The story gets its name as it involves elemental masters. Unlike ancient times where there were only four, or the periodic table or elementary particles like muons, photons, or electrons, these are elements like those of the ancient times, fire, earth, wind, and water, except extended on to using ten instead.

Fire is for anything above 50°C (122°F) such as lava, fires, and boiling water. The symbol is a flame.

Ice is the opposite of fire and refers to anything below 0°C (32°F) such as snow, liquid nitrogen or dry ice. The symbol is a snowflake.

Electric is for energy and electricity and includes anything mechanical and lightning bolts. The symbol is a lightning bolt.

Earth involves solids. It sometimes refers to hardness, six or above on Moh's Scale. The symbol is of rocks and mountains.

Chemical involves anything reactive, radiation, acids, or anything poisonous to most living things such as ammonia, or chlorine. The symbol is of a molecule of ammonia (NH_3).

Wind refers to gases, usually the atmosphere. It sometimes refers to friction. The symbol is of a tornado.

Water is for liquids, sometimes for pressure above 150 kilopascals ($\approx$22 psi). The symbol is the ocean and a rainstorm.

Light is anything good-natured such as those who save lives or a friendly spirit. The symbol is of two white sparkles.

Gravity is for force. The symbol is of an arrow pointing to a large object from a small one.

Dark is anything evil-natured such as demons, armed robbers, or murderers. The symbol is of two black sparkles.

Appendix 2: An explanation of the stats

Master Lavalent ! HP ☾	Origin: Virgo Supercluster, Local Group, Milky Way, Sol
Level: 5624 ▬▬	Earth of Fire, unknown, unknown
HP: 1.94724E10/	
4.06704E10 ▬▬	Strengths: Spell power, hit points, strength, intelligence, magic,
SP: 3.96559E09/	defense, speed, absorbs fire,status immunity, hard to find,
4.52899E09 ▬▬	electric, chemical, wind, gravity
Aura: ▬▬▬▬	Weaknesses: Water, ice, ranged accuracy, physical, dark
Age: 1.42953E17	

?	1.5		5.7 ★		4.3 ★		5.2 ★		3.3 ★
	4.2 ★		3.4 ★		4.2 ★		4.5 ★		5.6 ★
	3.6		5 ★		5.8 ★		3.9 ★		3.8
	5.9 ★	?	4 ★		3.8		5.8 ★		6.2 ★
	5.5 ★		1.7		2.5 ★		2.3		2 ★
	2.2 ★		1		4.7		3.5 ★		1.5

Physical attack	1,709,882	Magic attack	7,869,044	Strength	23,278,101
Melee accuracy	168	Magic efficiency	9.85453E09	Speed	179
Ranged accuracy	113	Magic accuracy	218	Hit points	4.06704E10
Physical defense	3,727,126	Magic defense	5,312,865	Spell power	4.52899E09
Physical evasion	92	Magic evasion	140	Level	5624
Actions/second	136	Magic potency	5.1692E09	Experience	1.91568E15

Stats as viewed on a window from a "full scan" spell

When a character casts the "full scan" spell, a window appears (shown above) showing a lot of in-depth details about the target "scanned". These include the stats, elemental and status defenses, and a few other things as well. Occasionally, they are mentioned in the story, but only vaguely. This part of the appendix explains what these all mean in greater detail.

There are five sections to the status window. From top to bottom, left to right, they are the primary stats, details, status defenses, elemental defenses, and the secondary stats.

Primary statistics

There are seven primary stats, found in the top left corner. The name is first. This is straight forward.

To the right of the name are icons representing status effects. Status effects are abnormal changes in an object's properties, good or bad. In the above case, it has "low HP" and "stop".

Level is an indication of overall power. For every 500 levels higher than someone else of the same species, they are relatively ten times as powerful. There is no upper limit, unlike RPGs. A being on level 1600 is relatively 100 times more powerful than another on 600. The "bar" to the right indicates how much progress has been made toward the next level filling from left to right. The left side is red (FFFF0000) and the right side is green (FF00C000). Yellow (FFFFFF00) is at the exact halfway point.

HP, hit points, is one's health. The more HP an enemy has, the harder it is to defeat it, as it can take more damage before dying. A bar identical to the one for level is present, but based on the current HP value (the top) over the maximum (bottom). When at or below 50%, the whole HP text becomes the color at the far edge of the bar, yellow at 50% fading to red at 0%.

SP, spell power, is one's magic energy. Spell power is used to cast spells. The more SP someone has, more powerful spells can be cast and more often. See appendix 3 for further details on spells. The bar and text-color-changing for spell power works exactly the same as that for HP, only it's for SP instead.

Aura is how good or evil the target's soul is. It uses a bar different but similar to the others. The entire bar is more than twice as wide and is always filled. A white (FFFFFFFF) arrow marker below it marks where their aura is at. The left has black (FF000000). This fades to red (FFFF0000), yellow (FFFFFF00), green (FF00C000), then white (FFFFFFFF). Each "checkpoint" is equidistant. Black is for pure evil, red for moderate evil, yellow for neutral, green for moderate good, and white for pure good.

Age is how old the object is, in seconds. There are about 31,556,926 seconds in a year. For a close approximation, for every million seconds, there are about 11 days, 13 3/4 hours (11 1/2). It's about 32 years for every billion seconds.

Secondary statistics

These are the 15 secondary stats, three are of the primary stats. They show the overall ability of the target and are split among three groups in columns of six. From left to right, they are physical, magical, and general. All of these are located at the bottom and span across the entire width of the window.

Physical (the left column):
Physical attack – the power of one's physical attacks. The higher this is, the more HP damage one can deal from a physical attack. A value of 50,000 means one can do 50,000 HP damage, ignoring resistance and critical hits, though with a slight 5% variation.
Melee accuracy – accuracy of non-projectile-based physical attacks. This includes things like hands, spears, swords, axes, or baseball bats. Accuracy can exceed 100%. The higher this is, the more likely one's attack will hit its target. A value of 90 means a 90% chance of striking the target, ignoring evasion.
Ranged accuracy – accuracy of projectile-based physical attacks. This applies to weapons such as guns or a bow and arrow. Accuracy can exceed 100%. This works the same way as melee accuracy though the size and distance of the target plays a role.
Physical defense – resistance to physical damage. This reduces the amount of HP damage received. The higher this is, physical attacks do less HP damage. If the enemy's physical attack was 50,000 and this was 30,000, 20,000 HP damage is expected. If defense is higher than attack, damage is usually zero.
Physical evasion – probability one will evade (dodge) a physical attack. Evasion can exceed 100%. The higher this is, the less likely one will be hit. If the enemy's accuracy was 90 and this was 20, the enemy has a 70% chance of a successful hit.
Actions per second – maximum rate of making actions. A swing of the sword, the punching of the fist, or the casting of a spell are based on this (spells have exceptions and are more complicated). The higher this is, the more often one can strike their target. Spells and special skills offset this.

Magical (the center column):
Magic attack – the power of one's magic. Since spells have their own base attack power, this stat is based on blaster of the first spell level. The higher this is, the more HP damage one can do on an enemy from magic attacks; it works like physical attack.
Magic efficiency – efficiency with spell-power usage. The higher this is, the less spell power is needed to cast the same spell. Increasing this to a value 100 times greater cuts spell power consumption to 10% of what it was.

Magic accuracy – accuracy with casting spells. Spells have the same accuracy regardless of the target's range or size. Accuracy can exceed 100%. The higher this is, the more likely a spell will hit its target. Status effect spells often have accuracy penalties.
Magic defense – resistance to magic damage. This works exactly like physical defense, except it applies to magic attacks.
Magic evasion – probability one will evade (dodge) a magical attack. Evasion can exceed 100%. This works exactly like physical evasion, except it applies to magic attacks.
Magic potency – magic potential. As this increases, casting speed and likelihood of a successful cast increase. When high, spells cast quickly (up to the action rate, with an exception) but when low, spells frequently fail and cast very slowly. Making this 100 times higher makes spells cast up to 10 times faster and are 100 times more likely to succeed in execution (as opposed to failing).

General (the right column):
Strength – Maximum mass, in kilograms, one can lift. If this is 30, one can lift up to 30 kilograms at normal gravity.
Speed – maximum rate overall position can be changed. It is based on the primary movement (running for humans, sliding with snakes, etc.) and is in meters per second at the greatest potential. The higher this is, the more distance can be covered in the same time period and the more likely one can escape from battle. A value of 10 indicates that one's maximum speed is 10 meters per second (about 22 3/8 mph).
Hit points – see the primary stats for details.
Spell power – see the primary stats for details.
Level – see the primary stats for details.
Experience – used to gain levels. Level increases by one when this passes a certain point. For every 500 levels higher, 10 times more experience is required for a level up though the amount per level increases very gradually.

Elemental defense
Elemental defense, found above the secondary stats, involve the weakness, resistance, immunity, or absorption of the ten

elements (ordered from worst to best), represented by icons. The elements and their symbols are explained in appendix 1.

The number is what the physical and magic defense are multiplied by when hit by something of the given element. A red star with a "W" indicates weakness (base damage is doubled and base defense is halved), a yellow star with an "I" indicates immunity (no damage is done), and a green star with an "A" indicates absorption (evasion and defense are ignored but damage becomes HP restoration (cure)). If no star is present, it indicates resistance. The higher the number, the more resistant the target is to the element. If the target's defense was 100 and resistance is 1.5, defense would be treated as if it was 150.

Status defense

Status defense – weakness, resistance, or immunity to status effects – is above the elemental defense. They work in a similar way as elemental defense, but don't use absorption. The icons, from left to right, top to bottom (ordered from best to worst – the first five are neutral status effects, the others are negative), are as follows: vanish, fear, berserk, charmed, magic mirror, sleep, SP leak, energy barrier, immobilized, poison, slow, distracted, blind, dizzy, stop, doomed, confusion, defenseless, stone, and fatal. Status defense lessens both the duration and likelihood of being hit with it. Only neutral and negative status effects have resistance. The chance of successfully adding a status effect depends on the chance of hitting the target (evasion is ignored if beneficial), the status effect's accuracy offset (0 if beneficial, 5 to 60 if otherwise), the caster's magic attack, the spell level, and the target's magic defense. The latter three determines duration. Spell level determines intensity (level five means intensity five).

Details

This section lists other basic details about the target in words. The "origin" section starts from the super cluster, cluster, galaxy, and star on the first row and narrows down to the planet, country or region, then state or sub-region on the second. The strengths and weaknesses follow, which serves as a quick summary, starting from the most intense in the group to the least intense.

Appendix 3: How the spell system works

Spells commonly use three terms: spell series, spell level, and spell name. We'll use "fire3" as an example. The number (3) is the spell level and the part before it (fire) is the spell series. The spell series and spell level, when put together, is the spell name, or commonly referred to as just the spell (fire3). If no number is at the end, then it's a level one spell.

Every spell within a series has the same effects, with slight changes. For example, as spell level increases with the water series, more water appears. For fire, the fire gets a bit hotter and bigger. Water90 has the same basic effect as water, but water90 involves several thousand gallons of water instead of just nine, but how it appears and behaves is unchanged. Even within the same spell level, there are still very slight differences – spells aren't perfect thanks to quantum fluctuations. Some spells, however, don't change, such as status effect spells.

Spells have upgrades. Upgrades refer to stronger versions of the same basic spell with improved efficiency and attack power, but take longer to cast. For example, the fire series upgrades into flare, fire storm, then plasma ball. "Plasma ball 4" is about as powerful as fire13, uses slightly less SP, but takes 3 5/8 times longer to cast. With each upgrade, the effects get more intense. At the third grade level and above, with rare exceptions, (fire storm in the fire example), time stops except for the effects.

Many spells scale with their targets. A larger target has larger versions of the effects. Knuckles may get something 10 inches in diameter whereas a human may get it at 28 inches because Knuckles is much smaller than humans.

In addition, many spells have the effects play many times, especially those without time stopping and fades. Cast fire on one target and a single flame bursts over it. Cast fire on five targets and five flames burst out, one for each target, and with the same effects. Cast plasma ball on one target and the effects of the explosions occur. Cast it on five targets, and the effects are exactly identical, but only one instance plays.

Appendix 4: The various popups

When something is attacked or healed in a battle in an RPG, some number or text pops out, of various colors, usually two, sometimes three. My story has a lot of this, but includes some elements not used in RPGs, and some are just expanded on.

Popups can be either numbers, the most common, or text. Less than a billion, numbers have commas if at least 10,000. If they reach a billion, they are formatted as "1.12345E12". This means that the actual value is a 1 followed by 12 other digits before the decimal. Written out, this is 1,123,450,000,000, about 1 1/8 trillion. It's easier to read "5.70584E68" than a 5 followed by 68 other digits before the decimal (try ultimara6's once).

Text appears too. The most common is from status effects. Casting "blind14" often results in a gray "14 blind" popping out of the target. The number indicates the intensity and the text indicates the status effect involved. There are exceptions to this though: casting "blind20" right after causes a gray "6 blind" to pop out instead of a gray "20 blind" – the status effect is being intensified by 6 which is what the popup means. Others, like "missed!", "immune", and "no effect" are fairly rare.

The seven colors used

There are several colors of numbers used, each with different meaning. Here are the seven colors used and what they mean:

Red (FFFF4040): HP damage. The "missed!", "immune", and "no effect" popups are also this same color.
Blue (FF4040FF): HP damage from a critical hit. Critical hits are rare hits that deal 1.5 to 4 times the damage than normal with the upper end being less common than the lower end.
White (FFFFFFFF): HP damage from a supercritical hit. A hit that deals 3 to 16 times more damage than normal is a supercritical hit. The upper end, too, is less common than the lower end.
Green (FF40FF40): HP recovery or status effect degradation. Status effect degradation (reduced intensity), whether a beneficial one or otherwise, uses green popups.

Gray (FF808080): The addition or intensification of a status effect, beneficial or otherwise.

Gold (FFFFC040): Sudden SP recovery.

Black (FF000000): Sudden SP loss. Casting spells does not cause these to appear – it's being used, not lost.

How popups move and behave

All popups always face the caster or attacker (the screen in the story) and have their base position directly above the top of the horizontal center of the target (with rare exceptions). They are of the "Tahoma" font, bold, only 90% as wide, font size 160, and extend a half inch back. The size is constant regardless of distance and the orientation and base position never change once they appear, even if the target moves or vanishes.

All but the green and gold colors behave like a bouncing ball. They rise at 1/8 normal gravity to 9.518 inches above the starting point. When they reach the base position (the point where the popup first appears), it bounces back up at half the speed getting 25% as high. Upon returning to the base position, the speed is halved again, but the popup fades away in 100 milliseconds by becoming increasingly transparent. It is completely faded away at the base position. The bouncing effect lasts for 1.1 seconds.

The green and gold popups rise at a constant nine inches per second for 1.1 seconds, fading away during the last tenth.

When several popups appear at once on a single target, they appear separated by 100 milliseconds. When popups from the same action (even if different values) pop out of multiple targets, they pop out at the same time. For example, casting "barrier7" on targets A and B causes a gray "7 defense up" to pop out of targets A and B. A gray "7 magic shield" pops out of both at the same time 100 milliseconds later with the previous ones still there. Color or type doesn't make any difference in this behavior. If two actions that result in a popup are done separately, the popup appears at the moment the action is executed. That is, if caster A casts "barrier7" on a target then caster B casts "hasten5" on it, with B executing 25 milliseconds later, "7 defense up" appears upon A's execution, "5 haste" appears 25 milliseconds later and "7 magic shield" appears 75 milliseconds after that.

Appendix 5: What numerical colors mean

Because I describe things best using numbers, including colors, I need to explain it. We'll use C0804020 as an example.

Breaking up the numerical color
All numerical colors have four parts: opacity, red, green, then blue. In the example color, the opacity, "C0", is 75.3% (using the tables below). The red, "80", is 128, green "40", is 64, and blue "20" is 32. This makes a dark brown color. By using the tables below and inputting this into any image-editing program (ignoring opacity), you can see what the color really is.

From working on animations, I have a habit of snapping to multiples of 16 (where the last digit is always a zero, except 255, the highest), except if there's too much of a visual difference (I'd go with multiples of 8 instead) or if calculations tell me otherwise.

Color values (for red, green, and blue)

Col	Val	Col	Val	Col	Val	Col	Val	Col	Val	Col	Val
00	0	10	16	20	32	30	48	40	64	50	80
60	96	70	112	80	128	90	144	A0	160	B0	176
C0	192	D0	208	E0	224	F0	240	FF	255		

Opacity (as a percentage)

Val	Opa	Val	Opa	Val	Opa	Val	Opa	Val	Opa	Val	Opa
00	0.0	10	6.3	20	12.5	30	18.8	40	25.1	50	31.4
60	37.6	70	43.9	80	50.2	90	56.5	A0	62.7	B0	69.0
C0	75.3	D0	81.6	E0	87.8	F0	94.1	FF	100.0		

A true-color reference
A quick reference chart to 729 colors showing them in steps of 32 is on the back of the book. Within a block, red increases from left to right and green increases from top to bottom. Blocks left to right, top to bottom (as you'd read this book) is increasing blue. Because printers print colors as dark as 3/5 as bright as they should be, I did experiments to get as close as possible.

Appendix 6: Formula list

If you don't like math, feel free to skip this appendix.

Some behaviors are simple and don't need explaining. Some, however, are complex, especially acceleration during a glide while pitching. This section explains this and others important to the story. Unlike traditional math which uses single-letter variables in a special format, I use the C programming style which has major readability advantages. Variables always have capital letters for the first word of each, but without spacing and often shortened (e.g. "StartSpeed" or "RandNum"). Function names are always lowercase (e.g. "sqrt" (square root) or "cos" (cosine)). The "^" indicates powers, like in spreadsheets (e.g. $2^3 = 8$).

Pitching while gliding

With level gliding, or pitching straight up or down, the acceleration in the direction of travel is easy. It's when the angle is oblique that the motion is awkward and getting the final result involves six formulas, five used!

Used: while any character glides.

If pitching up (errors if pitching down):
Accel = (((1-sin(PitchAngle))-1)*-1)^0.654317989965143*-20;

If pitching down (errors if pitching up):
Accel = (sin(PitchAngle)*-1)^0.654317989965143*20;

In both cases (to include the effects of banking):
Accel *= abs(cos(BankAngle));

For the vertical descent rate (two feet per second when level):
VertDescent = (15/11) * cos(PitchAngle) +
(sin(PitchAngle)*cos(PitchAngle)*BaseSpeed);

For the vertical speed (the speed going up and down):
VertSpeed = sin(PitchAngle)*BaseSpeed -
(cos(PitchAngle)*VertDescent);

For the horizontal speed (the speed horizontally (over the map)):
HorizSpeed = sqrt(BaseSpeed^2-VertSpeed^2);

Accel – acceleration in the glide's direction (in mph per second)
sin – the sine function
PitchAngle – the angle of the pitch (this is positive if pitching up)
BankAngle – the angle of a bank (left/right turn; 0 when level)
abs – the absolute value function
cos – the cosine function
VertDescent – the speed of the vertical descent
BaseSpeed – the current diagonal speed (acceleration applied)
VertSpeed – vertical speed
HorizSpeed – horizontal speed
sqrt – the square root function

Notes: I had to spend two hours fiddling with numbers in a spreadsheet to get this formula. One of the first two formulas must be used, based on when they are used. The "0.654318" number is the value at which, at maximum speed, one glides perfectly level, which occurs at an angle near 6.827994177089°. Also note that gliding cannot occur below 2 feet per second. Use a sine and cosine function on the horizontal speed to get the Z and X speeds (respectively – 0° is due north like on a compass).

Rate of turning while banking in a glide
     When banking (changing the heading), the rate at which turning is done is based on how sharp the banking is.

Used: when characters bank while in a glide
TurningRate = sin(BankAngle)*90;

TurningRate – how fast the horizontal turning is in degrees per second (add if turning right, subtract if turning left)
sin – the sine function
BankAngle – the angle of the bank, in degrees (0 when level)

Notes: This is used throughout the story.

Critical hit randomization

Critical hits are explained in appendix 4. They involve random damage from 1.5 to 4 times that of normal. For when this is used, simply multiply the base range given by this result.

Used: when lots of numbers pop out at once, for popup's values
CritDmgVar = (RandNum^2)*2.5+1.5;

CritDmgVar – critical [hit] damage variation
RandNum – a random number from and including 0 to 1

Notes: This is only needed during scene 10.

Speed busher fireball speed

Speed's "speed busher" is a special skill that turns destroyed objects into fireballs that move at extreme speed. The speed they start at is dependent solely on the object's mass.

Used: when Speed's speed busher destroys a target

Note: 6437 m/s, 1200 kg mass base

Speed = sqrt(96,000,000,000*RandNum/Mass);

Speed – the resulting speed, in meters per second, that the fireball starts moving at
RandNum – a random number from and including 0.95 to 1.05
Mass – the object's mass, in kilograms

Notes: The 96 billion value is the kinetic energy, in joules, a tremendous amount of energy (about that of running a 100-watt bulb continuously for 11.1 days).